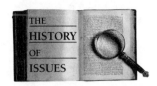

Drug Abuse

Other Books in the History of Issues Series:

Drug Abuse

Kelly Barth, Book Editor

GREENHAVEN PRESS

An imprint of Thomson Gale, a part of The Thomson Corporation

Detroit • New York • San Francisco • New Haven, Conn. • Waterville, Maine • London

Christine Nasso, *Publisher*
Elizabeth Des Chenes, *Managing Editor*

© 2007 The Gale Group.

Star logo is a trademark and Gale and Greenhaven Press are registered trademarks used herein under license.

For more information, contact:
Greenhaven Press
27500 Drake Rd.
Farmington Hills, MI 48331-3535
Or you can visit our Internet site at http://www.gale.com

Articles in Greenhaven Press anthologies are often edited for length to meet page requirements. In addition, original titles of these works are changed to clearly present the main thesis and to explicitly indicate the author's opinion. Every effort is made to ensure that Greenhaven Press accurately reflects the original intent of the authors. Every effort has been made to trace the owners of copyrighted material.

Cover photograph © Eric Travers/Pascal Le Floch/epa/Corbis.

ISBN-13: 978-0-7377-2007-5
ISBN-10: 0-7377-2007-7

2007932781

Contents

Chapter 1: The Early Drug Abuse Debates

Chapter 2: The War on Drugs

According to Herbert Fingarette, labeling alcoholism a disease leads to a gross oversimplification of a complex and multifaceted problem.

Chapter 5: Drug Abuse Today

Foreword

In the 1940s, at the height of the Holocaust, Jews struggled to create a nation of their own in Palestine, a region of the Middle East that at the time was controlled by Britain. The British had placed limits on Jewish immigration to Palestine, hampering efforts to provide refuge to Jews fleeing the Holocaust. In response to this and other British policies, an underground Jewish resistance group called Irgun began carrying out terrorist attacks against British targets in Palestine, including immigration, intelligence, and police offices. Most famously, the group bombed the King David Hotel in Jerusalem, the site of a British military headquarters. Although the British were warned well in advance of the attack, they failed to evacuate the building. As a result, ninety-one people were killed (including fifteen Jews) and forty-five were injured.

Early in the twentieth century, Ireland, which had long been under British rule, was split into two countries. The south, populated mostly by Catholics, eventually achieved independence and became the Republic of Ireland. Northern Ireland, mostly Protestant, remained under British control. Catholics in both the north and south opposed British control of the north, and the Irish Republican Army (IRA) sought unification of Ireland as an independent nation. In 1969, the IRA split into two factions. A new radical wing, the Provisional IRA, was created and soon undertook numerous terrorist bombings and killings throughout Northern Ireland, the Republic of Ireland, and even in England. One of its most notorious attacks was the 1974 bombing of a Birmingham, England, bar that killed nineteen people.

In the mid-1990s, an Islamic terrorist group called al Qaeda began carrying out terrorist attacks against American targets overseas. In communications to the media, the organization listed several complaints against the United States. It generally opposed all U.S. involvement and presence in the Middle East. It particularly objected to the presence of U.S. troops in Saudi Arabia, which is the home of several Islamic holy sites. And it strongly condemned the United States for supporting the nation of Israel, which it claimed was an oppressor of Muslims. In 1998 al Qaeda's leaders issued a fatwa (a religious legal statement) calling for Muslims to kill Americans. Al Qaeda acted on this order many times—most memorably on September 11, 2001, when it attacked the World Trade Center and the Pentagon, killing nearly three thousand people.

These three groups—Irgun, the Provisional IRA, and al Qaeda—have achieved varied results. Irgun's terror campaign contributed to Britain's decision to pull out of Palestine and to support the creation of Israel in 1948. The Provisional IRA's tactics kept pressure on the British, but they also alienated many would-be supporters of independence for Northern Ireland. Al Qaeda's attacks provoked a strong U.S. military response but did not lessen America's involvement in the Middle East nor weaken its support of Israel. Despite these different results, the means and goals of these groups were similar. Although they emerged in different parts of the world during different eras and in support of different causes, all three had one thing in common: They all used clandestine violence to undermine a government they deemed oppressive or illegitimate.

The destruction of oppressive governments is not the only goal of terrorism. For example, terror is also used to minimize dissent in totalitarian regimes and to promote extreme ideologies. However, throughout history the motivations of terrorists have been remarkably similar, proving the old adage that "the more things change, the more they remain the same." Arguments for and against terrorism thus boil down to the same set of universal arguments regardless of the age: Some argue that terrorism is justified to change (or, in the case of state terror, to maintain) the prevailing political order; others respond that terrorism is inhumane and unacceptable under any circumstances. These basic views transcend time and place.

Similar fundamental arguments apply to other controversial social issues. For instance, arguments over the death penalty have always featured competing views of justice. Scholars cite biblical texts to claim that a person who takes a life must forfeit his or her life, while others cite religious doctrine to support their view that only God can take a human life. These arguments have remained essentially the same throughout the centuries. Likewise, the debate over euthanasia has persisted throughout the history of Western civilization. Supporters argue that it is compassionate to end the suffering of the dying by hastening their impending death; opponents insist that it is society's duty to make the dying as comfortable as possible as death takes its natural course.

Greenhaven Press's The History of Issues series illustrates this constancy of arguments surrounding major social issues. Each volume in the series focuses on one issue—including terrorism, the death penalty, and euthanasia—and examines how the debates have both evolved and remained essentially the same over the years. Primary documents such as newspaper articles, speeches, and government reports illuminate historical developments and offer perspectives from throughout history. Secondary sources provide overviews and commentaries from a more contemporary perspective. An introduction begins each anthology and supplies essential context and background. An annotated table of contents, chronology, and index allow for easy reference, and a bibliography and list of organizations to contact point to additional sources of information on the book's topic. With these features, The History of Issues series permits readers to glimpse both the historical and contemporary dimensions of humanity's most pressing and controversial social issues.

Introduction

The debate over how to manage the problems associated with drug abuse has become increasingly contentious with each passing century. A look at some of the most recent statistics reveals that the debate over how best to manage substance use and abuse will remain one of the most compelling of the twenty-first century as well. The 2004 National Survey on Drug Use and Health revealed that in America alone, more that 46 percent of the population twelve or older reported having used an illegal drug in their lifetime. Also, the survey found that one hundred thousand deaths annually can be directly traced to alcohol consumption. In addition to alcohol, the numbers of people addicted to other "legal" drugs, such as cigarettes and prescription medications, continue to remain steady or increase. The substance abuse discussion has mainly centered around two primary questions. First, does the substance abuser have control over his problem? The second and perhaps more contentious question surrounding drug abuse is whether the problem is best managed by reforming the addict or by attempting to prohibit or control the source of his addiction.

The idea that certain individuals were particularly vulnerable to alcohol and less able than others to resist it originated with the ancient Greeks and Romans. Historical records indicate that these ancient governments even offered state-sponsored treatment to those suffering from what was perceived then as chronic drunkenness. Indeed, some texts even refer to drinking as a sickness not only of the body but of the spirit as well, suggesting that humans have long understood some people's tendency to abuse alcohol and other substances in response to personal problems or emotional pain. Not all societies were as compassionate.

Though they initially saw alcohol as a gift from God providing medicinal benefits and a purified beverage, the American colonists slowly began to view those who misused alcohol as evil. In a 1673 sermon entitled "Woe to Drunkards," Puritan preacher Increase Mather made a clear distinction between drink itself and the members of his community who abused it: "Drink is in itself a good creature of God and to be received with thankfulness, but the abuse of drink is from Satan, the wine is from God, but the Drunkard is from the Devil." One reason for the increased concern about alcohol could be that town drunks became a more common sight as the distillation process was perfected and hard liquor became a more popular drink than the less potent, fermented beverages of beer and wine.

As the colonies became ruled less by strictly religious governments than secular ones, societal norms became more difficult to agree upon and enforce. Nevertheless, in the years leading up to the American Revolution, colonists began to see alcohol abuse as a threat to the stability of the new and somewhat fragile emerging country. A number of them publicized their concerns.

In these publications were some of the earliest articulations of the concept of addiction as a disease. Philanthropist and social reformer Anthony Benezet, in 1774, published a treatise, "The Mighty Destroyer Displayed," that decried the evils of drink. In it he directly challenged the long-held Christian belief that alcohol was a gift from God. Following the publication of Benezet's treatise, the Methodists and Quakers began discouraging members from either producing or consuming hard liquor. Another social reformer, Dr. Benjamin Rush, published, "Inquiry Into the Effects of Ardent Spirits on the Human Mind and Body." The 1784 pamphlet suggests that people could possibly develop addictions to alcohol and that, with increased drinking over time, some people would become unable to stop. A signer of the Declaration of Independence who is considered one of America's most prominent medical experts, Rush never advocated complete abstinence for all; however, he did provide medical support to Benezet's unproven hunch that a person could be afflicted by a "drinking disease." By the mid-1800s, the idea that addiction was a disease that required treatment had attained a toehold in American thought.

Addiction Is Viewed as a Disease State

With the acceptance of the idea that substance abuse was a disease, came a sense that society must also begin to assist the "drunkard" in dealing with his problem as they would anyone else suffering from a debilitating illness he had no control over. In fact, though still firmly convinced that addiction to drink indicated moral weakness, Dr. Rush went on to suggest that places called "sober houses" be established to shelter and care for drunkards. Physician Samuel Woodward proposed that asylums be established to treat drunkards, who, he suggested, might have inherited a special vulnerability to alcohol. He believed that if an alcohol abuser understood that he drank to assuage guilt or pain, he could then face the truth about himself and begin the process of recovery. Woodward was beginning to articulate one of the most troubling paradoxes of substance abuse: In the addictive substance lies the addict's greatest curse and his greatest consolation.

As social reformers and physicians increasingly arrived at this new understanding—that substance abusers suffered from a disease—a profile of the addict took root. He was a person who had a biological addiction to a certain substance. He had an increased biological tolerance for this substance and could not stop using it where others could. Also, the medical problems that an addict faced seemed to follow a set and fairly predictable progression. In 1849, Swedish physician Magnus Huss made the strongest case yet for this new medical understanding of alcohol addiction with the publication of his book

Chronic Alcohol Illness. His documentation of delirium tremens and the effects of excessive alcohol consumption on the organs of an abuser revealed a profile of symptoms associated with chronic alcohol exposure, a profile that could no longer be ignored.

Along with this new emphasis on medical explanations rather than moral or religious vices came an increasing compassion for substance abusers. Aid societies were formed to address the needs of alcoholics in particular. Formed in reaction against incarceration of drunkards (as alcoholics were called at the time), these organizations strove to provide a place where the social and emotional needs of a drunkard could be acknowledged and addressed. They emphasized total abstinence from alcohol and the sharing of stories and mutual support to help alcoholics remain sober. Among these precursors to Alcoholics Anonymous (AA) were the Fraternal Temperance Society and the Washingtonians. Such groups reached out to those judged irredeemable by the church. One of the Washingtonians' founders, the Reverend Joel Parker, described the group's origins this way, "God raised up reformers from among themselves and now the multiplied and moving tales of woes and sins, and recoveries of poor, lost drunkards, are telling with amazing power upon hearts that were accounted to be beyond the reach of the gospel." In fact, many of these organizations banned members of the clergy from attending lest they squelch important, healing discussion among the alcoholics.

In the mid-1800s, a class of painkillers called narcotics, derived from opium, came to rival alcohol as an addictive substance. These drugs, such as morphine, were prescribed to cure a whole host of illnesses and sold in over-the-counter remedies as cough syrups and sleep and digestive aids. Many unwitting people became dependent upon them. As addiction numbers increased, so did societal intolerance of the problem. As had alcoholics, those addicted to narcotics were initially stigmatized as morally weak and sinful. Eventually, however, the new medical theories about addiction influenced societal perceptions and narcotics addiction came to be viewed as a medical condition with predictable and treatable symptoms.

A growing number of physicians began to search for ways to increase their own knowledge about addictions and derive new methods for treating them. Some of these doctors—most notably Joseph Parrish and Willard Parker—grouped those addicted to alcohol, opium, morphine, and other substances under the term inebriates. In 1870 they, and the founders of several asylums and homes created to treat inebriety, founded the American Association for the Cure of Inebriety (later named the Association for the Study of Inebriety) in Binghamton, New York. Though these doctors did not completely reject the idea that substance abuse was something people could and should voluntarily refrain from, they did believe that some individuals developed such acute problems with substance abuse that they no longer had control over them. Never before had there been such an organized attempt to influence national opinion toward an understanding of addiction as a chronic medical problem in need of as much compassion and treatment as any other.

Return to Temperance and the Move Toward Prohibition

Not everyone adhered to the idea that addiction was a disease. In the 1880s, a prominent critic of the idea, Chicago physician C.W. Earle, and a growing number of others insisted that a move away from a discussion of vice simply led to further substance abuse and irresponsibility. Even some leaders of the new treatment centers for inebriety began to question that the disease concept of addiction had a basis in medical fact. Dr. Robert Harris, of the Franklin Reformatory for Inebriates in Philadelphia, spoke out strongly that the disease concept of addiction undermined important religious standards about personal choice and morality. To say people were simply victims of their bodies' response to a substance, he believed, relieved them of an essential sense of personal accountability and freedom to change. The fact that few medical cures to addiction had proven effective in treating alcoholics cast further suspicion on the disease concept. Earle's and Harris's sentiments chimed well with another movement gaining in strength across the nation. The temperance movement would shift attention away from a medical approach to addiction, treatment, and even the addict himself and toward a prohibition of substances and a call for wholesale abstinence.

By the turn of the twentieth century, the temperance movement had captured the hearts and minds of the majority of Americans concerned about the problem of substance abuse. Prevailing opinion held that Prohibition, the banning of all alcohol production and sale in the United States, was the only way to control substance abuse. Members of the Women's Christian Temperance Union (WTCU), an organization headed by social reformer Frances Willard, are largely credited for this shift in public opinion. Willard galvanized an army of people that, among other things, established "reform clubs," or groups of recovering alcoholics who met regularly to encourage one another to remain sober. As Mark Edward Lender and James Kirby Martin describe the strong influence of the WTCU in their book *Drinking in America*: "Gospel temperance [of the WTCU] became a national phenomenon, and claims that it had saved thousands for sobriety and for God by the late 1870's are entirely believable." Though the WTCU and other Christian reform groups did show compassion toward alcoholics and their families, they insisted that complete abstinence was the only way to ensure recovery. Support for the idea that addiction was a disease waned as a direct result of the influence of temperance groups. Their insistence that excessive drinking was a sin against God forgiven and reversible only by an addict's voluntarily religious conversion directly contradicted the earlier understanding of alcoholism and other substance abuse as a disease over which the addict had little control.

By the early part of the twentieth century, the general public had all but abandoned the rising medical explanation for addiction, and the United States was charting a direct course toward Prohibition. Its advocates insisted that if the source of addiction were removed then the addict would have little choice but to turn to God, the church, and other reform organizations for help. Though Prohibition became official with passage of the Eighteenth Amendment to the Constitution, it ultimately failed. Despite the fact that Prohibition correlated directly with a drop-off in mortality rates from cirrhosis of the liver and other disorders associated with alcohol abuse, enforcing abstinence proved far more difficult and ultimately ineffective than anyone could have imagined. In 1933, Prohibition was overturned by the Twenty-first Amendment to the Constitution.

Though Prohibition failed, this did not mean an end to addicts seeking a spiritual solution to their addiction problems. In the 1930s, alcoholics again turned to religious groups as a way toward recovery. Many of these groups, however, took a far less rigid, judgmental approach to encouraging abstinence than the evangelical temperance groups had. The Oxford Group, for example, emphasized the broader idea of a healthy, balanced spiritual life as an antidote to addiction rather than an emphasis on the addict's sinful nature. From this less specifically evangelical Christian approach emerged Alcoholics Anonymous (AA) and the twelve-step program of recovery and personal accountability. Many offshoots using a similar model of group sharing and a commitment to abstinence arose throughout the twentieth century such as Jewish Alcoholics, Narcotics Anonymous, and Chemically Dependent People and Significant Others. Most of these groups still offer substantial help to addicts to this day.

The 1940s witnessed a resurgence of the idea that alcoholism and other addictions could be classified as a disease. As such, addicts' symptoms could be categorized, their medical and hereditary histories traced, and treatment options planned. The groundbreaking research of E.M. Jellinek at the Yale University Center of Alcohol Studies inspired this renewed interest, which culminated in his 1960 paper, *The Disease Concept of Alcoholism.*

Jellinek's colleagues also conducted research into addiction and established clinics in urban areas in the East to further the treatment and prevention of alcoholism. Most significantly, the center established medical science as the proper venue for addressing the addiction. Once again, the theory that addicts had a disease rather than weak moral fiber helped to remove the stigma many alcoholics faced. In response to this ideological shift, closeted addicts began turning to organizations like AA and other treatment centers in unprecedented numbers.

The Government Weighs In

The '60s and '70s, an era of social protest and civil unrest, witnessed an associated increase in drug use and experimentation that caused the U.S. government to begin to take its own official positions and action on the issue of substance abuse. In 1971, President Richard Nixon established the National Commission on Marihuana and Drug Abuse, which he hoped would determine marijuana was a dangerous drug that should be deemed strictly illegal. Despite his commission's findings to the contrary, Nixon established harsh laws regulating marijuana possession and use. Throughout his administration, he took a strong stance against illegal drugs of all kinds and worked to establish harsh penalties for their use. He is credited with first calling America's antidrug policies, the War on Drugs. During the Jimmy Carter administration, the government briefly took a less punitive approach to drug use and even made moves toward legalizing marijuana.

The 1980s saw a return to a more conservative approach to drug use and an era of increased penalties and harsh anti-drug legislation. The Ronald Reagan administration accelerated the War on Drugs by crafting the Anti-Drug Abuse Act of 1986, a bill that put in place tough penalties and mandatory minimum sentences for the sale of even small amounts of cocaine. He and his wife Nancy also spearheaded the highly publicized Just Say No campaign designed to keep kids from using drugs. The George H.W. Bush administration added even more fuel to America's antidrug efforts by appointing ultraconservative William Bennett as head of the Office of National Drug Control Policy. During Bennett's tenure, the national dialogue around addiction again shifted toward morality. Drug use was once again stigmatized. During Bennett's term as drug czar, the government launched military operations against other countries to control their illegal drug trade with the United States. Bennett also ensured that harsh fines and long prison terms for even minor drug offenses became the norm. Generally, drug use remained stable or rose during this period, signaling to critics that attempting to control supply was an ineffective way to address drug abuse.

Bennett's conservative antidrug policies created a groundswell of opposition even among social conservatives. His critics maintained that using such extreme measures to control drug supplies siphoned money from treatment, rehabilitation, and prevention programs proven effective in fighting drug abuse. Organizations and think tanks such as the National Organization for the Reform of Marijuana Laws (NORML) formed to oppose the U.S. War on Drugs. Some even blamed the illegality and harsh penalties for exacerbating and creating the problems associated with drug abuse. In a speech to the New York Bar Association in the summer of 1995, conservative columnist William F. Buckley phrased the concern about Bennett's policies this way: "The cost of the drug war is many times more painful in all its manifestations than would be the licensing of drugs combined with intensive education of non-users and intensive education designed to warn those who experiment with drugs." Joseph McNamara, former chief of police of Kansas City, Missouri, added his voice of opposition as well:

> It was my own experience as a policeman trying to enforce the laws against drugs that led me to change my attitude about drug-control policy. . . . I was a willing foot soldier at the start of the modern drug war, pounding a beat in Harlem. During the early 1960s, as heroin use spread, we made many arrests but it did not take long before cops realized that arrests did not lessen drug selling or drug use.

When advocates of the Drug War cited decreases in the use of certain drugs in response to harsh antidrug policies, critics pointed out that as long as there were untreated, uneducated, and uninformed addicts, there would also be large numbers of producers and suppliers waiting with the next drug that would meet their cravings.

Struggling Toward Consensus

The disease concept of addiction prevailed until the 1980s, when large numbers of people in the medical and treatment profession began to question its validity. One prominent disease-concept critic Herbert Fingarette says in his book, *Heavy Drinking*, "The overall theme that must guide social policies in heavy drinking is that we are not dealing with an illness but with an activity that—like bad diet, lack of exercise or smoking—tends to cause illness." Consensus now seems to be that the problems of addiction are far too complex to be solved by a one-size-fits-all explanation. A complex mix of circumstantial, cultural, hereditary, and social factors may in fact interact to cause a person to abuse substances.

Though people may disagree over whether drug addiction is a disease or not, most in the religious, medical, and treatment communities agree that the behavior should be curtailed and that the addict should be able to choose from a wide array of solutions to his problems. In fact, the last couple of decades have witnessed a renewed focus on ensuring that adequate treatment options exist for addicts and that education be provided to new users to prevent them from joining the ranks of the chronically addicted. For example, President George W. Bush's Access to Recovery program has provided increased legitimacy to faith-based programs that in the past had received little or no federal funding because of their religious status. The philosophy behind such funding has been that no matter what the medium of recovery, if the program effectively helps addicts regain a sense of health and personal responsibility and if it allows them to live meaningful lives then it should be applauded and assisted. Though religious-based recovery may not be preferred or effective for some, it may be entirely appropriate for others.

Though the War on Drugs rages on, general agreement exists that until the needs of addicts are properly addressed, no amount of supply reduction measures will have measurable results. According to most experts, the only lasting solutions appear to be those that approach each substance abuser as an individual with responsibility for his choices and the freedom to choose a life free from addiction. Many agree that an approach that provides a mix of compassion and accountability and that acknowledges the vulnerabilities within us all is the only sort that appears destined to work.

CHAPTER 1

The Early Drug
Abuse Debates

Chapter Preface

Since the earliest recorded history humans have consumed mood-altering substances, or drugs. Numerous references to wine exist in ancient texts such as the Hebrew Bible and the Koran. Many cultures used psychoactive substances as a part of sacred ceremonies. For example, according to the histories of Herodotus, the Scythians, an ancient nomadic people who occupied present-day Iran, placed wild cannabis on heated rocks inside tents. They then leaned into and inhaled the smoke to increase the merriment before ceremonial dances. Humans also perfected the cultivation of plants with psychoactive effects. Natives of South American tribes, for example, grew coca, from which cocaine is derived, and chewed the leaves as a mild stimulant. Medieval apothecary gardeners in Europe accumulated a large body of knowledge about medicinal plants, many of which, if taken in large enough quantities, could alter mood.

With this increasing knowledge came a growing fear and moral unease. Though people knew that many of these substances had great power to heal, they also came to understand they had the power to cause addictions and even death. As botanist and author Michael Pollan writes in his book, *The Botany of Desire*, humans have had to carefully assess the dangers of the plants in their gardens: "Some heal; others douse or calm or quiet the body's pain. But most remarkable of all, there are plants in the garden that manufacture molecules with the power to change the subjective experience of reality we call consciousness."

By becoming increasingly skilled in the production and use of psychoactive substances, humans opened a proverbial Pandora's box. Perfecting the distillation process by the seventeenth century made alcohol even more potent and more addictive. Equipped with an ever-increasing understanding of chemistry in the nineteenth century, pharmacists were able to patent medicines containing cocaine, heroin, and morphine. Initially, these drugs seemed to have not only great therapeutic potential but also an impressive power to enhance mental functioning. An unanticipated result of the drugs, however, was an associated rise in addictions to them. While many of these medicines were intended for use as temporary painkillers and sleep aids, people quickly found they could not function without them. For example, soldiers treated with morphine to help them endure the pain of their injuries became hopelessly addicted.

It did not take long for people to recognize the unintended danger of these substances and the need to regulate them. Specifically, the U.S. government passed legislation that required pharmaceutical companies to label the contents of their medications. It also banned nonprescription drugs that contained highly addictive substances such as cocaine. An underground illegal drug trade arose to supply the great need for the drugs that people could no longer acquire legally.

The tide of opinion also turned against alcohol. The move to prohibit its production and sale gained in strength at the turn of the twentieth century. Temperance and religious groups called Prohibitionists organized and eventually succeeded in influencing the nation's leaders to pass Prohibition, the Eighteenth Amendment to the Constitution.

Americans soon discovered that Prohibition had its drawbacks. A culture of criminal activity arose to meet the nation's continuing demand for alcohol. People built stills and sold their liquor on the black market. Alcohol was smuggled from other countries. An increasing number of speakeasies, or places where alcohol was sold illegally, sprang up around the country as well.

Prohibition garnered many opponents who called for its repeal. Compassionate treatment for alcoholics and enforceable laws governing the legal sale of liquor, they maintained, was the only answer to the problem of excessive drinking. Prohibition's opponents prevailed; in 1933 prohibition was repealed with the passage of the Twenty-first Amendment to the Constitution.

Cocaine Has Therapeutic Potential

Sigmund Freud

In his experimentation with the newly discovered alkaloid co-caine, Austrian neurologist Sigmund Freud was highly impressed with its effect on the mind and its potential use as a medicine. He presented the following paper in March 1885 at a meeting of the Psychiatric Society in Vienna, Austria. In it, he describes the therapeutic effects of cocaine on people treated for exposure and its ability to greatly enhance mental capacity and endurance in him and all others he administered it to. He expresses great ex-citement about the drug's potential use as a way to ease with-drawal from other addictive substances such as alcohol and mor-phine. Freud also says he is encouraged that, in his numerous experiments, cocaine never caused addiction.

Last summer I made a study of the physiologic action and therapeutic use of cocaine. I am now speaking to you be-cause I believe that some points in this area may also be of interest to a psychiatric society. In this talk, I have excluded entirely the external use of cocaine, which has been intro-duced so successfully into ophthalmology and is also so valu-able in other branches of practical medicine. We are interested only in the effects of cocaine when it is administered inter-nally.

With the conquest of the lands of South America by the Spaniards, it became known that the leaves of the coca plant were used by the natives there as a source of enjoyment, and that the effects of coca, according to the most reliable infor-mants, lay chiefly in a remarkable increase in efficiency. It is easy to understand, therefore, why great expectations were aroused in Europe when the Novara [Austrian ship used to circumnavigate the globe from 1857–59] expedition brought a quantity of coca leaves to Europe, and Niemann, one of [German chemist Friedrich] Wöhler's pupils in Göttingen, prepared a new alkaloid, cocaine, from them. Since then, numerous experiments have been performed with this substance, as well as with the leaves themselves, in order to obtain results similar to the effects of coca on the Indians, but the over-all results of these efforts have been a great disappointment and a tendency to question the credibility of the reports from the lands where coca grows. I do not wish to go into any details here about the probable reasons for these failures, but there are some findings even from those times (60 and 70 years ago [early 1800s]) that indicate a heightening of efficiency by cocaine. In the winter of 1883, Dr. [Theodor] von Aschenbrandt reported that Bavarian soldiers who had become fatigued as a result of exposure to such exhausting factors as overexertion, heat, and so forth recovered after they had received very small amounts of cocaine hydrochloride. Perhaps my only merit lies in the fact that I gave credence to these reports. They prompted me to study the effects of coca on my own person and on others.

Cocaine Increases Mental Functioning

I can describe the effects of cocaine when taken internally as follows: If one takes a minimally active dose (0.05 to 0.10 g) while in excellent health and does not expect any special exertion thereafter, one can hardly perceive any surprising effect. It is different, however, if this dose of cocaine hydrochloride is taken by a subject whose general health is impaired by fatigue or hunger. After a short time (10–20 minutes), he feels as though he had been raised to the full height of intellectual and bodily vigor, in a state of euphoria, which is distinguished from the euphoria after consumption of alcohol by the absence of any feeling of alteration. However astonishing this effect of ingestion of coca may be, the absence of signs that could distinguish the state from the normal euphoria of good health makes it even more likely that we will underestimate it. As soon as the contrast between the present state and the state before the ingestion of cocaine is forgotten, it is difficult to believe that one is under the influence of a foreign agent, and yet one is very profoundly altered for four to five hours, since so long as the effects of the drug persist, one can perform mental and physical work with great endurance, and the otherwise urgent needs of rest, food, and sleep are thrust aside, as it were. During the first hours after cocaine, it is even impossible to fall asleep. This effect of the alkaloid gradually fades away after the aforesaid time, and is not followed by any depression.

In my paper "On Coca," I have given several examples of the disappearance of legitimate fatigue and hunger, etc., which I observed largely among colleagues who had taken cocaine at my request. Since that time, I have made many similar observations, among them that of a writer who for weeks before had been incapable of any literary production and who was able to work for 14 hours without interruption after taking 0.1 g of cocaine hydrochloride. I could not fail to note, however, that the individual disposition plays a major role in the effects of cocaine, perhaps a more important role than with other alkaloids. The subjective phenomena after ingestion of coca differ from person to person, and only few persons experience, like myself, a pure euphoria without alteration. Others already experience slight intoxication, hyperkinesia [excessive body movement], and talkativeness after the same amount of cocaine, while still others have no subjective symptoms of the effects of coca at all. On the other hand, heightened functional capacity appeared much more regularly as a symptom of the action of cocaine, and I directed my efforts toward an objective demonstration of the latter, perhaps through changes in values that are readily determined in the living subject and that relate to physical and mental functional capacity. . . .

I now come to the two points that are of direct psychiatric interest. Psychiatry is rich in drugs that can subdue over-stimulated nervous activity but deficient in agents that can heighten the performance of the depressed nervous system. It is natural, therefore, that we should think of making use of the effects of cocaine that we have described above in the forms of illness that we interpret as states of weakness and depression of the nervous system without organic lesions. As a matter of fact, cocaine has been used since its discovery against hysteria, hypochondria, etc., and there is no shortage of reports of individual cures obtained with it. . . . On the whole, it must be said that the value of cocaine in psychiatric practice remains to be demonstrated, and it will probably be worthwhile to make a thorough trial as soon as the currently exorbitant price of the drug becomes more reasonable.

Cocaine Helps with Withdrawal from Other Drugs

We can speak more definitely about another use of cocaine by the psychiatrist. It was first discovered in America that cocaine is capable of alleviating the serious withdrawal symptoms observed in subjects who are abstaining from morphine and of suppressing their craving for morphine. The *Detroit Therapeutic Gazette* has published in recent years a whole series of reports on morphine and opium withdrawals that were achieved with the aid of cocaine, from which it may be concluded, for example, that the patients did not require constant medical surveillance if they were directed to take an effective dose of cocaine whenever they felt a renewed craving for morphine. I myself have had occasion to observe a case of rapid withdrawal from morphine under cocaine treatment here, and I saw that a person who had presented the most severe manifestations of collapse at the time of an earlier withdrawal now remained able, with the aid of cocaine, to work and to stay out of bed, and was reminded of his abstinence only by his shivering, diarrhea, and occasionally recurring craving for morphine. He took about 0.40 g of cocaine per day, and by the end of 20 days the morphine abstinence was overcome. No cocaine habituation set in; on the contrary, an increasing antipathy to the use of cocaine was unmistakably evident. On the basis of my experiences with the effects of cocaine, I have no hesitation in recommending the administration of cocaine for such withdrawal cures. . . . On several occasions, I have even seen cocaine quickly eliminate the manifestations of intolerance that appeared after a rather large dose of morphine, as if it had a specific ability to counteract morphine. . . .

I know very well that cocaine appears to be of no value in certain cases of withdrawal treatment, and I am prepared to believe that there are differences in the individual reactions to the alkaloid. Finally, I believe that I should mention that the American physicians have seen fit to report on the cure or palliation of the craving for alcohol in alcoholics.

Common Pain Relievers Can Cause Widespread Addiction

Ian Scott

The nineteenth century saw the development of many narcotics from plants. Fledgling pharmaceutical companies helped these drugs find their way into the public's hands in the form of pain-killers, cough syrups, and other medicinal remedies. In the following 1998 article, Ian Scott, professor of biological sciences at the University of Wales, Aberystwyth, traces the history of these narcotics and their fall from favor. He reports that by the turn of the century, it had become apparent to doctors and governments alike that despite initially seeming helpful, these substances were also highly addictive. Scott points out that by the time countries like the United States removed the medicines containing these narcotics from drugstore shelves, millions of people already had serious addictions. Regulating the substances quickly created a subculture of drug abuse and a lucrative illegal drug trade.

In 1898 a German chemical company [Bayer] launched a new cough medicine called 'Heroin'. A hundred years later, this drug is flooding illegally into Britain in record amounts. The latest Home Office [British government division designed to protect the public] annual figures show a 40 per cent increase in police seizures of heroin. The National Criminal Intelligence Service believes that up to 80 per cent of the heroin currently entering Britain is controlled by Turkish organised criminals based in London and the South East. How, then, did nineteenth-century science come to bequeath this notorious drug of abuse to twentieth-century crime?

In 1863 a dynamic German merchant called Friedrich Bayer (1825–76) set up a factory in Elberfeld to exploit new

Ian Scott, "A Hundred Year Habit," *History Today*, vol. 48, June 1998, pp. 6–8. Reproduced by permission.

chemical procedures for making colourful dyes from coal-tar. German coal-tar dye manufacture expanded rapidly, surpassing English or French production six-fold by the mid-1870s. In the mid-1880s, however, price conventions and raw material availability deteriorated in the German dye industry, so the Bayer company invested in scientific research to diversify its product range. In 1888, a new substance synthesised by Bayer chemists became the company's first commercial medicine.

Synthetic chemical medicines were something new. In the early years of the nineteenth century, medicines had been prepared using crude natural materials like opium, the dried milky juice of poppy seed pods. A young German pharmacist called Friedrich Serturner (1783–1841) had first applied chemical analysis to plant drugs, by purifying in 1805 the main active ingredient of opium. Recalling Morpheus, the Greek god of dreams, Serturner gave his drug the name 'morphium', which later became morphine. Perhaps appropriately, the discoverer of morphine was in due course nominated for academic honours; by the author of 'Faust', [Johann] Goethe himself.

The possibility of obtaining morphine and other pure drugs from plants brought commercial reward for entrepreneurs such as Georg Merck (1825–73), who turned his family's seventeenth-century pharmacy in Darmstadt into a major supplier of these new products. Morphine was widely used for pain relief in the American Civil War and the Franco-Prussian War, in combination with the hypodermic syringe, which was invented in 1853. In contrast to the old crude preparations, precisely measured doses of the new purified drugs could be administered. Furthermore, drug action in the body could be more scientifically investigated. Pharmacology therefore developed rapidly not least in Germany.

As part of the Prussianisation of Alsace-Lorraine [region of northeast France] following the Franco-Prussian War, a well-equipped institute was built in Strasbourg in 1872 for the eminent German pharmacologist Oswald Schmiedeberg (1838–1921). One of Schmiedeberg's many talented pupils, Heinrich Dreser (1860–1924), ended up as head of the pharmacological laboratory at the product-hungry Bayer Company in Elberfeld.

Now that plant-derived drugs were available in purified form, chemists could modify them to form new molecules that might prove more effective, or perhaps safer to use. In the late 1890s, Dreser and his colleagues adopted this strategy to produce for Bayer two of the most famous drugs in the world today. Heroin, made by adding two acetyl [alcohol compound] groups to the morphine molecule, was followed a year later by another acetyl derivative of a painkiller from plants; the second natural drug was salicylic acid and the Bayer derivative was named 'Aspirin'.

Highly Addictive Drugs Were Thought Therapeutic

Ironically from today's perspective, heroin took its name from the adjective heroisch (heroic) sometimes used by nineteenth-century German doctors for a powerful medicine. Dreser presented his new drug as a cough, chest and lung medicine to the Congress of German Naturalists and Physicians in 1898. Painful respiratory diseases such as pneumonia and tuberculosis ('consumption') were then the leading causes of death, and in the days before antibiotics or the BCG vaccine [Bacillus Calmette Guérin, used to fight tuberculosis], doctors could only prescribe narcotics to alleviate the sufferings of patients who otherwise could not sleep. There was, therefore, considerable interest in the highly effective new drug. Today, heroin is known to be a more potent and faster acting painkiller than morphine because it passes more readily from the bloodstream into the brain. Heroin was praised in a number of early clinical trials, and was rapidly adopted in medical establishments in many countries. Bayer advertised the drug in German, English, Italian, Russian and other languages.

Heroin was prescribed in place of morphine or codeine (another constituent of opium, isolated in 1832). In a typical early report of 1898, G. Strube of the Medical University Clinic of Berlin tested oral doses of 5 and 10 mg of heroin on fifty phthisis [a wasting disease] patients and found it effective in relieving their coughs and producing sleep. He noted no unpleasant reactions; indeed the patients liked it and continued to take the heroin after he ceased to prescribe it. The addictive potential of heroin's parent, morphine, was only too well known, and evidence steadily emerged that the new drug was not the hoped-for improvement in this respect. Horatio C. Wood Jr. reported in 1899 that heroin dosages had to be increased with usage to remain effective. Such was the preoccupation with morphine addiction, however, that some doctors, such as A Morel-Lavallee in 1902, even advocated treatment by heroin in 'demorphinisation'. This practice was criticised by J. Jarrige in 1902, who by then had observed that heroin withdrawal symptoms were even worse than those of morphine.

By 1903 the writing was on the wall: in an article in the *Alabama Medical Journal* entitled 'The Heroin Habit Another Curse', G.E. Pettey declared that of the last 150 people he had treated for drug addiction, eight were dependent on heroin. Nevertheless, other physicians remained reluctant to abandon this highly effective drug. In 1911, J.D. Trawick could still lament in the *Kentucky Medical Journal.* 'I feel that bringing charges against heroin is almost like questioning the fidelity of a good friend. I have used it with good results.'

The United States was the country in which heroin addiction first became a serious problem. By the late nineteenth century, countries such as Britain and Germany had enacted pharmacy laws to control dangerous drugs, but under the US Constitution individual states were responsible for medical regulation. Late in the century some state laws required morphine or cocaine to be prescribed by physician, but drugs could still be obtained from bordering states with laxer legislation. Moreover, this era was the peak of a craze for over-the-counter patent medicines that were still permitted to contain these drugs. At the turn of the century [1900] it is believed that over a quarter of a million Americans (from a population of 76 million) were addicted to opium, morphine or cocaine.

After years of resistance, American patent medicine manufacturers were required by the federal Pure Food and Drug Act of 1906 accurately to label the contents of their products. These included 'soothing syrups' for bawling babies, and 'cures' for chronic ills such as consumption or even drug addiction, which previously had not declared (and sometimes denied) their content of opium, cocaine or cannabis. Consumers by this time were becoming fearful of addictive drugs, so the newly labelled patent medicines either declined in popularity or removed their drug ingredients. (The pre-eminent survival from this era is a tonic beverage from Atlanta called 'Coca-Cola'.) Bayer's 1899 launch of Aspirin, moreover, had made available a safe and effective painkiller to replace opium for everyday use.

In 1914 President Woodrow Wilson signed the Harrison Narcotic Act, which exploited the federal government's power to tax as a mechanism for finally enabling federal regulation of medical transactions in opium derivatives or cocaine. The main impetus for national drug laws in the US was diplomatic. As today, China was seen as the greatest emerging market, to which the Americans sought improved access. To help the massive Chinese opium problems, the US had led an international campaign culminating in the Hague Opium Convention of 1912, which required signatories to enact domestic legislation controlling opium trade. After the First World War, the Hague Convention was added to the Treaty of Versailles, requiring the British Dangerous Drugs Act of 1920, despite the absence of a serious drug problem in this country.

Heroin Quickly Became a Problem

The now familiar association of youthful heroin abusers with underworld suppliers was first noted in New York, where illicit availability was probably greatest due to the proximity of many of the chemical companies that then distributed heroin. In 1910, New York's Bellevue Hospital made its first ever admission for heroin addiction. In 1915, it admitted 425 heroin addicts, who were, according to the *Psychiatric Bulletin of the New York State Hospitals*, 'in many instances members of gangs who congregate on street corners particularly at night, and make insulting remarks to people who pass. It was noted that 'in practically every case the drug had been tried by one of the members of the gang who then induced the other members to try it'. These early heroin users were mostly between seventeen and twenty-five years old, and took the drug by sniffing.

New York addiction specialist A. Lambert in 1924 described heroin addiction as a 'vice of the underworld' acquired by the young through 'vicious associations'. American drug abusers were completely dependent on black market sources soon after 1919, when legal interpretation of the Harrison Act outlawed medical prescription of narcotics to maintain addicts. At this stage, heroin increased in popularity among drug dealers, who appreciated its black market qualities as a compact and powerful substance that could easily be adulterated. Another development at this time was the discovery by addicts of the enhanced euphoric effects when heroin was injected with the hypodermic syringe.

During the early 1920s a number of New York addicts supported themselves by collecting scrap metal from industrial dumps, so earning the label 'junkies'. Less savoury behaviour by heroin addicts was, however, causing concern to the authorities and public. Dr Lambert claimed that 'heroin destroys the sense of responsibility to the herd'. Heroin addiction was blamed for a number of the 260 murders that occurred in 1922 in New York (which compared with seventeen in London). These concerns led the US Congress to ban all domestic manufacture of heroin in 1924.

Two years later, however, US Narcotic Inspector SL. Rakusin declared that heroin seemed 'more plentiful than it ever was before'. Organised criminals were still obtaining heroin produced by legitimate pharmaceutical manufacturers in Western Europe, and later Turkey and Bulgaria, until restrictive policies of the League of Nations drove heroin manufacture largely underground by the early 1930s. An exception was militarist Japan and its occupied territories, where pharmaceutical firms produced heroin on a massive scale for the Chinese market until the end of the Second World War. Since then heroin has effectively belonged to the realm of international crime.

Prohibition of Alcohol Must Be Upheld

William Fraser McDowell

Spurred by antialcohol crusaders such as Carrie Nation, in 1919 the U. S. government ratified the Eighteenth Amendment to the Constitution, Prohibition, which outlawed the production, sale, or consumption of alcohol. Large numbers of people flouted the amendment. Alcohol-related crimes became more than federal, state, and local law enforcement officers could manage. Some officials even began accepting bribes from alcohol producers, sellers, and consumers in exchange for not arresting them. Even among nondrinkers, talk began of repealing the amendment since widespread violations of it crossed all social and economic boundaries. Still many wanted the amendment in place, so much so that a delegation gathered in Washington, D.C., in 1923 for the Citizenship Conference. The following keynote address by Methodist Episcopal bishop William Fraser McDowell expresses the delegation's collective fear that lack of respect for the amendment threatened not only the Constitution but also the power of law in the United States. Though passion from its proponents was great, Prohibition was overturned with passage of the Twenty-first Amendment in 1933.

The people of Washington [D.C.] proudly welcome you all to your own city. Every American living outside of this District has two homes, the one in which he lives and pays or evades taxes, and the other this capital which belongs to the entire nation. To this place many forces and influences naturally flow, some good, some bad; some noble, some base. From it go many laws, some wise, some unwise, some beneficial, some doubtful. On the whole, life at the capital of the na-

William Fraser McDowell, "Opening Address," in *Law vs. Lawlessness: Addresses Delivered at the Citizenship Conference, Washington, DC, October 13, 14, 15, 1923.* Edited by Fred B. Smith. New York: Fleming H. Revell, 1924. Reproduced by permission.

tion keeps about the same level as that maintained through-out the nation itself. If the tone of life at large be low, it will show itself here in a life that is off the true key of national well-being. If the morale of the states and their citizens be slack, if their devotion to law and ideals be weak, the capital will be a sorry spectacle for men and not fit for angels to look upon at all. You are come up for these few days from all over the country not for a festival, a pageant or a ceremonial. Washington is happily familiar with such gatherings of her people from everywhere and proudly lends her spacious ways to their use. But you are come for sober work, as serious men and women, to consider the very life of the Republic. For forces are at work, as you know, that tend to destroy, that if not arrested *will* destroy, the nation itself. This is no holiday visit you are making, but is an earnest gathering of earnest people for solemn, brave business. And you are come not as partisans, not as Republicans or Democrats, but as citizens and patriots. After Concord and Lexington, in our early his-tory, Patrick Henry [American statesman and orator 1736–1799] sent word to Massachusetts: "I am not a Virginian, I am an American." And that spirit made the young Republic.

We here, today, belong to many parties, represent many creeds, have in our veins the blood of many nations, but all of us are Americans with resolution in our hearts and a common purpose in our wills. The American people love liberty. They would fight and die for it. Some of them would do nearly anything except the one thing necessary to secure and pre-serve it. For there can be no liberty except liberty based upon law, upon law secured by orderly and proper process, and obeyed everywhere and by everybody. If we love liberty as our fathers did, we must perpetuate it against all foes by an unfal-tering devotion to the Constitution and the law. We cannot deceive ourselves. We are in a fight today, not for an indi-vidual measure, but through a particular issue, for the very existence of the Constitution, of the Union, of the Govern-ment.

A mighty evil, mad with its own power, purple with its own greed, and red with its own defiance of right and law is doing its worst to destroy civil liberty, religious freedom, order under law, and the security of any right under the flag. For if lawlessness at this point be not destroyed it will destroy obedience to law at all other points, and with it the very nation itself. We have the eternal principle of the divided house right before our eyes again. The nation cannot exist half slave and half free, half drunk and half sober, half wet and half dry, half under law and half above it, half obedient and half defiant. We have many classes in the United States. We have no classes that are exempt from the laws of the United States. We have many sections in our common country. But the flag flies over all alike, the laws of the country extend to all alike. We have many laws that we do not all or always like, but we have no classes that are privileged to choose whether they will regulate their obedience by their tastes or by their skill in defiance. Liberty under law is matched by the fundamental principle of equality before the law. That way our life as a nation lies. Any other way is the way to national death. And already we have too much bad blood, too many dangerous germs in our system.

We are always having elections. We are within a year of our supreme quadrennial election. Usually we are interested in measures and policies, in taxes and tariffs, in finances and transportation, in prices and wages. And all this is well, but our current elections and our next great election center in the essential principle of government itself. "Therefore," as George William Curtis said, a half-century ago, "there must be no doubt about our leaders. They must not prevaricate, or stand in the fog, or use the language of the demagogue to deceive the public while they seek public favor." If they are for the Constitution, let them be for it, and not half way for it and half way against it. The enforcement of laws must be in the hands of men who believe in the laws they are sworn to enforce and who will neither falter in their duty nor palter with their consciences. They must be men whose palms will not itch for bribes, whose tongues will not blister with lies, whose arms will not be palsied with fear, whose minds will not be clouded with evasions.

We have had a long war to gain what we now have. We have not the slightest intention of yielding now the victory we have won in the long struggle. The liquor traffic all along the long line of battle has always maintained a criminal attitude toward every law designed to regulate it. It now strikes at law itself. We know that the evasion of one law, whether by favored groups, or by large numbers leads straight to anarchy and contempt for all law. A public wrong is not a private right for any man or group of men in the republic.

Therefore, we are summoned and have come up to enlist anew in the great fight for freedom under law, for decency and a sober life under the flag, for the obedience of all classes to all laws while those laws stand in constitution and statute. Shall the saloon come back into our homes through the front door? No, ten thousand times no. Then in the name of decency let it not come back through the cellar door or the back door. Shall it come back through the upper world, with the approval of our best citizens upon its return? Then in the name of honor let it not come back through the underworld of our life, with only the blessing of criminals and law breakers upon it.

Tonight, you will see the white dome of the Capitol yonder as it shines in its high splendor. While you are here, you will see again the Washington shaft piercing the sky, and perhaps, for the first time, the monument to Lincoln in its majestic beauty. Citizens of the republic, coming from your homes to your capital, let us here highly resolve that there shall be no compromise with lawlessness and no nullification of law anywhere within our borders. To such resolution Washington solemnly bids you welcome.

We have heard a good deal about making the world safe for democracy. But a lawless democracy is not safe for the world. Our task is the creative task of making a democracy that is strong within itself and that can go anywhere. Grim old Thomas Carlyle [Scottish essayist and historian, 1775–1881] was always asking: "Wilt thou be a hero or a coward?" And a living journalist has declared that there is a hero and a coward in each one of us. Probably this is true of the nation itself. It is for us in these days and the days that follow to give the right answer to Carlyle's question, remembering that nothing is good enough which is not as good as it can be.

On a certain avenue in this city three men live in near neighborhood to one another. One of them you will hear with delight on Monday when the brilliant Senator from Idaho [William E. Borah] speaks upon this question: "Shall the Constitution of the United States Be Nullified?" Another of the three living in the same block is now speaking. This one brings his own remarks to a conclusion and a climax by a quotation from the third, who is really the first of these neighbors. He said: "It is now the duty of every good citizen, no matter what his previous opinion of the wisdom or the expediency of the amendment, to urge and vote for all reasonable and practical legislative measures adapted to secure the enforcement of this amendment. Those who oppose the passage of practical measures to enforce the amendment, which itself declares the law and gives to Congress the power and duty to enforce it, promote the non-enforcement of this law and the consequent demoralization of all law. Such a course is unpatriotic, and is not playing the game of self-government fairly."

And with this declaration from William Howard Taft, son of Yale University, formerly President of the United States [1909–1913] and now its Chief Justice, I bid you take up your high and solemn task. For that, you are welcome to the capital of your country.

Prohibition Is Not the Solution to Alcohol Abuse

J.A. Homan

Not all Christians believed that Prohibition was the answer to alcohol abuse. In fact, even clergymen wrote sermons and pamphlets decrying Prohibition as an evil in itself. The Reverend J.A. Homan wrote, mass produced, and distributed the following pamphlet in 1910 as an indictment of the Prohibition laws in effect at a time when the nation was moving toward a constitutional amendment banning all production and consumption of alcohol in every state. Homan maintains this tactic would cause more crime and illegal activity than it prevented. The way to control alcohol abuse, he says, is to enact and enforce strong laws controlling the legal sale of alcohol.

In seeking for the best solution of the drink problem, the experience of European countries should be carefully noted, for they have the failures and successes of many centuries behind them. Their unanimous voice favors a strict license law and not prohibition. Prohibition is not much more than a half century old, purely an American product, and it is already acknowledged a failure save by its adherents, whose prejudices have blinded them to the truth. There is but one question in the controversy, and it is: "Which restricts the evils of intemperance more, prohibition or license?" The answer is easily found. . . . Testimony past and present; stubborn facts, gathered by men without bias in the interest of psychological and sociological science; official statistics that defy contradiction; the very admissions of prohibitionists, reluctantly made, all go to prove that prohibition is not an effective method of dealing with and restricting the evils of alcoholic abuse.

J.A. Homan, "A National License Law," in *Prohibition: The Enemy of Temperance.* Cincinnati, OH: Christian Liberty Bureau, 1910, pp. 111–114.

Prohibition Is Doomed to Fail

The Subcommittee of the Committee of Fifty [a group of scholars assembled to study alcohol abuse] composed of Chas. W. Eliot, President Emeritus of Harvard University, Seth Low and James C. Carter, who had this subject under investigation in several States, reached the following conclusion: "Prohibitory legislation has failed to exclude intoxicants completely even from districts where public sentiment has been favorable. In districts, where public sentiment has been adverse or strongly divided, the traffic in alcoholic beverages has been sometimes repressed or harassed, but never exterminated, or rendered unprofitable. *In Maine and Iowa (during the prohibition period) there have always been counties and municipalities in complete and successful rebellion against the law.* Prohibition has, of course, failed to subdue the drinking passion, which will forever prompt resistance to all restrictive legislation."

But listen to what this report has to say about the concomitant evils of prohibitory legislation: "The efforts to enforce it during forty years past have had some unlooked-for effects on public respect for courts, judicial procedure, oaths and law in general, and for officers of the law, legislators and public servants. The public have seen law defied, a whole generation of habitual law-breakers schooled in evasion and shamelessness, courts ineffective through fluctuations of policy, delays, perjuries, negligences and other miscarriages of justice, officers of the law double-faced and mercenary, legislators timid and insincere, candidates for office hypocritical and truckling, and office-holders unfaithful to pledges and to reasonable public expectation." And with this flood of public misdemeanors and corruption, there was nothing to show that the evils of intoxicating drink had been abated, as is clear from the conclusions of the Committee: "Whether it has or has not reduced the consumption of intoxicants and diminished drunkenness is a matter of opinion, and opinions differ widely. No demonstration on either of these points has been reached, or is now attainable, after more than forty years of observation and experience."

Perhaps the day is not far distant when the subject of the restriction and regulation of the liquor traffic, or its prohibition, will come up for consideration before the American people in the draft of a national law. It will then be of the utmost importance to steer clear of extremists, and keep only the common welfare in view. A national license law would undoubtedly give uniformity to a system of control, and take the problem out of State politics, where it has so long been a bone of contention between the two great parties, to the detriment of the temperance cause.

Prohibition Creates Its Own Evils

If [only] the money spent for the past thirty years and more by the prohibition and saloon factions in tossing between them the short-lived adjustments of the liquor problem had been converted into a gospel temperance fund. . . . How absolutely ridiculous to spend millions of money in political contests that in the end will make more drunkards, blight more lives and ruin more homes! It is a fact that nothing has done so much for the propagation of intemperance as intemperate legislation, and no legislation is quite so intemperate as prohibition.

In an interview published in the *New York Freeman's Journal* a few months ago, [the archbishop of Baltimore] Cardinal [James] Gibbons says that prohibition is an excess as much as intemperance. "Liquor," he reasons earnestly, "would be sold just as much under prohibition laws as under well-regulated license. The consequence is that liquor would be sold contrary to law, instead of in accord with the law. When a law is flagrantly violated it brings legislation into contempt. It creates a spirit of hypocrisy and deception; it induces men to do insidiously and by stealth what they would otherwise do openly and above board. Yet all good men, all good citizens, are in favor of temperance. But you can not, by legislation or by civil action, compel any man to the performance of good and righteous deeds. High license, I think, is the only solution of the liquor problem. The infliction of fines upon the violators of the law for the first offense, and the withdrawal of the license or even imprisonment for the subsequent infractions, would be proper punishment."

It might be desirable to make the human race one vast total abstinence society if it were possible to eradicate the almost universal taste of man for alcohol, but such a result could only be accomplished by education, and not by legislation. From the Christian standpoint it could not be done without the assistance of divine grace to each individual. But even then total abstinence would necessarily be a voluntary self-imposed restraint, and not a duty or obligation, such as temperance is essentially always. It will not be questioned, however, that an efficient self-control and such qualities as make up strong character and for the attainment of the highest ideals, are best acquired without the shackles of prohibitory laws. Some physiologists, who are directly concerned only with the hygienic phase of the problem, call attention to the importance of this fact. Thus Dr. John J. Abel, of Johns Hopkins University, concludes his review of the pharmacological action of alcohol by saying: "It is a question well worth considering, whether the continued presence of alcoholics in the world is not more conducive, in the long run, to the evolution of an efficient self-control, than would be their total abolition."

The object of all laws in the end must be to accomplish the greatest amount of good for the greatest number, and no law can accomplish this that does not take into account the social needs of man and the rights of human liberty.

Drugs Can Enhance
Religious Experience

Huston Smith

Humans have long ingested or smoked sacred plants to deepen the meaning of religious ceremonies and rituals. In the following article, Huston Smith, writer and then comparative religion scholar at Massachusetts Institute of Technology, defends the practice as a legitimate avenue to inducing or enhancing religious experience. The article appeared in the early 1960s when America's illegal drug culture was finding a stronghold, especially on college campuses, and so many of Smith's theological contemporaries quickly rejected such drug use and the resulting experiences as inauthentic. Smith maintains, however, that such experiences and visions can be deeply enlightening. He concludes here that though religious experiences must not be separated from the practice of a recognized religion, a devout person intent on using drugs to deepen his or her religious faith can and should do so.

Until six months ago, if I picked up my phone in the Cambridge [Massachusetts] area and dialed KISS-BIG, a voice would answer, "If-if." These were coincidences: KISS-BIG happened to be the letter equivalents of an arbitrarily assigned telephone number, and I.F.I.F. represented the initials of an organization with the improbable name of the International Federation for Internal Freedom. But the coincidences were apposite to the point of being poetic. "Kiss big" caught the euphoric, manic, life-embracing attitude that characterized this most publicized of the organizations formed to explore the newly synthesized consciousness-changing substances; the organization itself was surely one of the "iffy-est" phenomena to appear on our social and intellectual scene in some time. It

Huston Smith, "Do Drugs Have Religious Import?" *The Journal of Philosophy*, vol. LXI, September 3, 1964, pp. 517–24, 528–30. Copyright © 1964 by The Journal of Philosophy, Inc. Reproduced by permission of the publisher and the author.

produced the first firings in Harvard's history, an ultimatum to get out of Mexico in five days, and "the miracle of Marsh Chapel," in which, during a two-and-one-half-hour Good Friday service, ten theological students and professors ingested psilocybin [a hallucinogen] and were visited by what they generally reported to be the deepest religious experiences of their lives.

Despite the last of these phenomena and its numerous if less dramatic parallels, students of religion appear by and large to be dismissing the psychedelic drugs that have sprung to our attention in the '60s as having little religious relevance. The position taken in one of the most forward-looking volumes of theological essays to have appeared in recent years— *Soundings*, edited by A. R. Vidler—accepts [professor of theology at Oxford] R. C. Zaehner's *Mysticism Sacred and Profane* as having "fully examined and refuted" the religious claims for mescalin [cactus-derived hallucinogen] which Aldous Huxley sketched in *The Doors of Perception*. This closing of the case strikes me as premature, for it looks as if the drugs have light to throw on the history of religion, the phenomenology of religion, the philosophy of religion, and the practice of the religious life itself.

Use of Drugs for Religious Purposes Has a Long History

In his trial-and-error life explorations man almost everywhere has stumbled upon connections between vegetables (eaten or brewed) and actions (yogi breathing exercises, whirling-dervish dances, flagellations) that alter states of consciousness. From the psychopharmacological standpoint we now understand these states to be the products of changes in brain chemistry. From the sociological perspective we see that they tend to be connected in some way with religion. If we discount the wine used in Christian communion services, the instances closest to us in time and space are the peyote of The Native American

[Indian] Church and Mexico's 2000-year-old "sacred mush-rooms," the latter rendered in Aztec as "God's Flesh"—striking parallel to "the body of our Lord" in the Christian eucharist. Beyond these neighboring instances lie the *soma* [intoxicating juice of a plant] of the Hindus, the *haoma* and hemp of the Zoroastrians, the Dionysus of the Greeks who "everywhere . . . taught men the culture of the vine and the mysteries of his worship and everywhere [was] accepted as a god," the *benzoin* [medicinal resin] of Southeast Asia, Zen's tea whose fifth cup purifies and whose sixth "calls to the realm of the immortals," the *pituri* [nicotine-based drug] of the Australian aborigines, and probably the mystic *kykeon* that was eaten and drunk at the climactic close of the sixth day of the Eleusinian myster-ies. There is no need to extend the list, as a reasonably com-plete account is available in [French theologian] Philippe de Félice's comprehensive study of the subject, *Poisons sacrés, ivresses divines* [Sacred Poisons Divine Raptures].

More interesting than the fact that consciousness-changing devices have been linked with religion is the possibility that they actually initiated many of the religious perspectives which, taking root in history, continued after their psychedelic origins were forgotten. [French philosopher, Henri-Louis] Bergson saw the first movement of Hindus and Greeks toward "dynamic religion" as associated with the "divine rapture" found in intoxicating beverages; more recently Robert Graves [British author], Gordon Wasson [amateur American bota-nist], and Alan Watts [British expert in comparative religion] have suggested that most religions arose from such chemically induced theophanies. Mary Barnard [professor of religion of the University of Michigan] is the most explicit proponent of this thesis. "Which . . . was more likely to happen first," she asks, "the spontaneously generated idea of an afterlife in which the disembodied soul, liberated from the restrictions of time and space, experiences eternal bliss, or the accidental discovery of hallucinogenic plants that give a sense of euphoria, dislocate the center of consciousness, and distort time and space, making them balloon outward in greatly expanded vistas?" Her own answer is that "the [latter] experience might have had . . . an almost explosive effect on the largely dormant minds of men, causing them to think of things they had never thought of before. This, if you like, is direct revelation." . . .

Phenomenology attempts a careful description of human experience. The question the drugs pose for the phenomenology of religion, therefore, is whether the experiences they induce differ from religious experiences reached naturally, and if so how.

Even the Bible notes that chemically induced psychic states bear *some* resemblance to religious ones. Peter had to appeal to a circumstantial criterion—the early hour of the day—to defend those who were caught up in the Pentecostal experience against the charge that they were merely drunk: "These men are not drunk, as you suppose, since it is only the third hour of the day" (Acts 2:15); and Paul initiates the comparison when he admonishes the Ephesians not to "get drunk with wine . . . but [to] be filled with the spirit" (Ephesians 5:18). Are such comparisons, paralleled in the accounts of virtually every religion, superficial? How far can they be pushed?

Not all the way, students of religion have thus far insisted. With respect to the new drugs, Prof. R. C. Zaehner has drawn the line emphatically. "The importance of Huxley's *Door of Perception*," he writes, "is that in it the author clearly makes the claim that what he experienced under the influence of mescalin is closely comparable to a genuine mystical experience. If he is right, . . . the conclusions . . . are alarming." Zaehner thinks that Huxley is not right, but I fear that it is Zaehner who is mistaken.

There are, of course, innumerable drug experiences that have no religious feature; they can be sensual as readily as spiritual, trivial as readily as transforming, capricious as readily as sacramental. If there is one point about which every student of the drugs agrees, it is that there is no such thing as the drug experience *per se*—no experience that the drugs, as it were, merely secrete. Every experience is a mix of three ingredients: drug, sex (the psychological make-up of the individual), and setting (the social and physical environment in which it is taken). But given the right set and setting, the drugs can induce religious experiences indistinguishable from experiences that occur spontaneously. Nor need set and setting be exceptional. The way the statistics are currently running, it looks as if from one-fourth to one-third of the general population will have religious experiences if they take the drugs under naturalistic conditions, meaning by this conditions in which the researcher supports the subject but does not try to influence the direction his experience will take. Among subjects who have strong religious inclinations to begin with, the proportion of those having religious experiences jumps to three-fourths. If they take the drugs in settings that are religious too, the ratio soars to nine in ten.

How do we know that the experiences these people have really are religious? We can begin with the fact that they say they are. The "one-fourth to one-third of the general population" figure is drawn from two sources. Ten months after they had had their experiences, 24 per cent of the 194 subjects in a study by the California psychiatrist Oscar Janiger characterized their experiences as having been religious. Thirty-two per cent of the 74 subjects in [the] ... study reported, looking back on their LSD experience, that it looked as if it had been "very much" or "quite a bit" a religious experience; 42 per cent checked as true the statement that they "were left with a greater awareness of God, or a higher power, or ultimate reality." The statement that three-fourths of subjects having religious "sets" will have religious experiences comes from the reports of sixty-nine religious professionals who took the drugs while the Harvard project was in progress.

In the absence of (a) a single definition of religious experience acceptable to psychologists of religion generally and (b) fool-proof ways of ascertaining whether actual experiences exemplify any definition, I am not sure there is any better way of telling whether the experiences of the 333 men and women involved in the above studies were religious than by noting whether they seemed so to them. But if more rigorous methods are preferred, they exist; they have been utilized, and they confirm the conviction of the man in the street that drug experiences can indeed be religious. In his doctoral study at Harvard University, Walter Pahnke worked out a typology of religious experience (in this instance of the mystical variety) based on the classic cases of mystical experiences as summarized in Walter Stace's *Mysticism and Philosophy*. He then administered psilocybin to ten theology students and professors in the setting of a Good Friday service. The drug was given "double-blind," meaning that neither Dr. Pahnke nor his subjects knew which ten were getting psilocybin and which ten placebos to constitute a control group. Subsequently the reports the subjects wrote of their experiences were laid successively before three college-graduate housewives who, without being informed about the nature of the study, were asked to rate each statement as to the degree (strong, moderate, slight, or none) to which it exemplified each of the nine traits of mystical experience enumerated in the typology of mysticism worked out in advance. When the test of significance was applied to their statistics, it showed that "those subjects who received psilocybin experienced phenomena which were indistinguishable from, if not identical with . . . the categories defined by our typology of mysticism."

Many Have Been Skeptical of Drugs' Religious Usefulness

With the thought that the reader might like to test his own powers of discernment on the question being considered, I insert here a simple test I gave to a group of Princeton students following a recent discussion sponsored by the Woodrow Wilson Society:

> Below are accounts of two religious experiences. One occurred under the influence of drugs, one without their influence. Check the one you think was drug-induced.
>
> I
>
> Suddenly I burst into a vast, new, indescribably wonderful universe. Although I am writing this over a year later, the thrill of the surprise and amazement, the awesomeness of the revelation, the engulfment in an overwhelming feeling-wave of gratitude and blessed wonderment, are as fresh, and the memory of the experience is as vivid, as if it had happened five minutes ago. And yet to concoct anything by way of description that would even hint at the magnitude, the sense of ultimate reality ... this seems such an impossible task. The knowledge which has infused and affected every aspect of my life came instantaneously and with such complete force of certainty that it was impossible, then or since, to doubt its validity.
>
> II
>
> All at once, without warning of any kind, I found myself wrapped in a flame-colored cloud. For an instant I thought of fire ... the next, I knew that the fire was within myself. Directly afterward there came upon me a sense of exultation, of immense joyousness accompanied or immediately followed by an intellectual illumination impossible to describe. Among other things. I did not merely come to believe, but I saw that the universe is not composed of dead matter, but is, on the contrary, a living Presence; I became conscious in myself of eternal life. ... I saw that all men are immortal: that the cosmic order is such that without any preadventure all things work together for the good of each and all; that the foundation principle of the world ... is what we call love, and that the happiness of each and all is in the long run absolutely certain.

On the occasion referred to, twice as many students (46) answered incorrectly as answered correctly (23). . . . [The first account occurred under the influence of drugs.]

Why, in the face of this considerable evidence, does Zaehner hold that drug experiences cannot be authentically religious? There appear to be three reasons:

1. His own experience was "utterly trivial." This of course proves that not all drug experiences are religious; it does not prove that no drug experiences are religious.

2. He thinks the experiences of others that appear religious to them are not truly so. Zaehner distinguishes three kinds of mysticism: nature mysticism, in which the soul is united with the natural world; monistic mysticism, in which the soul merges with an impersonal absolute; and theism, in which the soul confronts the living, personal God. He concedes that drugs can induce the first two species of mysticism, but not its supreme instance, the theistic. As proof, he analyzes Huxley's experience as recounted in *The Doors of Perception* to show that it produced at best a blend of nature and monistic mysticism. Even if we were to accept Zaehner's evaluation of the three forms of mysticism, Huxley's case, and indeed Zaehner's entire book, would prove only that not every mystical experience induced by the drugs is theistic. Insofar as Zaehner goes beyond this to imply that drugs do not and cannot induce theistic mysticism, he not only goes beyond the evidence but proceeds in the face of it. [Anthropologist] James Slotkin reports that the peyote Indians "see visions, which may be of Christ Himself. Sometimes they hear the voice of the Great Spirit. Sometimes they become aware of the presence of God and of those personal shortcomings which must be corrected if they are to do His will." . . .

3. There is a third reason why Zaehner might doubt that drugs can induce genuinely mystical experiences. Zaehner is a Roman Catholic, and Roman Catholic doctrine teaches that mystical rapture is a gift of grace and as such can never be re-

duced to man's control. This may be true; certainly the empirical evidence cited does not preclude the possibility of a genuine ontological [concerning the nature of being] or theological difference between natural and drug-induced religious experiences. At this point, however, we are considering phenomenology rather than ontology, description rather than interpretation, and on this level there is no difference. Descriptively, drug experiences cannot be distinguished from their natural religious counterpart. When the current philosophical authority on mysticism, W. T. Stace, was asked whether the drug experience is similar to the mystical experience, he answered, "It's not a matter of its being *similar* to mystical experience; it *is* mystical experience."

What we seem to be witnessing in Zaehner's *Mysticism Sacred and Profane* is a reenactment of the age-old pattern in the conflict between science and religion. Whenever a new controversy arises, religion's first impulse is to deny the disturbing evidence science has produced. Seen in perspective, Zaehner's refusal to admit that drugs can induce experiences descriptively indistinguishable from those which are spontaneously religious is the current counterpart of the seventeenth-century theologians' refusal to look through [astronomer and physicist] Galileo's telescope or, when they did, their persistence on dismissing what they saw as machinations of the devil. When the fact that drugs can trigger religious experiences becomes incontrovertible, discussion will move to the more difficult question of how this new fact is to be interpreted. . . .

Drugs Induce Religious Experience, Not Religious Belief

Suppose that drugs can induce experiences indistinguishable from religious experiences and that we can respect their reports. Do they shed any light, not (we now ask) on life, but on the nature of the religious life?

One thing they may do is throw religious experience itself into perspective by clarifying its relation to the religious life as a whole. Drugs appear able to induce religious experiences; it is less evident that they can produce religious lives. It follows that religion is more than religious experiences. This is hardly news, but it may be a useful reminder, especially to those who incline toward "the religion of religious experience"; which is to say toward lives bent on the acquisition of desired states of experience irrespective of their relation to life's other demands and components.

Despite the dangers of faculty psychology, it remains useful to regard man as having a mind, a will, and feelings. One of the lessons of religious history is that, to be adequate, a faith must rouse and involve all three components of man's nature. Religions of reason grow arid; religions of duty, leaden. Religions of experience have their comparable pitfalls, as evidenced by Taoism's struggle (not always successful) to keep from degenerating into quietism, and the vehemence with which Zen Buddhism has insisted that once students have attained *satori* [a state of intuitive illumination], they must be driven out of it, back into the world. The case of Zen is especially pertinent here, for it pivots on an enlightenment *experience—satori*, or *kensho*—which some (but not all) Zennists say resembles LSD. Alike or different, the point is that Zen recognizes that unless the experience is joined to discipline, it will come to naught:

> Even the Buddha . . . had to sit . . . Without *joriki*, the particular power developed through *zazen* [seated meditation], the vision of oneness attained in enlightenment . . . in time becomes clouded and eventually fades into a pleasant memory instead of remaining an omnipresent reality shaping our daily life. . . . To be able to live in accordance with what the Mind's eye has revealed through *satori* requires, like the purification of character and the development of personality, a ripening period of *zazen*.

If the religion of religious experience is a snare and a delusion, it follows that no religion that fixes its faith primarily in substances that induce religious experiences can be expected to come to a good end. What promised to be a short cut will prove to be a short circuit; what began as a religion will end as a religion surrogate. Whether chemical substances can be helpful *adjuncts* to faith is another question. The peyote-using Native American Church seems to indicate that they can be; anthropologists give this church a good report, noting among other things that members resist alcohol and alcoholism better than do nonmembers. The conclusion to which evidence currently points would seem to be that chemicals *can* aid the religious life, but only where set within a context of faith (meaning by this the conviction that what they disclose is true) and discipline (meaning diligent exercise of the will in the attempt to work out the implications of the disclosures for the living of life in the everyday, common-sense world).

Nowhere today in Western civilization are these two conditions jointly fulfilled. Churches lack faith in the sense just mentioned; hipsters lack discipline. This might lead us to forget about the drugs, were it not for one fact: the distinctive religious emotion and the emotion that drugs unquestionably can occasion . . . the phenomenon of religious awe—seems to be declining sharply. As Paul Tillich said in an address to the Hillel Society at Harvard several years ago:

> The question our century puts before us [is]: Is it possible to regain the lost dimension, the encounter with the Holy, the dimension which cuts through the world of subjectivity and objectivity and goes down to that which is not world but is the mystery of the Ground of Being?

Tillich may be right; this may be the religions question of our century. For if (as we have insisted) religion cannot be equated with religious experiences, neither can it long survive their absence.

THE
HISTORY
OF
ISSUES

CHAPTER 2

I The War on Drugs

Chapter Preface

In many countries, illegal drugs rank high on the list of threats to public health and security. The United States has approached this threat as it would any other enemy of the public good—by waging war against it. Though U.S. leaders have agreed that America needed to fight drug abuse, they have disagreed over battle strategy.

America's War on Drugs officially began in 1971 when President Richard Nixon, who believed a tough stance against drugs was the only way to control them, created a new governmental position called drug czar. He appointed Dr. Jerome Jaffe to the post and charged him with the task of addressing what he feared could be an explosion of drug abuse as thousands of Vietnam War veterans returned home with heroin addictions. As drug czar, Jaffe oversaw the Special Action Office for Drug Abuse Prevention. In 1973, the Nixon administration created the Drug Enforcement Agency (DEA). Throughout Nixon's tenure in the White House, he continued to advocate for strict federal regulation of all drugs, even the easily obtainable and commonly used marijuana. He maintained his vigilance against marijuana even after a commission he organized to examine the dangers of the drug found it presented relatively little threat to users and to the nation as a whole.

As the war raged on, those waging it had to reassess the real nature of the enemy and how best to fight it. For example, during the Gerald Ford and Jimmy Carter administrations in the mid to late 1970s, the battle shifted away from so-called soft drugs such as marijuana and toward more dangerous ones such as cocaine and heroin. President Carter even recommended that federal penalties for marijuana possession be lifted.

By the 1980s, however, drug use had reached such high levels—especially that of crack cocaine—that the government felt the time for leniency had passed. President Ronald Reagan and his wife Nancy began a highly publicized campaign called Just Say No, which targeted young people with the message that they could halt America's drug problems by refusing to use them. Reagan also created the Anti-Drug Abuse Act of 1986, a bill that put in place tough penalties and mandatory minimum sentences for the sale of even small amounts of cocaine. As a result, ever-increasing numbers of poor African Americans, who were more likely to sell cocaine in small quantities than other ethnic groups, flooded the prison system. In 1988, Reagan created the Office of National Drug Control Policy (ONDCP) to set the National Drug Control Strategy (NDCS).

ONDCP would continue to play a crucial role in the George H.W. Bush administration. In fact, its leader William Bennett, the man Bush appointed as drug czar, took an aggressive approach to dealing with drug abuse. Highly critical of what he considered the overly lenient policies of previous administrations, Bennett painted the drug problem with a moral brush. Under his leadership, the government stigmatized drug use. He also ordered costly military strikes against smuggling operations in other countries. Critics accused Bennett of spending a disproportionate amount of money on such "supply reduction" instead of funding drug abuse prevention and treatment initiatives.

Since Bennett's tenure, the ONDCP now headed by John Walters has continued to struggle to find the best approach to controlling drugs. However, as University of Nevada at Reno professor Gary L. Fisher says in his book *Rethinking Our War on Drugs*, the approach has changed insignificantly despite promises and power shifts in Congress and the White House. Both parties, he says, have followed "similar paths" and neither has gained any ground in the war.

Commission's Report Should Take a Hard Stance Against Marijuana

Richard Nixon and Raymond P. Shafer

In the following transcripts of a 1971 conversation with Raymond P. Shafer, the man he had appointed to head his National Commission on Marihuana and Drug Abuse, President Richard Nixon relays his concerns about marijuana use in the United States. He encourages Shafer to ensure that the commission's report would spell out what he perceived to be the serious threat marijuana posed to the nation's effort to control drug abuse. Throughout the conversation, Nixon expresses great concern that the commission will not take a hard enough position and that the resulting report will sound lenient and permissive concerning marijuana use.

Richard Nixon: "When will the marijuana one [report from the National Commission on Marihuana and Drug-Abuse] come out?"

Raymond P. Schafer: "The marijuana [report] will come out in March '72. In other words we are coming into the final phases of it now, we've had all of our public hearings. We have not, we have nine more informal hearings."

Nixon: "You've had all your public hearings already?"

Shafer: "All of the public hearings, yes, and, uh, we've . . . had several informal hearings, we have nine more of those. . ."

Nixon: "Hard to find anybody who isn't on the stuff?"

Shafer: "Uh, no. [unintelligible] Over 75 percent of the [unintelligible] are white, and, uh, and under 18, almost 85 percent, which I [unintelligible]."

Richard Nixon and Raymond P. Shafer, "Oval Office Conversation 568–4," September 9, 1971. www.csdp.org/research/nixonpot.txt.

Nixon: "It's now becoming a white problem."

Shafer: "It's almost, it's a real tragedy. Well look, the thing, the thing is, we're, we've been a very low profile commission as you know from the very beginning. We didn't go through the whole folderol and, uh—"

Nixon: "How long have you been operating, uh, I don't know."

Shafer: "Well, you appointed us, the last day of January [1971]. We organized on February the Fifth, but we didn't get any money until the end of March."

Nixon: "So you didn't start till then."

Shafer: "No, we, uh, were in operation April, April, because, uh—"

Nixon: "And so your hearings began."

Shafer: "Right. You very carefully, uh, gave us some money in advance before Congress acted to give us any money, you gave us some money out of your contingency fund. And uh, when we got our, uh, uh, money, then, uh, we were able to move in high gear. I want to thank you very much for the fact that all the money that we've requested has been approved. I've been working closely with [Secretary of Labor] George Schultz and, uh, and Congress has approved what we asked for which is, uh, really uh, extraordinary. But we've uh, we've got a tiny morale problem as uh, you may or may not know, and that's one of the reasons why I wanted to see you, get what we're doing into proper perspective so that, uh we won't have to go through this again. We had a [unintelligible] that, you know, that Congress would, some of your enemies in Congress would like to use this as a, a [unintelligible] and we're not going to let that happen if we can possibly avoid it."

Egil "Bud" Krogh: "How would they use that as, as a [unintelligible]."

Shafer: "Well, when the Commission was first formed you know, there's criticism in part of the press about the fact that we're old and conservative and that we were put together by a

President to merely tow the party line and the attitudes of uh, [unintelligible]. Then secondly, Mike Sonnenreich, who's our executive director [of the Presidential Commission on Marijuana] and doing a very excellent job came from . . . the Department of Justice and those people from the scientific community thought that, uh, they should, uh—" . . .

Nixon: "The thing about, let me say that the thing I'm, I really feel concerned about is this, that uh, Ray, is, that I know you were a former prosecutor, uh. The difficulty with the whole commissions, you set them up, is that, uh, you're going to [suffer?] them, you know, we've had so many discredited committees, [unintelligible] screwing off in every different direction, so forth. I'm sure you understand. This is an area of course where we, we don't, I mean there's an awful lot of stuff [drug czar under Nixon] Dr. [Jerome "Jerry"] Jaffe's the first to admit and he's a real expert in his field, that we don't know all the answers. However, I have a strong firm conviction which I have expressed and which I won't change, about the, about the, the, the situation [unintelligible] about marijuana, in, in two areas. One, about its legalne-, about legalizing which some would do. Second however, now on the other hand, my, my attitude toward penalties on marijuana, is uh, very powerful. I talked with District Attorney on [unintelligible] and all the rest, and to take somebody that's smoked some of this stuff, put him into a jail with a bunch of hardened criminals, is [silly?], that's absurd."

Shafer: "Absolutely yes."

Nixon: "There must be different ways than jail. I think that's your experience, is it not? Have you talked to, uh, what's his name up there, uh—"

"[Then district attorney of Philadelphia and current Pennsylvania senator] Arlen Specter." . . .

Nixon: "Specter's got a remarkable crime program, where, where, where basically they don't even get records."

Jerome Jaffe: "Uh, we've been working on it, we've been working on it."

Nixon: "Almost like probation, give them probation before uh, before indictment."

Jaffe: "Uh, Illinois has just passed a similar bill."

Nixon: "They do the same thing?"

Jaffe: "In effect we sentence people to a school, for six months. They have to come every Saturday, they've been doing this. It was initiated by the uh, by the uh district attorney and that ultimately if they haven't been rearrested and if they carried out the sentence appropriately, they don't, they're not criminalized, and yet it's not legalized."

Nixon: "What you have here is a very interesting live situation, where there is a certain [unintelligible] through the country, that, heh, on the one hand want to make smoking illegal, cigarette smoking illegal and marijuana legal. Now, that's what I mean, that doesn't make any damned sense now. I mean, probably if we repeat what that didn't help its best aspects everything shouldn't do anything shouldn't need it, but uh, you know if they're going to [unintelligible]. On the marijuana thing, I have very strong feelings that that's, uh the, best final, uh, analysis, that once you start down that road, uh, the chances of going further down that road are greater. I'm aware some disagree with that, but uh, the uh, and also we have some people that are, frankly promoting it. They're not good people. The whole marijuana, uh—"

Shafer: "I understand that, let, let me answer, not answer, at least discuss with you the points that you've raised because this is crucial to what we're attempting to do."

Nixon: "Mm-hmm."

Shafer: "National commissions have not been in very excellent repute, but we—" . . .

Shafer: "And, uh, when you asked me to take this job I hesitated in fact, did not, uh, see I could see clouds of what happened with the [Pennsylvania governor William] Scranton, uh, Scranton Commission [a Nixon-appointed independent panel that declared the 1970 National Guard shootings of student antiwar protesters at Kent State unnecessary and inexcusable, which was a blow to the Nixon administration], I thought that was a disgrace. I told [U.S. attorney general], John Mitchell that and I think he passed it on to you. I thought that the things that arose before—" . . .

The Report Must Not Create National Controversy

Shafer: "And, uh, and third, I said that if I would take it of course I had to have your support but that we were going to play it low . . . profile, we were not going to have a great lot of hoopla and we would do nothing that would in any way embarrass you or the Administration because in the long run that's going to hurt the country, if we have a Commission that just comes through with a report that, that, that creates controversy and gives fodder for the newspapers to, to, to create a lot of conflict, that, they're not [unintelligible]. So we've been very careful on that. And secondly, I think that I am able to say without qualification that you have a commission here that you yourself have appointed, that they are very intelligent, they are well-known in their own fields and in their own communities and they're not going to do anything such as happened in previous Commission reports."

Nixon: "Good."

Shafer: "And insofar as legalization, I think the thing that has caused us the greatest problem was your statement in San Clemente [California]—which is a part of your strong convictions, naturally you expressed them as you felt them. But you used the word legalization, and, the way I answered it was, 'Look, we're a national commission, we're going to take a look at the whole picture, we know that the president is interested in what we're doing, is concerned about the problem, and, uh, we've never had a chance to discuss what he means by legalization. If he means, uh, removing all controls, or if [unintelligible] simple possession, these are things that can be worked out at a later date. We're going ahead and make our studies, and I know that he is wholeheartedly behind us because of everything that he has done. That does not mean that he's going to agree with everything which we say, but, that he knows that these are men of, uh, integrity, men and women of integrity who wanted to do something for their country.'"

Nixon: "Mm-hmm, mm-hmm."

Shafer: "Now, what, what happened on this when this statement was made, several members of the commission called up and said, well we may as well, give up. I said No, that isn't right, the President has his own, uh, convictions on this and he isn't going to tell the Commission what to say or what not to say."

Nixon: "Come out with a different view." . . .

Shafer: "Well, yes, but sure, the point is, that, I mean, say what they say, what the Commission is doing is, is, is following [unintelligible], and in fact, the, the confidential report that I had prepared to give you to Bud so that you, you've maybe even seen it—"

Nixon: "Yeah."

Shafer: "—gives clearly the direction that we're going, and I think that that should relieve your mind, uh, uh, insofar as your personal convictions or so. We don't want you to say, Well I've got a great commission, anything they say we'll follow; well of course not, that's ridiculous."

Nixon: "No, no. [unintelligible], to look at it."

Shafer: "Now on the hand we are a national commission, certain, with the, really the first commission going in to this particular problem of long-range action on the whole field of drug abuse that the United States has ever had. We're, we're, we're conducting a national survey that's never been done before."

Nixon: "Mm, hmm."

Shafer: "With clear, you know, [unintelligible] going to get tough. But at the present time, we have about a million nine [hundred dollars], we're going to need, uh, seven, we don't know how much but we have uh, but the point was that we were initially authorized one million but Congress was so interested in it that they upped the authorization to four, but we're going to get five, and the total amount is what about 3.7?" . . .

Nixon: "Will you take polls and do a lot of—"

Shafer: "We're going to have a survey put out by one of the fine outfits out of Princeton, uh, not Gallup, but Research Associates, they're a very good, uh, outfit. And they're willing to do this uh, uh problem of marijuana attitudes, then we're going into the whole field of what is the extent of marijuana. We have all kinds of figures, anywhere from 8 million up to 40 million." . . .

Shafer: "What we're trying to do, we don't [unintelligible], we don't believe, that, that uh, that there should be, uh, given to the people the combination of the use of a dangerous substance—"

Nixon: "With respectability [unintelligible, both Nixon and Shafer speaking at same time]."

Shafer: "We don't want to give it respectability, and we will not be—"

Nixon: "Like uh, almost, almost anything in the drug field, it's making it respectable, just make sure you don't. That's fine, if they, I, there's some person, he can try anything, maybe even heroin, and get away with it."

Shafer: "Well sure."

Nixon: "It won't work with kids."

Shafer: "One of our, one of our doctors on our, uh, on our Commission is uh, is one of the finest pharmacologists in the nation, Dr. [Maurice] Seevers of Michigan. Jerry knows him very well, he has his own [unintelligible], he talks about heroin, he says you can smoke a little, er, take a little heroin and, uh, and get away with it. It's the idea that it becomes a [unintelligible]. What we want to do is to be sure that we don't give approval, the approval of society. We're interested in—"

Nixon: "Right."

Shafer: "—public health."

Nixon: "Very important, very important."

Shafer: "I can't say that publicly—"

Nixon: "Not just, not just physical health."

Shafer: "And, and we're not, we're not just interested in the, uh, pure pharmacological effects of these drugs. We're looking at the whole social picture."

Nixon: "Good."

Shafer: "We want to de-mythologize marijuana so that the kids aren't going out experimenting with it because they think it's great stuff. And uh, [unintelligible Shafer and others talking at once]. I think, I think that we've gone into this thing as, uh deeply as, as uh, any commission could. [unintelligible], I'm, I'm having a great time learning, and, uh, we, we have individuals, but what we need from you is your, uh, public support, as a commission, not from the standpoint that you're going to accept what we say but that here is a commission that is working on a problem that cuts across the cross-section of every, uh, family in, in the nation, next, next to your economy, and incidentally I think that what you've done in that regard is excellent." . . .

Shafer: "Next to the economy, and also the winding down of the [Vietnam] war which I don't think will be a particular issue next year and I think you agree with me there. I think the problems of drug abuse will be a political issue. And, while our report isn't going to give you a platform, it's going to be the thing that will, uh, bring us the kind of victory you want, but it can be a source of possible embarrassment and that's why I don't want to have, give any ammunition to the, those who would like to use it against you."

Krogh: "So far you're staying away from any possible endorsement of legalization of marijuana."

Shafer: "Absolutely, absolutely."

Nixon: "I would keep in mind that, you [unintelligible], you would run too strongly against the public tide, but suppose it ought to be done."

Shafer: "Well, I understand that."

Nixon: "You're just, you have a, a great problem."

Shafer: "We have, we have, uh, four Congressmen on the Commission, uh, two Republicans, two Democrats, and, at least one of the, the opposition would like to, uh, to uh, take over. We've prevented that. Uh, and uh, I think that we've got the Commission moving in the right direction. We, we're, we're, we're seeking unanimity, I think we're going to have that, and we're staying away from that, that, that quote legalization endquote syndrome that could create, uh, very—"

Nixon: "You see, the thing that is so terribly important here is that it not appear that the Commission's frankly just a bunch of do-gooders, I mean, they say well they're a bunch of old men who don't understand, that's fine, I wouldn't mind that, but, but if they get the idea you're just a bunch of do-gooders that are going to come out with a quote soft on marijuana report, that'll destroy it, right off the bat. I think there's a need to come out with a report that is totally, uh, uh, oblivious to some obvious, uh, differences between marijuana and other drugs, other dangerous drugs, there are differences. And also that you don't go into the matter of, uh, penalties and that sort of thing, as to whether there should be uniformity in penalties, whether in courts, I'd much rather have uniformity than diversity, but uh, different approaches. I'd say look, everywhere, hell, in Texas they put them in jail for six years."

Shafer: "Well, longer than that, you can get 99 years up in North Dakota." . . .

Shafer: "Well the Act, the Act of 1970, the, the drug abuse act of, er narcotics control act of 1970 is the best thing that has hit the country, best, this is the best thing that has hit the country in the narcotics field. And it is, and, the Commission is wholeheartedly behind that, I, I give you that assurance. We're going to, we're going to [unintelligible] the shots at marijuana, scientific shots, and after all, three of the members of our commission, our advisors, uh, to Jerry—Dr. [Henry] Seevers, Dr. Farnsworth, and uh Dr. [Dana] Brill, they're three of the foremost medical men in the country. And so you can rest assured that we're not going to go off half-cocked, we're not a bunch of stupid, you know?"

Nixon: "Well, I know about you, you know, but I know your problem of course, Ray,—"

Shafer: "But I'm, I'm, I'm—"

Nixon: "Keep your Commission in line."

Shafer: "I'm going to keep the Commission in line and one of the things that I can do it is to raise their morale—"

Nixon: "Mm-hmm."

Shafer: "—is to, to have them assured. In fact, they asked me to come see you because they're concerned."

Nixon: "Well let me ask you, how close is your contact with Krogh and Jaffe?"

Shafer: "Well we have a, we have a very excellent—" . . .

Nixon: "—but you work with the staff."

Shafer: "I have not had a chance to meet with Jerry [Jaffe] as much as I would like to be and I think that we will be doing more things together—"

Nixon: "I think that would be a good idea, you see, we're given him a very broad, uh, uh, assignment here and uh, and uh I think, I think, he's uh, how, how do you feel, would you like to say a word about the Commission, what uh, what our attitude should be?"

Jaffe: "Well, soon as I can stop behaving like a one-armed paperhanger we're going to have more and more contact, uh—"

Nixon: "Would you say it's a bunch of do-gooders?"

Jaffe: "In this interim, gearing up, I, I probably share the, part of the responsibility for not linking up with . . . other—"

Nixon: "Let's try to do that, shall we? After all, it is a commission that's spending three and a half million dollars, it will have enormous impact when it hap- happens. And of course, the problem in this field is, uh, the acceptability among those, I mean it's a question, it doesn't make a damn bit of difference what we say about drugs, if people want them, they think it's all proper, they're going to use them, they're going to find ways to get it. And, uh, I think the most, the most important, uh, function of the Commission really is education, using, using the [unintelligible] lead the country a little about this thing, whether this is just a, uh, is, is, as you say mythology, misdirect, etc., on both sides. Some of it, some of it is that maybe marijuana is, uh, is, [unintelligible] saying those are the worst things that can happen, and others [unintelligible]."

Shafer: "Well, Mr. President. Well, I hate to make broad statements, but I think that this is going to be one of the most far-reaching reports that, uh, has come out of a national commission—"

Nixon: "How many members do you have in this Commission?"

Shafer: "We have nine provided by you and four Congressmen, that's thirteen."

Nixon: "Nine appointed, er, public members, how many are doctors?"

Shafer: "There are four doctors. Four doctors."

Nixon: "Four doctors, the other men we know as [hippies?], [unintelligible]. Well I think what we really need here, let me suggest this, first you go back to your Commission and tell them we had a talk and that, we uh, we, I believe the work of the Commission is enormously important, naturally I can't endorse in advance the Administration cannot, what its finding are, not knowing what you're going to find. But I urge the

Commission to dig and delve deeply and particularly I, I, I think that in this field more than anything else, we need lots of men on the job, and, in this field we need, above everything else, men on the job for the purpose of educating the public. I think your, uh, maybe your low profile men is fine up to this point but when your report comes out, it's going to be very high profile, it should be, and I think it would be probably helpful, probably helpful if we could have some good consultation at that time."

Shafer: "Oh there will be."

Nixon: "In other words, because if we don't have, what I think they have, Ray, is same that happened once. Well now Scranton, with it, did well, himself, but his staff ran away with the thing, you know, and it was a turbulent time. But you see, and, and he's [unintelligible], but you're enough of a pro to know that for you to come out with something that would run counter to what the Congress feels and what the country feels and what we're planning to do, would make your Commission just look bad as hell. And I think in, I think that, and on the other hand, you could probably render a great service, that doesn't mean we're going to tell you what it's going to be, but we're going into this too, see, and naturally the whole, we're looking into it from the White House, from the Jaffe group and we're going to be into it, the, naturally from the Justice Department and the HEW [Department of Health, Education, and Welfare], you know, and all the rest."

Shafer: "One thing we're stepping—"

Nixon: "Most of them are stepping on each other—"

Shafer: "—and we should know that. There are thirteen different agencies and that's—"

Nixon: "That has been, I've said that and I told Jaffe when he came in here that, we're [unintelligible], and I don't think he's been able to do much yet, but, and the Defense Department's, everybody's in it, and nobody's doing it well.

That's part of the problem. So we'll be very interested in your recommendations in that respect. But let me just say one. Don't go to HEW."

Shafer: "Oh for heaven's sakes, no—"

Nixon: "Don't go to HEW. Well we might, we might have big problems with HEW too. The difficulty that, that, well, Bureau, as an old prosecutor, and, uh, as an old prosecutor, I, I, I don't mind somebody putting in J. Edgar Hoover's [FBI director from 1922 to 1974] hands, but, the, I, I come down very [heartily] on the side of putting in, uh, hard-headed doctors, rather than a bunch of muddle-headed psychiatrists."

Shafer: "Well you've, you've hit on—"

Nixon: "They're all muddle-headed. You know what I mean?" . . .

Commission Must Take a Hard Line Against Drugs

Nixon: "Too many of them are, I mean, their, they get so that their hearts run their brains, and it should be the other way around, most of the time."

Shafer: "Our operation, our operations are going to complement each other very well because we're working on the long-range blueprint for the things that are the people of the United States on a total policy—health policy, social policy, and, and as well as, uh—"

Nixon: "I think [unintelligible], I think they have enormous respect, and I think we ought to try to play [unintelligible, participants speak at same time], and I think, and I urge, I urge strongly that the Jaffe office have the very closest contact with the Commission, maintaining of course your independence and theirs. They have to because Ray [unintelligible], but on the other hand, you could [unintelligible], and they're all trying to find the answer and maybe there aren't a hell of a lot [unintelligible]. You agree?"

Jaffe: "Yes. I think there are different emphases. They're long-term but focusing right now on, marijuana. We're responding with action to the crisis of heroin and other drugs—"

Shafer: "We, uh, we're on the, we're on the hard drugs end. Well we just came back from Belgium. We're not in marijuana so much. We came back from Amsterdam, er Holland, and Belgium, and England. And one of the things that we were looking into in England primarily was the kind of methadone [drug used to break heroin addiction] treatment that, that Jerry is interested in, because we want, we think that this is an excellent approach and we're out in the field getting first-hand knowledge—"

Krogh: "That reinforces what we're doing terrifically too."

Shafer: "No, I'd, uh, there's no reason in the world why this couldn't be, uh, worked out. Uh, in substance, just exactly what you want to, have happen, and it has to work in a [unintelligible] too, for the benefit of the general public, and this is what—"

Nixon: "Read an amusing story, [unintelligible] was telling me,—"

Shafer: "I have an amusing story too—"

Nixon: "Uh, it is uh, this is a father and son, got, got arrested [unintelligible], his father says, you [unintelligible]. [unintelligible] a couple more weeks you know he says, our, says you know I'm working my garden and everything, father says ok, father says well, uh, maybe the kid couldn't [unintelligible] that day, go out and work in the garden. He found out that the little son of a bitch was growing marijuana, had to wait for the crop to come in. It's an absolute true story. But, I, I, I believe having said all I have, I have a tremendous [unintelligible], I see these kids, and we've all, we've all, uh, grown up, and, there was smoking, there was alcohol, there's a lot of other things people do. . . ."

Nixon: "But anyway. . . . by golly, the thing to do now is to alert the country to the problem and say now, this far no farther, and I think that that's you want to do, is take a strong line."

Shafer: "I think this can be done, and I think that uh, the report that comes out will be, uh, something that we can, uh, wholeheartedly embrace. . . ."

Marijuana Is Not a Major Health Threat

Raymond P. Shafer

After months of study by experts from the fields of medicine and psychology, the National Commission on Marihuana and Drug Abuse, organized by President Richard Nixon, published a report on its findings. At the time of its publication in 1972, many people were concerned about the rise in marijuana use. Many others, however, believed that marijuana represented a relatively minor problem compared to other illegal drugs being sold and used. The following conclusion of the report reveals that the commission shared the opinion that, though its use should hardly be encouraged, marijuana played a relatively minor role in the nation's larger drug problem. Shafer maintains that the nation's overzealous legislation against marijuana should be toned down in light of the relatively minor threat it presented. Nixon quickly rejected the commission's findings.

We have carefully considered the spectrum of social and legal policy alternatives. On the basis of our findings, . . . we have concluded that society should seek to discourage use, while concentrating its attention on the prevention and treatment of heavy and very heavy use. The Commission feels that the criminalization of possession of marihuana for personal use is socially self-defeating as a means of achieving this objective. We have attempted to balance individual freedom on one hand and the obligation of the state to consider the wider social good on the other. We believe our recommended scheme will permit society to exercise its control and influence in ways most useful and efficient, meanwhile reserving to the individual American his sense of privacy, his sense of indi-

Raymond P. Shafer, "A Final Comment," in *Marijuana, a Signal of Misunderstanding: The Official Report of the National Commission on Marihuana and Drug Abuse.* 1972, pp. 210–11.

viduality, and, within the context of an interacting and inter-dependent society, his options to select his own life style, val-ues, goals and opportunities.

Marijuana Is Not a Serious Drug Problem

The Commission sincerely hopes that the tone of cautious re-straint sounded in this Report will be perpetuated in the de-bate which will follow it. For those who feel we have not pro-ceeded far enough, we are reminded of Thomas Jefferson's advice to George Washington that "Delay is preferable to er-ror." For those who argue we have gone too far, we note [American jurist] Roscoe Pound's statement, "The law must be stable, but it must not stand still."

We have carefully analyzed the interrelationship between marihuana the drug, marihuana use as a behavior, and mari-huana as a social problem. Recognizing the extensive degree of misinformation about marihuana as a drug, we have tried to *demythologize* it. Viewing the use of marihuana in its wider social context, we have tried to *desymbolize* it.

Considering the range of social concerns in contemporary America, marihuana does not, in our considered judgment, rank very high. We would *deemphasize* marihuana as a prob-lem.

The existing social and legal policy is out of proportion to the individual and social harm engendered by the use of the drug. To replace it, we have attempted to design a suitable so-cial policy, which we believe is fair, cautious and attuned to the social realities of our time.

Individuals Can Stop Drug Abuse

Ronald Reagan and Nancy Reagan

Republican president Ronald Reagan revitalized the War on Drugs policy initiated during the Richard Nixon presidency. To reveal that his administration would make fighting drugs a top priority, Reagan arranged for his wife, Nancy, to appear on national television in September of 1986 to launch her now famous, Just Say No campaign with the following address. The campaign's simple catchphrase was designed to empower individual children and their families to break the cycle of addiction by preventing their initial exposure to drugs. The Just Say No campaign was one of the more visible of the many antidrug initiatives put in place by the Reagan administration. By the end of Reagan's second term, drug use among high school students was on the decline, though there is no way to prove that this was a result of Nancy Reagan's campaign.

T*he President.* Good evening. Usually, I talk with you from my office in the West Wing of the White House. But tonight there's something special to talk about, and I've asked someone very special to join me. Nancy and I are here in the West Hall of the White House, and around us are the rooms in which we live. It's the home you've provided for us, of which we merely have temporary custody.

Nancy's joining me because the message this evening is not my message but ours. And we speak to you not simply as fellow citizens but as fellow parents and grandparents and as concerned neighbors. It's back-to-school time for America's children. And while drug and alcohol abuse cuts across all generations, it's especially damaging to the young people on

Ronald Reagan and Nancy Reagan, "Just Say No Address to the Nation," September 14, 1986. www.medaloffreedom.com/RonaldReaganJustSayNo.htm.

whom our future depends. So tonight, from our family to yours, from our home to yours, thank you for joining us. . . .

From the early days of our administration, Nancy has been intensely involved in the effort to fight drug abuse. She has since traveled over 100,000 miles to 55 cities in 28 States and 6 foreign countries to fight school-age drug and alcohol abuse. She's given dozens of speeches and scores of interviews and has participated in 24 special radio and TV tapings to create greater awareness of this crisis. Her personal observations and efforts have given her such dramatic insights that I wanted her to share them with you this evening.

Nancy.

Drugs Affect Everyone

Mrs. Reagan. Thank you. As a mother, I've always thought of September as a special month, a time when we bundled our children off to school, to the warmth of an environment in which they could fulfill the promise and hope in those restless minds. But so much has happened over these last years, so much to shake the foundations of all that we know and all that we believe in. Today there's a drug and alcohol abuse epidemic in this country, and no one is safe from it—not you, not me, and certainly not our children, because this epidemic has their names written on it. Many of you may be thinking: "Well, drugs don't concern me." But it does concern you. It concerns us all because of the way it tears at our lives and because it's aimed at destroying the brightness and life of the sons and daughters of the United States.

For 5 years I've been traveling across the country—learning and listening. And one of the most hopeful signs I've seen is the building of an essential, new awareness of how terrible and threatening drug abuse is to our society. This was one of the main purposes when I started, so of course it makes me happy that that's been accomplished. But each time I meet with someone new or receive another letter from a troubled person on drugs, I yearn to find a way to help share the message that cries out from them. As a parent, I'm especially concerned about what drugs are doing to young mothers and their newborn children. Listen to this news account from a hospital in Florida of a child born to a mother with a cocaine habit: "Nearby, a baby named Paul lies motionless in an incubator, feeding tubes riddling his tiny body. He needs a respirator to breathe and a daily spinal tap to relieve fluid buildup on his brain. Only 1 month old, he's already suffered 2 strokes."

Now you can see why drug abuse concerns every one of us—all the American family. Drugs steal away so much. They take and take, until finally every time a drug goes into a child, something else is forced out—like love and hope and trust and confidence. Drugs take away the dream from every child's heart and replace it with a nightmare, and it's time we in America stand up and replace those dreams. Each of us has to put our principles and consciences on the line, whether in social settings or in the workplace, to set forth solid standards and stick to them. There's no moral middle ground. Indifference is not an option. We want you to help us create an outspoken intolerance for drug use. For the sake of our children, I implore each of you to be unyielding and inflexible in your opposition to drugs.

Changing Attitudes Will Fight Drugs

Our young people are helping us lead the way. Not long ago, in Oakland, California, I was asked by a group of children what to do if they were offered drugs, and I answered, "Just say no." Soon after that, those children in Oakland formed a Just Say No club, and now there are over 10,000 such clubs all over the country. Well, their participation and their courage in saying no needs our encouragement. We can help by using every opportunity to force the issue of not using drugs to the point of making others uncomfortable, even if it means making ourselves unpopular.

Our job is never easy because drug criminals are ingenious. They work everyday to plot a new and better way to steal our children's lives, just as they've done by developing this new drug, crack. For every door that we close, they open a new door to death. They prosper on our unwillingness to act. So, we must be smarter and stronger and tougher than they are. It's up to us to change attitudes and just simply dry up their markets.

And finally, to young people watching or listening, I have a very personal message for you: There's a big, wonderful world out there for you. It belongs to you. It's exciting and stimulating and rewarding. Don't cheat yourselves out of this promise. Our country needs you, but it needs you to be clear-eyed and clear-minded. I recently read one teenager's story. She's now determined to stay clean but was once strung out on several drugs. What she remembered most clearly about her recovery was that during the time she was on drugs everything appeared to her in shades of black and gray and after her treatment she was able to see colors again.

So, to my young friends out there: Life can be great, but not when you can't see it. So, open your eyes to life: to see it in the vivid colors that God gave us as a precious gift to His children, to enjoy life to the fullest, and to make it count. Say yes to your life. And when it comes to drugs and alcohol just say no.

Drug War Is Fought on Many Fronts

The President. I think you can see why Nancy has been such a positive influence on all that we're trying to do. The job ahead of us is very clear. Nancy's personal crusade, like that of so many other wonderful individuals, should become our national crusade. It must include a combination of government and private efforts which complement one another. Last month I announced six initiatives which we believe will do just that.

First, we seek a drug-free workplace at all levels of government and in the private sector. Second, we'll work toward drug-free schools. Third, we want to ensure that the public is protected and that treatment is available to substance abusers and the chemically dependent. Our fourth goal is to expand international cooperation while treating drug trafficking as a threat to our national security. In October I will be meeting with key U.S. Ambassadors to discuss what can be done to support our friends abroad. Fifth, we must move to strengthen law enforcement activities such as those initiated by Vice President [George H.W.] Bush and Attorney General [Edwin] Meese. And finally, we seek to expand public awareness and prevention.

In order to further implement these six goals, I will announce tomorrow [September 15, 1986] a series of new proposals for a drug-free America. Taken as a whole, these proposals will toughen our laws against drug criminals, encourage more research and treatment and ensure that illegal drugs will not be tolerated in our schools or in our workplaces. Together with our ongoing efforts, these proposals will bring the Federal commitment to fighting drugs to $3 billion. As much financing as we commit, however, we would be fooling ourselves if we thought that massive new amounts of money alone will provide the solution. Let us not forget that in America *people* solve problems and no national crusade has ever succeeded without human investment. Winning the crusade against drugs will not be achieved by just throwing money at the problem.

Key to Victory Is the Will of the People

Your government will continue to act aggressively, but nothing would be more effective than for Americans simply to quit using illegal drugs. We seek to create a massive change in national attitudes which ultimately will separate the drugs from the customer, to take the user away from the supply. I believe, quite simply, that we can help them quit, and that's where you come in.

My generation will remember how America swung into action when we were attacked in World War II. The war was not just fought by the fellows flying the planes or driving the tanks. It was fought at home by a mobilized nation—men and women alike—building planes and ships, clothing sailors and soldiers, feeding marines and airmen; and it was fought by children planting victory gardens and collecting cans. Well, now we're in another war for our freedom, and it's time for all of us to pull together again. So for example, if your friend or neighbor or a family member has a drug or alcohol problem, don't turn the other way. Go to his help or to hers. Get others involved with you—clubs, service groups, and community organizations—and provide support and strength. And, of course, many of you've been cured through treatment and self-help. Well, you're the combat veterans, and you have a critical role to play. You can help others by telling your story and providing a willing hand to those in need. Being friends to others is the best way of being friends to ourselves. It's time, as Nancy said, for America to Just Say No to drugs.

Those of you in union halls and workplaces everywhere: Please make this challenge a part of your job every day. Help us preserve the health and dignity of all workers. To businesses large and small: we need the creativity of your enterprise applied directly to this national problem. Help us. And those of you who are educators: Your wisdom and leadership are indispensable to this cause. From the pulpits of this spirit-filled land: we would welcome your reassuring message of redemption and forgiveness and of helping one another. On the athletic fields: You men and women are among the most beloved citizens of our country. A child's eyes fill with your heroic achievements. Few of us can give youngsters something as special and strong to look up to as you. Please don't let them down.

And this camera in front of us: It's a reminder that in Nancy's and my former profession and in the newsrooms and production rooms of our media centers—you have a special opportunity with your enormous influence to send alarm signals across the Nation. To our friends in foreign countries: We know many of you are involved in this battle with us. We need your success as well as ours. When we all come together, united, striving for this cause, then those who are killing America and terrorizing it with slow but sure chemical destruction will see that they are up against the mightiest force for good that we know. Then they will have no dark alleyways to hide in.

Drugs Undermine Freedom

In this crusade, let us not forget who we are. Drug abuse is a repudiation of everything America is. The destructiveness and human wreckage mock our heritage. Think for a moment how special it is to be an American. Can we doubt that only a divine providence placed this land, this island of freedom, here as a refuge for all those people of the world who yearn to breathe free?

The revolution out of which our liberty was conceived signaled an historical call to an entire world seeking hope. Each new arrival of immigrants rode the crest of that hope. They came, millions seeking a safe harbor from the oppression of cruel regimes. They came, to escape starvation and disease. They came, those surviving the Holocaust and the Soviet gulags [labor camps]. They came, the boat people [from Southeast Asia] chancing death for even a glimmer of hope that they could have a new life. They all came to taste the air redolent and rich with the freedom that is ours. What an insult it will be to what we are and whence we came if we do not rise up together in defiance against this cancer of drugs.

And there's one more thing. The freedom that so many seek in our land has not been preserved without a price. Nancy and I shared that remembrance 2 years ago at the Normandy American [World War II] Cemetery in France. In the still of that June afternoon, we walked together among the soldiers of freedom, past the hundreds of white markers which are monuments to courage and memorials to sacrifice. Too many of these and other such graves are the final resting places of teenagers who became men in the roar of battle.

Look what they gave to us who live. Never would they see another sunlit day glistening off a lake or river back home or miles of corn pushing up against the open sky of our plains. The pristine air of our mountains and the driving energy of our cities are theirs no more. Nor would they ever again be a son to their parents or a father to their own children. They did this for you, for me, for a new generation to carry our democratic experiment proudly forward. Well, that's something I think we're obliged to honor, because what they did for us means that we owe as a simple act of civic stewardship to use our freedom wisely for the common good.

Americans Must Stand Against Drugs

As we mobilize for this national crusade, I'm mindful that drugs are a constant temptation for millions. Please remember this when your courage is tested: You are Americans. You're the product of the freest society mankind has ever known. No one, ever, has the right to destroy your dreams and shatter your life.

Right down the end of this hall is the Lincoln Bedroom. But in the Civil War that room was the one President [Abraham] Lincoln used as his office. Memory fills that room, and more than anything that memory drives us to see vividly what President Lincoln sought to save. Above all, it is that America must stand for something and that our heritage lets us stand with a strength of character made more steely by each layer of challenge pressed upon the Nation. We Americans have never been normally neutral against any form of tyranny. Tonight we're asking no more than that we honor what we have been and what we are by standing together.

Mrs. Reagan. No we go on to the next stop: making a final commitment not to tolerate drugs by anyone, anytime, anyplace. So, won't you join us in this great, new national crusade?

The President. God bless you, and good night.

Penalties Must Be Harsh to Curtail Drug Use

William Bennett

William Bennett, drug czar under President George H.W. Bush, offers no apology for taking the hardest line possible against drug use in the following chapter from his 1992 book, The De-Valuing of America. *He says that waging a war against drugs is a moral imperative that previous administrations had failed to obey. By downplaying the real dangers of drugs to people, especially children, previous government officials laid the foundations for widespread drug abuse. The chapter chronicles how Bennett's forceful approach to dealing with the drug problem directly challenged and angered those officials who flirted with legalization as a solution. Bennett insists that legalization amounts to an admission of defeat and precedes even more moral decay.*

Harlem Hospital's neonatal intensive care unit is not very big but a very busy place. Too busy. It is a place that treats babies born addicted to cocaine. Neonatal units weren't intended to care for drug addicts. But in large American cities, a lot of them do. In the spring of 1989 the doctors in Harlem Hospital's neonatal intensive care unit told me that the word on the streets was that if you were pregnant and you wanted an easy delivery, cocaine—especially crack cocaine—would help. Crack is free-base cocaine; when smoked, it is extremely potent.

What the doctors told me was true: crack would ease the pain of delivery, though the baby would often be born prematurely, at six months or earlier, sometimes weighing a pound or two, with a bulb head and Popsicle limbs. And many times,

William J. Bennett, from *The De-Valuing of America*. New York: Summit Books, 1992. Copyright © 1992 by William J. Bennett. Abridged by permission of Simon & Schuster Adult Publishing Group.

the baby would be born a cocaine addict. These infants—
"cocaine babies" in the modern-day lexicon—are so tiny and
vulnerable that they look barely human. And apart from their
size, the exposure to cocaine often causes them pain, irritabil-
ity, anxiety, and constant, uninterrupted crying.

When I had my first look at a cocaine baby in April of
1989, I thought about the child Elayne and I were expecting
the following month. In one of the rooms at the hospital I
saw tiny babies linked up to elaborate monitoring and support systems. For each baby there was a nurse, doctor, or
paramedic nearby, constantly monitoring the baby's well-
being. When you see infants like this, the real stakes in the
drug war become most evident.

Children Are the Ultimate Victims

The word on the street was also that the crack high could be
sustained if the crack was sprayed with insect repellent. "There
are more ways they find to destroy themselves than we can
imagine," the head of the pediatric clinic told me. "The street
chemists are pretty good in their way. They don't pay any attention to what the long-term consequences are, but they
come up with novel ways of giving people bigger 'hits' and
higher 'highs.'"

I had returned home to the city of my birth, to one of the
greatest cities in the world, to a hospital with some of the best
technology in the world, and watched doctors and nurses do
their damnedest to keep up with what human beings had
done to themselves and to their babies.

A crack house is a small, dark hellhole where people gather
to smoke cocaine for a day or two. The typical scene is one of
human waste, degradation, and abuse, of people sprawled out
on their high, or "crashing" afterward. Food and garbage are
littered everywhere. Often human excrement and puddles of
urine are found around the room. And, as the police will tell
you, there are sometimes children living in the midst of all

this. Children do their best to maintain some sense of order in their lives, often leaving crack houses in the morning to seek refuge at school during the day. But they still have to come back home.

A police officer once told a colleague of mine about going into an apartment after receiving a call from a neighbor and finding two young children. They had been there by themselves for three days. When the police entered, the young girl was holding on to the hand of her older brother. The boy said, "This is my sister and my mother told me to take care of her." He was trying manfully to do his best. While the police were there, the mother came in with a roll of money in her hand. She had been out selling her body to get the money to support not her children but her crack habit.

I heard of a six-month-old child who died of an overdose of crack. How does a six-month-old overdose on crack? Because its mother or father, we're not sure which, inhaled crack and then, to quiet the crying baby, blew the crack into its mouth.

And I read about a Detroit woman who owed money to her drug dealer and handed over her thirteen-year-old daughter as payment.

These things have happened, and still happen, in America. Experts on child abuse have told me time and again that dramatic increases in child abuse and neglect are often due to drugs. When people take crack they often become paranoid and violent, frequently taking their rage out on those who are closest and most defenseless—often a child, *in utero* or out. When the drug problem comes home, the children take the hardest blows.

Controlling Drug Abuse Is a Moral Imperative

Somewhere along the way, in the late 1960s and 1970s, part of America lost its moral bearings regarding drugs. Drugs were not only seen as a political statement of sorts but were also advertised as a path to self-discovery, self-expression, and liberation. In 1970 Charles A. Reich wrote *The Greening of America*, a best-selling book that was emblematic of the cultural tenor of the times. "The effect of psychedelic drugs does not end when the drug itself wears off," wrote Reich, "it is lasting in the sense that the user finds his awareness and sensitivity has increased, whether he is using drugs at the time or not. In other words, something has been learned."

Even some of those who disagreed with this view often did not know how to challenge it. It didn't help, of course, that drugs were blessed by the highest councils of government and in some quarters of elite opinion. Elaine Shannon, author of *Desperados*, recounts how in 1975 President [Gerald] Ford's Domestic Council Drug Abuse Task Force, chaired by Vice President Nelson Rockefeller, produced a white paper that dismissed marijuana as a minor problem and stated that "cocaine is not physically addictive." The panel recommended that the DEA [Drug Enforcement Administration] and U.S. Customs deemphasize investigations of marijuana and cocaine smugglers and give higher priority to heroin trafficking. That finding was acclaimed by a *Washington Post* editorial as "common sense . . . a welcome departure from the heroics of the past." And Dr. Peter Bourne, a psychiatrist who served as President [Jimmy] Carter's adviser on drugs, held that "cocaine is probably the most benign of illicit drugs currently in widespread use."

It was the collapse of institutional government authority, essentially giving permission to take drugs, that was largely responsible for the epidemic that eventually hit us. For almost two decades—and with catastrophic consequences—many forgot how to answer the question, "Why not drugs?" . . .

Getting Tough Causes a Stir

Toward the close of my tenure as Secretary of Education [1985–88], in a speech before the White House Conference on a Drug-Free America, I called for "a transformation of government policy to match, and build on, the transformation of public sentiment."

"We cannot win simply by doing more of the same," I said. "We must consider a qualitative change in how we conduct our war against drugs." Among other things, I called for heightened inspections of international cargo and mail, more prisons, higher fines, and, for parolees, longer probationary periods and regular drug tests.

But the real stir came when I argued for an expanded military role in the war on drugs: "As the greatest military and economic power in the world," I said, "we can do more to prevent criminals in foreign nations from growing and processing illegal drugs. It is to be hoped we can do this in collaboration with foreign governments, but if need be we must consider doing this by ourselves. And we should consider broader use of military force against both the production and shipment of drugs."

My remarks were the lead story that evening on NBC News. Correspondent Fred Francis reported that "the suggestion that the military be used to stop drug smuggling is based on the government's private admission that the war on drugs is lost; that only firepower and men in uniform can stop shipments. Secretary Bennett became the first senior official to indicate that if Latin American nations refuse to cooperate, then military intervention by the United States could be used to end cocaine smuggling."

As I sometimes did, I was free-lancing. I hadn't received White House clearance for my remarks, and I heard through back channels that my remarks caused heartburn among some members of the Domestic Policy Council, and especially at the Pentagon. But I was not troubled. We were at stalemate on this issue, and I felt that the most important thing was to move the debate (and, I hoped, policy) in a new and more aggressive direction. In the weeks following my remarks, the idea of the use of military force gained more and more adherents, both in the administration and on Capitol Hill. It didn't hurt that a few days before my speech, the public had already stated its support of greater use of the military, by a ratio of better than four to one.

This episode revealed a tactic I frequently used. I believed in what I said. But I would also try to throw out an idea with the intent of sparking a debate, to get the national conversation going in a new direction. The reason this is necessary is that there is an enormous inertia in government; thinking on policy matters is rutted, and if you hope to effect real change, you have to overcome the inertia. Sometimes this approach worked. This time it did.

In this particular case, I was speaking out of a good deal of frustration. Kids were dying on the street, neighborhoods were being torn apart, and the federal government was not taking an aggressive enough posture. We were reacting to events instead of initiating them. And there were administrative problems with the Drug Enforcement Policy Board, problems Attorney General [Edwin] Meese was working hard to correct.

In a long memo to Meese, I laid out what I thought were the deficiencies of our efforts. "The effectiveness of almost every action taken against a part of the [drug] problem (production, shipment, sale, and use) depends upon effective pressure simultaneously and continuously being applied, and maintained, on the other parts," I wrote. "I'm afraid our current structure isn't suited as well as it might be to the mounting of such comprehensive, sustained, and effective pressure." I offered specific suggestions for strengthening our fight against drugs in the areas of production and shipping, sanctions against drug pushers and users, education and treatment. I later heard that the memo was taken up with President [Ronald] Reagan, but no final decisions were made. I didn't know at the time that I would later have the opportunity to put some of these ideas into action.

To Understand the Drug Problem You Need a Street View

While waiting for confirmation as director of the Office of National Drug Control Policy, I thought I would get a jump on the job and do a little homework. I had scheduled a speech at a school in a Detroit suburb in February 1989, and through a friend arranged a tour of the drug zone.

I flew out early Sunday morning and spent three hours with the police in downtown Detroit. I thought it important to see what happens when drugs take control of an area, so I had the police take me to neighborhoods where the police said drug abuse involved more than a third of the residents. I went to housing projects that had deteriorated badly after becoming havens for crack dealers. We drove around corners and the police captain told me to look at a window to spot a "lookout" before he ducked his head down. We saw crack houses and small groups of young men on the corners quickly disperse as we came near them. The officers were giving me what became the standard police tour, standard in what was said as well as what I saw.

"We have a deadly serious issue on our hands," I said, following the tour. "It's compelling. This was fact-finding for me, very preliminary, to find out what people on the ground are facing. [The police] emphasized what I was looking at was the heart of the problem. Downtown Detroit is as bad as it gets anywhere."

The scene was familiar to almost every American who watches television: parts of an inner city resembling what the philosopher Thomas Hobbes described as "the state of nature," where life is "solitary, poor, nasty, brutish and short."

During the tour of downtown, one of the police officers accompanying me asked, "Why should a kid earn four bucks an hour at McDonald's when he can make two or three hundred dollars a night working drugs?"

"For a lot of reasons," I said on that first tour, as I was to say a hundred times after. The police officer had picked up this line of reasoning from the media. It became increasingly fashionable in some circles to wonder how we can expect *any* inner-city child not to succumb to the lure of peddling drugs. After all, the argument goes, jobs paying the minimum wage don't hold much appeal when youngsters have the opportunity to make $100 or $500 or $1,000 a day. Drugs are so pervasive, their allure so strong, the money so easily obtained, the draw of evil so powerful—and the power to resist evil so feeble—that we should simply face reality and surrender any quaint notion we continue to harbor about children resisting drugs. Not surprisingly, a lot of youngsters picked up on this argument.

On June 22, 1989, when President [George H.W.] Bush visited residents of New York's Covenant House (a home for children involved with drugs, prostitution, and crime), a teenage boy made the same argument to the President. "I'm not working for a hundred twenty-five dollars, a hundred and ten dollars, there's no way," he said. "For a whole week and sitting over a hot oven flipping hamburgers? One hundred dollars a week, that ain't no money. I can make a hundred dollars in fifteen minutes by dealing drugs."

Following his trip, the President called me. He was moved and deeply bothered by what he had seen and heard, as anyone would be. We talked for twenty-five minutes and discussed what the proper response should be.

Giving Up the Fight Is Fueled by Racism

It violates everything a civilized society stands for simply to throw in the towel and say, "Okay, we give up. It's not right that children use drugs, but we adults can't seem to do anything about it." Of course the lure of drug money can exert a tremendous pull. But responsible adults are supposed to pull back—to be better, and do better, and point to a better way. Inner-city parents who are trying to do right by their children, who are trying to shape their children's character, need allies. Those faraway commentators who excuse these children trample on the parents who are trying to teach good lessons. And when this "what can we do?" attitude trickles down to mayors and police captains and social workers, the situation gets much worse.

At the very time we need to affirm belief in things like individual responsibility, civic duty, and obedience to the law, too many segments of society are equivocating and sending mixed messages. This sort of moral enervation must be challenged. If people think poor black children aren't capable of moral responsibility, they should say so. I think otherwise. I *know* they are capable of it. I have seen that they are. The inner-city children who obey their parents and obey the law give witness to the lie. Most inner-city kids—including those living in or near drug markets—refuse to serve as drug runners. We should honor, support, and reinforce those youngsters.

We are witnessing the emergence of a new "invisible man" (the title of Ralph Ellison's classic novel) in American society. This new "invisible man" is the black inner-city citizen who doesn't "do" drugs. In fact, significant numbers of inner-city residents do *not* commit themselves to the drug world. Most blacks in our inner cities are law-abiding citizens who lead decent lives and disdain drugs; they are victims, not perpetrators, of drug crimes. Americans need to see that because, unfortunately, these citizens are almost invisible so far as much of public opinion is concerned.

In the place of the law-abiding black man and woman we have seen the emergence of a new, all too "visible man"—the black predator, the young, inner-city black male who terrorizes communities, preys on innocent victims, or is arrested in drug busts. The image of the "visible man" is given wide currency through the camera lens. Film report after film report sears images in our sensibilities: drugs, violence, the inner city, and blacks. These images and associations perpetuate a racial stereotype. We need to confront it immediately, directly, before this myth and these images harden into dogma.

Blaming the Government Does Not Solve the Problem

Moral surrender needs to be challenged for another very important reason: when adults don't teach children how to live responsible lives, they will become cynical and go astray. It's not surprising to discover that, left to their own devices, children will want everything, and they will want it all at once. One of the tasks of adults is to tell children, "You can't have everything all at once," and explain why. That used to be part of education; it still needs to be.

Drug dealers are teachers—malevolent teachers. They are teaching our children the terrible lesson that you can get it all at once—money, cars, gold chains, fancy clothes, and all the rest—and it doesn't matter how. That is one more compelling reason we need to remove drug dealers from our children's lives. They are teachers of a wicked lesson. This kind of wickedness will flourish if good men do nothing, or if they throw up their arms in despair, or (worse yet) if they give credence to the lie of hopelessness and fruitlessness.

I made this point while I was Secretary of Education in a debate I had on the "MacNeil/Lehrer Newshour" with Jesse Jackson [the civil rights leader, politician, and minister]. In discussing the causes of the drug problem, Jackson referred several times to the Gramm-Rudman Deficit Reduction Act on federal spending.

The program ended with a vigorous exchange between us.

"For those who are escaping pain, the pain of unemployment and lack of job training, the pain of family farm foreclosures, the pain of the threat of nuclear war, that's one level that we must grapple with," Jackson said.

"Let's keep politics out of it, Reverend Jackson," I said. "You know as well as I do . . . that this problem crosses sex lines, race lines, class lines, community lines. This is a problem throughout society, and I don't think we're going to get very far by suggesting this is . . . due to some kind of governmental policy. That just won't fly."

"Oh, I submit to you that when I talk with some of the farm children out in Omaha," Jackson said, "their sense of impotence, their sense of alienation is that the future is not very bright for them . . . and their lives are quite tied up with what they see as their future."

"Reverend Jackson," I began to interject.

"I've been with these inner-city youth who make a buck this way or get high to escape their pain," he went on. "And we would make a sad mistake to just deal with the fruit of alienation and not deal with the root of this problem."

"Well, Mr. Jackson," I replied, "as a Christian minister you know that you have to be very careful about indulging people when they want to put responsibility onto somebody else, and if sixteen- or seventeen- or eighteen-year-olds in possession of their faculties are blaming their addiction to drugs or their use of drugs on somebody else, I hope you're correcting them on the grounds of individual moral responsibility."

"Well, there's a valid balance," Jackson conceded.

If adult leadership doesn't stand for individual responsibility, how can we expect children to learn it? . . .

The War on Drugs Is Not a Lost Cause

When I took the job of director of the Office of National Drug Control Policy, there were many people (including a lot of my friends) who said that I was on a fool's errand. Even though the task was clear and the stakes high, they were convinced the war on drugs was a hopeless undertaking. Every which way I turned, I heard dire predictions. "Bennett has a daunting, some say hopeless, assignment," said one report. Another said, "This is a drug epidemic that seems beyond the reach of any government." *The New York Times* wondered whether I had taken on a "mission impossible." In 1989, a nationwide poll showed that an astonishing 64 percent of those interviewed identified drugs as the nation's leading problem— far ahead of the threat of nuclear war, pollution, or crime. The general climate of opinion, then, was that there was not much we could do, that we were done and damned before we even started. And the scenes most often seen on American television and most often talked about resembled what I saw in Detroit and Liberty City.

Clearly one of my central tasks was to change the psychology that gripped much of the media and, in turn, much of the American people. I had to reassure people that the war on drugs was not a lost cause. There were huge hurdles that we faced; few people had a better sense of the terrible problems we faced than I. But despair clearly was not an option. America had prevailed against monarchy, bigotry, a civil war, a great depression, Nazism, and the Cold War; it could certainly prevail against the drug epidemic, too. I hit the issue head-on: "It's way too soon to say [the drug war] is over, we lost, because we haven't really waged it yet," I said. "Public opinion at this time, at this hour, gives us perhaps the most valuable weapon we can have in this campaign to end the scourge of drugs."

"Mr. Bennett is in for the fight of his life, but more important, he is in for the fight of our children's lives," said Senator Alfonse D'Amato (R-New York). I girded myself for a tough battle. A few congressmen even encouraged me. "The thing that made [Bennett] troublesome at Education may make him very valuable in this position," said Senator Joe Biden. "He's never been afraid to pick a fight."

"Do you think you can restrain yourself?" asked Senator Howard Metzenbaum (D-Ohio), a longtime liberal critic of mine. "You've been a real loose cannon at times," he said.

"That's fair enough," I conceded. But I bristled at what I described as the notion that "I ought to disassemble my bully pulpit, put on my green eyeshades, and run numbers for a couple of years."

I went to work fast. I worked on the job twenty months, but it was probably the hardest, most intense twenty months of my life. (As Elayne [his wife] put it, I went from the American dream, education, to the American nightmare, drugs.) As with each job I took, I started by doing my homework, reading, talking to experts, and taking inventory. And one of the great things about a high-profile government job is that when you ask people for advice, they give it to you.

In room 180 of the Old Executive Office Building situated next to the White House, I held about a dozen meetings, lasting two to three hours each. Each meeting included ten to fifteen experts from a single field: law enforcement, treatment, education, religious leaders, community leaders, parents, and so on. My questions were the same to each group: What do we do? How should we wage a drug war? And how do we win one?

I chose the best-known and most respected people in their fields, without any regard to politics or ideology. I was struck by the high degree of agreement among those gathered. The operative words were "more" and "smarter": more and smarter efforts are needed, they said, in law enforcement, interdiction, treatment, prevention, and education.

One very good piece of advice came from Jack Mendelson, professor of psychiatry at the Harvard Medical School. On leaving the conference room, with his hat and coat on, he turned to me and said, "Remember the most important thing."

"What's that, Dr. Mendelson?" I asked.

"Remember," he said, "don't just do something—stand there." What he meant was something very subtle, but very important: Don't just put forward a good antidrug plan. In addition, make sure you stand up for the right things and, if necessary, be a lightning rod for criticism. Don't worry if the critics beat up on you. Most antidrug efforts will be made locally. But what the federal government can do that the localities cannot is to serve as a kind of national reference point. By standing up for certain things, you will encourage others to act. This fit in well with my own view that an essential part of governing consists of standing for the right things, giving voice to the right sentiments, praising the right actions of others and condemning the wrong ones. . . .

Legalization Would Only Worsen the Problem

The legalization debate presented me with a somewhat unusual situation. Throughout my public life, most of my battles had been against leading liberal voices. But on this issue, I drew criticism from the political right flank, including a number of prominent conservatives: William F. Buckley, free-market economist Milton Friedman, former Secretary of State George Shultz, and others. So legalization seemed respectable at both ends of the political spectrum.

At first, I resisted getting heavily involved in this debate. As I told a congressional committee, I was hired to wage the war, not to discuss whether it was worth fighting. That issue had already been resolved.

Some members of my staff and a few friends told me that the argument was impossible to ignore and that the more we engaged the debate, the more arguments we advanced against legalization, the more support we would get from the public. So I began to more directly and more publicly take on the issue of legalization, in interviews, speeches, public forums, and even on national television.

The legalization debate is for all intent and purposes over. But even to call it a "debate" suggests that the arguments in favor of drug legalization are rigorous, substantial and serious. At first glance some of the arguments sound appealing. But on further inspection one finds that at bottom they are nothing more than a series of unpersuasive and even disingenuous ideas that more sober minds recognize as a recipe for a public policy disaster.

Legalization removes the incentive to stay away from a life of drugs. Some people are going to smoke crack whether it's legal or illegal. But by keeping it illegal, we maintain the criminal sanctions that persuade most people that the good life cannot be reached by dealing drugs. And that's exactly why we have drug laws—to make drug use a wholly unattractive choice.

One of the clear lessons of Prohibition is that when we had laws against alcohol, there *was* less consumption of alcohol, less alcohol-related disease, fewer drunken brawls, and a lot less public drunkenness. And contrary to myth, there is no evidence that Prohibition caused big increases in crime.

I am not suggesting that we go back to Prohibition. Alcohol has a long, complicated history in this country, and unlike drugs, the American people accept alcohol. They have no interest in going back to Prohibition. But at least advocates of legalization should admit that legalized alcohol, which is responsible for some 100,000 deaths a year, is hardly a model for drug policy. As the [*Washington Post*] columnist Charles Krauthammer has pointed out, the question is not which is worse, alcohol or drugs. The question is, should we accept both legalized alcohol *and* legalized drugs? The answer is no.

If drugs were legalized, use would surely soar. In fact, we have just undergone a kind of cruel national experiment in which drugs became cheap and widely available: that experiment is called the crack epidemic. It was only when cocaine was dumped into the country, and a three-dollar vial of crack could be bought on street corners, that we saw cocaine use skyrocket—mostly among the poor and disadvantaged.

The price that American society would have to pay for legalized drugs would be intolerably high: more drug-related accidents at work, on the highway, and in the airways; bigger losses in worker productivity; hospitals filled with drug emergencies; more students on drugs, meaning more dropouts; more pregnant women buying legal cocaine, meaning more abused babies *in utero*. Add to this the added cost of treatment, social welfare, and insurance, and welcome to the Brave New World of drug legalization.

To listen to legalization advocates, one might think that street crime would disappear with the repeal of our drug laws. But our best research indicates that most drug criminals were into crime well *before* they got into drugs. Making drugs legal would subsidize their habit. They would continue to rob and steal to pay for food, for clothes, for entertainment. And they would carry on with their drug trafficking by undercutting the legalized price of drugs and catering to teenagers who (I assume) would be nominally restricted from buying drugs at the corner drugstore.

In my travels around the country I have seen nothing to support the legalizers' argument that lower drug prices would reduce crime. Virtually everywhere I have gone, police and DEA agents have told me that crime rates are highest where crack is cheapest.

If we did legalize drugs, we would no doubt have to reverse the policy, like those countries that had experimented with broad legalization and decided it was a failure. In 1975 Italy liberalized its drug law and now has one of the highest heroin-related death rates in Western Europe. One Italian government official told me that the citizens of Italy are eager to recriminalize the use of drugs. They had seen enough casualties.

And what about our children? If we make drugs more accessible, there will be more harm to children, direct and indirect. There will be more cocaine babies and more child abuse. Children after all are among the most frequent victims of violent, drug-related crimes—crimes that have nothing to do with the cost of acquiring the drugs. In Philadelphia in 1987 more than half the child-abuse fatalities involved at least one parent who was a heavy drug user. Seventy-three percent of the child-abuse cases in New York City in 1987 involved parental drug use.

And it would be disastrous suddenly to switch signals on our children in school, whom we have been teaching, with great effect, that drug use is wrong. Why, they will ask, have we changed our minds?

The whole legalization argument is based on the premise that progress is impossible. But there is now incontrovertible, unmistakable evidence of progress in the war on drugs (more about that in the next chapter). Now would be exactly the wrong time to surrender and legalize. . . .

Drug Abuse Degrades Humans

In the end drug use is wrong because of what it does to human character. It degrades. It makes people less than they should be by burning away a sense of responsibility, subverting productivity, and making a mockery of virtue.

Using drugs is wrong not simply because drugs create medical problems; it is wrong because drugs destroy one's moral sense. People addicted to drugs neglect their duties. The lure can become so strong that soon people will do nothing else but take drugs. They will neglect God, family, children, friends, and jobs—everything in life that is important, noble, and worthwhile—for the sake of drugs. This is why from the very beginning we posed the drug problem as a moral issue. And it was the failure to recognize the moral consequences of drug use that led us into the drug epidemic in the first place.

In the late 1960s, many people rejected the language of morality, of right and wrong. Since then we have paid dearly for the belief that drug use was harmless and even an enlightening, positive thing.

Drugs undermine the necessary virtues of a free society—autonomy, self-reliance, and individual responsibility. The inherent purpose of using drugs is secession from reality, from society, and from the moral obligations individuals owe their family, their friends, and their fellow citizens. Drugs destroy the natural sentiments and duties that constitute our human nature and make our social life possible. As our founders would surely recognize, for a citizenry to be perpetually in a drug-induced haze doesn't bode well for the future of self-government.

When all is said and done, the most compelling case that can be made against drug use rests on moral grounds. No civilized society—especially a self-governing one—can be neutral regarding human character and personal responsibility.

Criminalizing Drugs
Only Lengthens the War

Milton Friedman

*Throughout the 1980s, the argument about how to manage the
United States' growing drug problem reached a fever pitch. In
the following 1989 letter to President George H.W. Bush's drug
czar William Bennett, Milton Friedman condemns Bennett's
strategy of intensifying the war on drugs by increasing domestic
criminal penalties and military attacks on countries that smuggle
drugs into the United States. A senior research fellow at Stanford
University, Friedman asserts that, far from assuaging the nation's
drug problem, Bennett's decisions exacerbated it. He says that
only by decriminalizing drug use and diverting funds from the
failed and demoralizing effort to control them would funds be
available for treatment and rehabilitation of users. Treatment,
Friedman insists, is the only real and lasting solution to the
nation's drug problem.*

Dear Bill [Bennett],

In [English statesman] Oliver Cromwell's eloquent words,
"I beseech you, in the bowels of Christ, think it possible you
may be mistaken" about the course you and President [George
H.W.] Bush urge us to adopt to fight drugs. The path you
propose of more police, more jails, use of the military in foreign countries, harsh penalties for drug users, and a whole
panoply of repressive measures can only make a bad situation
worse. The drug war cannot be won by those tactics without
undermining the human liberty and individual freedom that
you and I cherish.

You are not mistaken in believing that drugs are a scourge that is devastating our society. You are not mistaken in believing that drugs are tearing asunder our social fabric, ruining the lives of many young people, and imposing heavy costs on some of the most disadvantaged among us. You are not mistaken in believing that the majority of the public share your concerns. In short, you are not mistaken in the end you seek to achieve.

Your mistake is failing to recognize that the very measures you favor are a major source of the evils you deplore. Of course the problem is demand, but it is not only demand, it is demand that must operate through repressed and illegal channels. Illegality creates obscene profits that finance the murderous tactics of the drug lords; illegality leads to the corruption of law enforcement officials; illegality monopolizes the efforts of honest law forces so that they are starved for resources to fight the simpler crimes of robbery, theft and assault.

Drugs are a tragedy for addicts. But criminalizing their use converts that tragedy into a disaster for society, for users and non-users alike. Our experience with the prohibition of drugs is a replay of our experience with the prohibition of alcoholic beverages.

I append excerpts from a column that I wrote in 1972 on "Prohibition and Drugs." The major problem then was heroin from Marseilles [city in France]; today, it is cocaine from Latin America. Today, also, the problem is far more serious than it was 17 years ago: more addicts, more innocent victims; more drug pushers, more law enforcement officials; more money spent to enforce prohibition, more money spent to circumvent prohibition.

Decriminalizing Drugs Would Solve a Host of Social Problems

Had drugs been decriminalized 17 years ago, "crack" would never have been invented (it was invented because the high cost of illegal drugs made it profitable to provide a cheaper version) and there would today be far fewer addicts. The lives of thousands, perhaps hundreds of thousands of innocent victims would have been saved, and not only in the U.S. The ghettos of our major cities would not be drug-and-crime-infested no-man's lands. Fewer people would be in jails, and fewer jails would have been built.

Colombia, Bolivia and Peru would not be suffering from narco-terror, and we would not be distorting our foreign policy because of narco-terror. Hell would not, in the words with which [American evangelist] Billy Sunday welcomed Prohibition, "be forever for rent," but it would be a lot emptier.

Decriminalizing drugs is even more urgent now than in 1972, but we must recognize that the harm done in the interim cannot be wiped out, certainly not immediately. Postponing decriminalization will only make matters worse, and make the problem appear even more intractable.

Alcohol and tobacco cause many more deaths in users than do drugs. Decriminalization would not prevent us from treating drugs as we now treat alcohol and tobacco: prohibiting sales of drugs to minors, outlawing the advertising of drugs and similar measures. Such measures could be enforced, while outright prohibition cannot be. Moreover, if even a small fraction of the money we now spend on trying to enforce drug prohibition were devoted to treatment and rehabilitation, in an atmosphere of compassion not punishment, the reduction in drug usage and in the harm done to the users could be dramatic.

This plea comes from the bottom of my heart. Every friend of freedom, and I know you are one, must be as revolted as I am by the prospect of turning the United States into an armed camp, by the vision of jails filled with casual drug users and of an army of enforcers empowered to invade the liberty of citizens on slight evidence. A country in which shooting down unidentified planes "on suspicion" can be seriously considered as a drug-war tactic is not the kind of United States that either you or I want to hand on to future generations.

CHAPTER 3

I The Legalization Debate

Chapter Preface

One of the great debates that arose during the twentieth century was over the legalization of drugs. Though it would not initially seem so, participants on either side of the debate have been and continue to remain in general agreement that substance abuse creates problems. However, they agree neither about the nature of the problems, nor about how to solve them.

Proponents of legalization maintain that the illegality of drugs is the very thing that has led to the problems associated with them. They maintain that government interference in an adult's decision to use drugs violates her basic civil rights. They also believe that making drugs illegal has forced both addicts and suppliers to find other, more dangerous means of keeping the supply flowing. Attempting to control the resulting illegal activity costs local, state, and federal law enforcements huge sums of money and time. Legalization advocates say that these resources could be much better spent on prevention, education, and treatment.

Critics of legalization say the proponents could not be more wrong. They believe that removing restrictions on drugs would have disastrous effects. Prohibiting the possession and free trade of drugs is the only floodgate against rampant drug abuse, especially among young people, they contend. The following quote from the National Drug Control Strategy of 1999 clearly spells out the polarization between the two groups: "Addictive drugs were criminalized because they are harmful; they are not harmful because they are criminalized. The more a product is available and legitimized, the greater will be its use."

It is clear that both sides of the legalization debate have convincing arguments. What may not be so clear, however, is how the government ranks drugs as legal or illegal in the first place. At present, the U.S. government classifies only a few drugs as strictly illegal. Those are: marijuana, heroin, and hallucinogens. Surprisingly, other drugs such as cocaine and pain medications containing opium-based drugs are in fact legal but strictly regulated. Also, alcohol, and the stimulants caffeine and nicotine remain legal for use without a prescription as well. The resulting message about drugs is mixed.

Critics of legalization often oversimplify it as a way to prevent discussion of the myriad workable, legal alternatives to wholesale prohibition of all illegal drugs. One such alternative, decriminalization, would allow law enforcement officials to take a reasonable, case-by-case look at the use of so-called soft drugs such as marijuana. Just as it is legal to possess and consume alcohol safely, the decriminalization of marijuana would allow people to smoke it for medical purposes or in safe recreational ways. However, those who drive high would face a penalty. Another alternative, harm reduction, could and has been used to limit the damage drugs cause individuals and the society in general. Needle exchange programs are good examples of harm reduction. Methadone maintenance clinics, where heroin addicts can receive regular doses of the synthetic opiate to ease the stress of withdrawal from heroin are another.

Disagreement over the issues surrounding drug legalization has caused division within the government and the general public for years. What seems necessary is an earnest discussion of reasonable solutions rather than a retreat to the same tired and polarized arguments. Such a discussion has yet to occur.

Legalizing Drugs Will
Cause More Deaths

Frank "Buzz" Trexler

In December 1993, the newly appointed surgeon general of the United States Joycelyn Elders made the bold statement in a National Press Club speech that legalizing drugs would markedly decrease drug-related crime and gang activity. Though legalization advocates across the country applauded her stand, many others were shocked and disheartened. In the following piece, pastor and newspaper editor Frank "Buzz" Trexler says that rather than diminish crime as Elders said it would, legalizing drugs would increase crime in communities already suffering the effects of drug abuse and would further encourage the self-destructive behavior of addicts. Trexler has to look no further than the recent drug-related death of his former college roommate for an example of the kind of devastation awaiting more and more people should drug legalization become national policy.

We buried Steve the day before Thanksgiving.

My former college roommate was less than two weeks past his 35th birthday when the battle came to an end—a time span that his mother referred to as 21 years of hell.

For you see, her only son Steve was good looking, humorous, intelligent—a one-time teacher with a master's degree from University of Tennessee—most likable and generous. In fact, as his dad would say after the funeral, "Steve would take in a dog." Visiting his house you might find a street person sleeping on the living room floor, or "a busload of California hippies" who took Steve up on his offer . . . to drop in any time.

Frank "Buzz" Trexler, "Funeral for a Friend Just Says No to Elders," *The Maryville Tennessee Daily Times*, December 9, 1993. Reproduced by permission.

But Steve, who grew up in the Baptist faith and gave his life to Jesus as a pre-teen, fought a demon familiar to many our age: drugs and alcohol.

Abuse Began with Marijuana and Beer

Looking at our 1974 high school yearbook, it's easy to recall the drug-filled atmosphere that permeated the times; the heavy waft of marijuana smoke and the reek of stale beer were familiar at teen parties. Chances are it was those two substances that introduced the inherently curious Steve to the drug scene.

When I caught up with him in 1978, we rented a house about a mile from the East Tennessee State University campus in Johnson City. Our grades counted us as "respectable," as we used to say tongue in cheek; our lifestyle raucous and incredibly anti-Christian. But that lifestyle has its spiritual and earthly costs.

In 1 Corinthians 13, the apostle Paul writes, "When I was a child I talked like a child, I thought like a child, I reasoned like a child. When I became a man, I put childish ways behind me."

In 1985, I gave my life to Christ and put the "childish ways behind me." The demons fled. Later, Steve would try to escape his own demons, but they seemed to only dig the talons in more deeply. (Maybe my demons were wimpy compared to his.)

A Rehabilitation Failure

In 1990, with the help of his parents and church, Steve entered a rehabilitation unit in North Carolina. Upon release, he came to stay with me and my family in Knoxville [Tennessee], hoping to find a job in his teaching profession. He stayed only a few days before returning home.

My advice as he left was to escape his "friends" and their scene. He said the rehab people told him the same. Apparently he ignored us all.

At the time of his death, Steve was again in rehabilitation—this time under court orders. He had been jailed as a co-conspirator in a drug buy, but the judge saw in Steve what many of us did and tried to help him.

By all accounts, Steve had been straight for "four or five months" until the Thursday before his death. One friend said Steve came to his house that Friday a bit high with two other men and told him twice in less than 10 minutes that he needed to talk. The friend said at the time it didn't seem urgent and failed to pursue it any further.

On Saturday, Steve worked a flea market with his dad, who later said when his only son left he somehow knew it would be their last moments together. "I watched him until he went out of sight."

That afternoon, those who saw him say Steve arrived "sideways" at a house being renovated by some acquaintances. At some point, they say, he passed out in the front yard and was being taken inside before being left done while the others reportedly went to a bar. When they returned, Steve was dead and his war was over. The cause of death has not been determined. But there is little doubt substance abuse played some part.

Some of those who gathered in the Upper East Tennessee cemetery the day of his funeral are likely fighting the same war. Gathering around the gravesite, they took on the appearance of walking wounded returning from battle.

Legalization Is Not the Answer

Surgeon General Joycelyn Elders suggested Tuesday [December 7, 1993] that legalizing drugs could help make America's streets safer. Responding to questions at a National Press Club luncheon after a speech decrying violence, Elders said 60 percent of violent crimes are drug- or alcohol-related.

"Many times they're robbing, stealing and all these things to get money to buy drugs," she said. "I do feel that we would markedly reduce our crime rate if drugs were legalized."

The nation's top doc and those of her ideological ilk who engage in the Bob Marley-esque [sounding like reggae musician Bob Marley] chant of "legalize it . . . legalize it" appear to have tunnel vision on this issue. Yes, drug gangs and their violence would likely disappear; maybe thefts would even drop in correlation to the reduced costs of drugs. But has the lack of prohibition cut down on alcohol-related deaths? The numbers tell a different story.

While Elders is off the wall, Lee P. Brown, the director of the Office of National Drug Control Policy at the White House, is on target: Legalization, he said, is "a formula for self-destruction" and would inflict "terrifying damage" on communities already torn apart by drugs.

If Elders and others would like to study the issue, they should stroll to the nearest cemetery. Or, better yet, walk a mile in Steve's shoes. He doesn't need them anymore.

Marijuana Has Medicinal Potential

Institute of Medicine

The last half of the twentieth century saw increased marijuana use and an associated debate over whether or not the drug represented a precursor to more dangerous addictions and should be illegal to possess, sell, or use. By the 1990s, marijuana opponents could no longer deny that it and other cannabanoid drugs did have some medicinal potential. The National Academy of Sciences' Institute of Medicine conducted extensive research and issued a 1999 report on the subject. Though the following chapter from the document does not advocate smoking marijuana for medicinal purposes, it does point to tetrahydrocannabinol (THC), a substance in marijuana, as a potentially powerful painkiller. The report does caution that development of THC as a drug is dependent on the medical establishment's willingness to invest the time and money to convert it to a form that does not have to be smoked.

Advances in cannabinoid science of the past 16 years have given rise to a wealth of new opportunities for the development of medically useful cannabinoid-based drugs. The accumulated data suggest a variety of indications, particularly for pain relief, antiemesis [relief of nausea and vomiting], and appetite stimulation. For patients such as those with AIDS or who are undergoing chemotherapy, and who suffer simultaneously from severe pain, nausea, and appetite loss, cannabinoid drugs might offer broad-spectrum relief not found in any other single medication. The data are weaker for muscle spasticity but moderately promising. The least promising cat-

119

egories are movement disorders, epilepsy, and glaucoma. Animal data are moderately supportive of a potential for cannabinoids in the treatment of movement disorders and might eventually yield stronger encouragement. The therapeutic effects of cannabinoids are most well established for THC [tetrahydrocannabinol], which is the primary psychoactive ingredient of marijuana. But it does not follow from this that smoking marijuana is good medicine.

Although marijuana smoke delivers THC and other cannabinoids to the body, it also delivers harmful substances, including most of those found in tobacco smoke. In addition, plants contain a variable mixture of biologically active compounds and cannot be expected to provide a precisely defined drug effect. For those reasons there is little future in smoked marijuana as a medically approved medication. If there is any future in cannabinoid drugs, it lies with agents of more certain, not less certain, composition. While clinical trials are the route to developing approved medications, they are also valuable for other reasons. For example, the personal medical use of smoked marijuana—regardless of whether or not it is approved—to treat certain symptoms is reason enough to advocate clinical trials to assess the degree to which the symptoms or course of diseases are affected. Trials testing the safety and efficacy of marijuana use are an important component to understanding the course of a disease, particularly diseases such as AIDS for which marijuana use is prevalent. The argument against the future of smoked marijuana for treating any condition is not that there is no reason to predict efficacy but that there is risk. That risk could be overcome by the development of a nonsmoked rapid-onset delivery system for cannabinoid drugs.

There are two caveats to following the traditional path of drug development for cannabinoids. The first is timing. Patients who are currently suffering from debilitating conditions unrelieved by legally available drugs, and who might find relief with smoked marijuana, will find little comfort in a promise of a better drug 10 years from now. In terms of good medicine, marijuana should rarely be recommended unless all reasonable options have been eliminated. But then what? It is conceivable that the medical and scientific opinion might find itself in conflict with drug regulations. This presents a policy issue that must weigh—at least temporarily—the needs of individual patients against broader social issues. Our assessment of the scientific data on the medical value of marijuana and its constituent cannabinoids is but one component of attaining that balance.

The second caveat is a practical one. Although most scientists who study cannabinoids would agree that the scientific pathways to cannabinoid drug development are clearly marked, there is no guarantee that the fruits of scientific research will be made available to the public. Cannabinoid-based drugs will become available only if there is either enough incentive for private enterprise to develop and market such drugs or sustained public investment in cannabinoid drug research and development. . . . Although marijuana is an abused drug, the logical focus of research on the therapeutic value of cannabinoid-based drugs is the treatment of specific symptoms or diseases, not substance abuse. Thus, the most logical research sponsors would be the several institutes within the National Institutes of Health or organizations whose primary expertise lies in the relevant symptoms or diseases. . . .

Conclusion: Scientific data indicate the potential therapeutic value of cannabinoid drugs, primarily THC, for pain relief, control of nausea and vomiting, and appetite stimulation; smoked marijuana, however, is a crude THC delivery system that also delivers harmful substances.

Recommendation: Clinical trials of cannabinoid drugs for symptom management should be conducted with the goal of developing rapid-onset, reliable, and safe delivery systems.

Recommendation: Clinical trials of marijuana use for medical purposes should be conducted under the following limited circumstances: trials should involve only short-term marijuana use (less than six months), should be conducted in patients with conditions for which there is reasonable expectation of efficacy, should be approved by institutional review boards, and should collect data about efficacy.

Recommendation: Short-term use of smoked marijuana (less than six months) for patients with debilitating symptoms (such as intractable pain or vomiting) must meet the following conditions:

- failure of all approved medications to provide relief has been documented,

- the symptoms can reasonably be expected to be relieved by rapid-onset cannabinoid drugs,

- such treatment is administered under medical supervision in a manner that allows for assessment of treatment effectiveness, and

- involves an oversight strategy comparable to an institutional review board process that could provide guidance within 24 hours of a submission by a physician to provide marijuana to a patient for a specified use.

Until a nonsmoked rapid-onset cannabinoid drug delivery system becomes available, we acknowledge that there is no clear alternative for people suffering from chronic conditions that might be relieved by smoking marijuana, such as pain or AIDS wasting. One possible approach is to treat patients as n-of-1 [patient treated with both the experimental drug and a placebo] clinical trials, in which patients are fully informed of their status as experimental subjects using a harmful drug delivery system and in which their condition is closely monitored and documented under medical supervision, thereby increasing the knowledge base of the risks and benefits of marijuana use under such conditions. We recommend these n-of-1 clinical trials using the same oversight mechanism as that proposed in the above recommendations.

Medical Marijuana Research Is Misleading

Joseph Califano Jr.

The national Institute of Medicine (IOM) indicated in its report, "Marijuana and Medicine: Assessing the Science Base," that marijuana is not a gateway drug, or one that would lead users to become addicted to stronger, harsher drugs. This official statement from the medical establishment of the United States added fuel to the debate over whether marijuana should be legalized. Many labeled its bold defense of marijuana as a relatively harmless substance with medicinal potential misleading. In the following 1999 New York Times *editorial: former secretary of Health, Education, and Welfare and the chairman of the National Center on Addiction and Substance Abuse, Joseph Califano Jr., also decries the report's inconsistencies. He points out that though it states there is no evidence to indicate marijuana use leads to further drug abuse, it does suggest that people who try marijuana and like it are more likely to abuse other drugs. Califano also accuses the IOM of ignoring statistics that show a direct correlation between teen marijuana use and future abuse of other drugs such as LSD, heroin, and cocaine.*

"FEDS GO TO POT" screamed the *New York Post* headline last week [March 18, 1999] after the Institute of Medicine [IOM] released its report "Marijuana and Medicine: Assessing the Science Base." The Associated Press [AP] reported that the IOM had found "there was no conclusive evidence that marijuana use leads to harder drugs."

A look at the actual report shows that these press accounts are misleading. Consider these words from the report: "Not surprisingly, most users of other illicit drugs have used marijuana first. In fact, most drug users begin with alcohol and nicotine before marijuana—usually before they are of legal age. In the sense that marijuana use typically precedes rather than follows initiation of other illicit drug use, it is indeed a 'gateway' drug. But because underage smoking and alcohol use typically precede marijuana use, marijuana is not the most common and is rarely the first, 'gateway' to illicit drug use."

Those are the words that precede the tentatively worded statement the AP paraphrased: "There is no conclusive evidence that the drug effects of marijuana are causally linked to the subsequent abuse of other illicit drugs." The report notes, however, that "people who enjoy the effects of marijuana are, logically, more likely to be willing to try other mind-altering drugs than are people who are not willing to try marijuana or who dislike its effects. In other words, many of the factors associated with a willingness to use marijuana are, presumably, the same as those associated with a willingness to use other illicit drugs." And the report recognizes "intensity" of marijuana use as increasing the risk of progression to other drugs.

The medical benefits and risks of marijuana—the subjects to which the report devotes most of its attention—are matters for doctors, scientists and the Food and Drug Administration. The potential of marijuana as a gateway drug is a matter of concern for teenagers, parents and policy makers.

The IOM's brief, three-page discussion of the gateway issue fails to discuss mounting statistical and scientific evidence that children who smoke pot are much likelier than those who don't to use drugs like cocaine, heroin and LSD. And the press coverage has been dangerously deceptive.

The Institute of Medicine study fails to discuss mounting scientific evidence that children who smoke pot are much likelier to use drugs like cocaine, heroin and LSD.

I have not read or heard in any news report the important finding that "the . . . interpretation . . . that marijuana serves as a gateway to the world of illegal drugs in which youths have greater opportunity and are under greater social pressure to try other illegal drugs . . . is the interpretation most often used in the scientific literature, and is supported by—although not proven by the available data."

The National Center on Addiction and Substance Abuse, which I head, analyzed the data from the Centers for Disease Control and Prevention's 1995 Youth Risk Behavior Survey of 11,000 ninth-through 12th graders, adjusting for other risk factors such as repeated acts of violence and sexual promiscuity.

The correlations are potent:

- Teens who drank and smoked cigarettes at least once in the past month are 30 times more likely to smoke marijuana than those who didn't.

- Teens who drank, smoked cigarettes, and used marijuana at least once in the past month are more than 16 times as likely to use another drug like cocaine, heroin or LSD.

To appreciate the significance of these relationships, consider this: The first Surgeon General's report on smoking and health found a nine to 10 times greater risk of lung cancer among smokers. The early returns from the monumental Framingham heart study found that individuals with high cholesterol were two to four times as likely to suffer heart disease.

The Report Downplays Real Risks

Most people who smoke pot do not move on to other drugs, but then only 5% to 7% of cigarette smokers get lung cancer. The point for parents and teens is that those youngsters who smoke pot are at vastly greater risk of moving on to harder drugs. CASA's [Center on Addiction and Substance Abuse] studies reveal that the younger and more often a teen smokes pot, the more likely that teen is to use cocaine. A child who uses marijuana before age 12 is 42 times more likely to use cocaine, heroin or other drugs than one who first smokes pot after age 16.

The IOM report also fails to discuss findings of recent scientific studies that suggest some of the reasons for this high correlation. Studies in Italy reveal that marijuana affects levels of dopamine (the substance that gives pleasure) in the brain in a manner similar to heroin. Gaetana DiChiara, the physician who led this work at the University of Cagliari, indicates that marijuana may prime the brain to seek substances that act in a similar way. Studies in the U.S. have found that nicotine, cocaine and alcohol also affect dopamine levels.

Nor does the IOM report mention studies at the distinguished Scripps Research Institute in California and Cumplutense University in Madrid which found that rats subjected to immediate cannabis withdrawal exhibited changes in behavior similar to those seen after withdrawal of alcohol, cocaine and opiates. *Science* magazine called this "the first neurological basis for a marijuana withdrawal syndrome, and one with a strong emotional component shared by other drugs." Alan Leshner, director of the National Institute on Drug Abuse, has estimated that at least 100,000 individuals are in treatment because of marijuana use. Most are believed to be teenagers.

Our concern should be to prevent teen drug use. We know that someone who gets to age 21 without smoking, using drugs or abusing alcohol is virtually certain never to do so. We have known for some time, as the IOM report confirms that marijuana harms short-term memory, motor skills and the ability to concentrate, attributes teenagers need when they are learning in school.

Parents, teachers and clergy need to send teens a clear message: Stay away from pot. The incompleteness of the IOM report and the press's sloppy summaries of it must not be permitted to dilute that message.

Tobacco Is Lethal, Addictive, and Legal

Anna Quindlen

Smokers and tobacco companies have long made the argument that cigarette smoking cannot be compared to drug abuse. Many of the arguments tobacco advocates use to make their case, however, are circular according to naturalist and writer Anna Quindlen. One of the most famous of such fallacies, she says, is that smoking should not be regulated because tobacco is a legal substance. Quindlen wrote the following 2000 editorial in response to a rising number of successful class action lawsuits filed against big tobacco companies for knowingly marketing a lethal substance to people, especially children. In it, she says there is no real difference between tobacco and illegal substances that endanger their users' lives except that tobacco has been protected by profit-hungry companies and politicians afraid of being seen as unfriendly to free enterprise if they confront the issue.

Imagine that millions of Americans are addicted to a lethal drug. Imagine that the Food and Drug Administration [FDA] has repeatedly ducked its responsibility by refusing to regulate that drug. And imagine that when the FDA finally does its duty, an appeals court decides that it cannot do so, that the drug is so dangerous that if the FDA regulated it, it would have to be banned.

Welcome to the topsy-turvy world of tobacco, where nothing much makes sense except the vast profits, where tobacco company executives slip-slide along the continuum from aggrieved innocence to heartfelt regret without breaking a sweat, and where the only people who seem to be able to shoot straight are the jurors who decide the ubiquitous lawsuits.

The most recent panel to do the right thing handed down a judgment of $145 billion on behalf of sick smokers in the state of Florida, the largest jury damage award in history. Lawyers for the tobacco companies thundered that the award would bankrupt them, yet the stock market scarcely shuddered. Experts said the amount would likely be reduced when cooler judicial heads prevailed.

The jurors—who gave up two years of their lives, listened to endless witnesses and yet were able to hammer the tobacco companies after deliberating only a few hours—could be forgiven if they felt they'd fallen down Alice's rabbit hole into Wonderland, where the Red Queen cries "Off with their heads" but no one is ever executed. Al Gore, for instance, inspired by the death of his own sister from lung cancer, insisted not long ago that he will do everything he can to keep cigarettes out of the hands of children. But he says he would never outlaw cigarettes because millions of people smoke. Here is a question: how many users mandate legality? What about the estimated 3.6 million chronic cocaine users, or the 2.4 million people who admit to shooting or snorting heroin?

I can almost feel all the smokers out there, tired of standing outside their office buildings puffing in the rain when once they could sit comfortably at their desks, jumping up and down and yelling, "Tobacco is different from illicit drugs!" Because it is legal? Now, there's a circular argument. A hundred years ago the sale of cigarettes was against the law in 14 states. The Supreme Court, which ruled earlier this year that the FDA did not have the power to regulate tobacco, upheld a Tennessee law forbidding the sale of cigarettes in 1900. The justices agreed with a state court that had concluded, "They possess no virtue but are inherently bad and bad only." At the time, Coca-Cola still contained cocaine and heroin was in cough syrups.

Since then the tables have turned. Tobacco companies spread political contributions around like weed killer on the

lawn in summer, although they've passed from their bipartisan period into an era when they support largely complicit
Republicans, who like free enterprise (and soft money) more
than they hate emphysema. (George W. Bush responded to a
question about the recent megasettlement by bemoaning a li-
tigious nation.) Responsibility-minded Americans accept the
argument that individuals have the right to poison themselves,
although studies showing that the vast majority of smokers
began as minors raise questions about informed consent. Official tobacco apologists spent years insisting their product did
not cause cancer, then that it was not addictive. Now they've
done a 180, arguing that since there is no such thing as a safe
cigarette, a government agency like the FDA, created to regulate the safety of products, cannot touch them.

If this sounds like having it both ways, that's because it is.
Philip Morris masquerades as a corporate Robin Hood by
making large contributions to nonprofit organizations, soup
kitchens, ballet companies, museums and shelters, being a
good citizen with the profits of a product that kills 400,000
people a year. And magazines, including this one, run articles
about the dangers of cigarettes in the same issues that adver-
tise them.

Even tobacco foes have fudged. When Dr. David Kessler
ran the FDA, he publicly concluded what everyone already
knew: that cigarettes are nothing more than a primitive delivery device for nicotine, a dangerous and addictive drug. But
the agency never took the obvious next step. The Food, Drug,
and Cosmetic Act forbids the sale of any drug that is not safe
and effective, and part of the FDA's mandate is to regulate devices. Cigarettes are a device. The drug they deliver is patently
unsafe. Ergo, cigarettes should be banned.

That's not going to happen in our lifetime, which is why
even a more aggressive FDA refused to take this to the limit.
Too many tobacco farmers, too many tobacco addicts; a right
to a livelihood, a right to a lifestyle. (Both of these arguments

131

hold for legalizing illicit drugs as well, but never mind.) "Pro-hibition" is a dirty word in America. But tobacco can in no way be compared to alcohol. Many people can and do drink safely and in moderation, while it is impossible to smoke without some pernicious health effects, and nearly all smokers can be described as addicts. But if cigarettes were outlawed, what to do with all those tobacco junkies? Nicotine clinics providing the patch, strong coffee and hypnotherapy?

Public-service announcements, catchy commercials for kids, settlements with the states to recover health-care costs: the tobacco companies, which once swore they were doing nothing wrong, are now willing to lose some ideological battles to win the war of the profit margin. One Philip Morris executive appearing at a recent conference even told Kessler, whose efforts to restrict sales and advertising aimed at children spawned a battle royal of billable hours, that he welcomed "serious regulation of the tobacco industry at the federal level." Now they tell us. Why shouldn't the Marlboro men play the angles? The public and the pol's have provided them with so many angles to play. Here is the bottom line: cigarettes are the only legal product that, when used as directed, cause death. The rest is just a puppet show in the oncology wing.

Vote over Marijuana Legalization Fuels National Debate

Ethan Nadelmann and John Walters

In 2002, citizens of the state of Nevada had the opportunity to vote on Question 9, an initiative that would legalize the private use of marijuana there. The months leading up to the vote provided heavy hitters on both sides of the issue the opportunity to raise their voices. The two individuals interviewed by CNN anchor Fredricka Whitfield could not have been further apart in their opinions over Question 9. Ethan Nadelmann, executive director of the Drug Policy Alliance, praises the ballot initiative as a way to divert the excessive money and police efforts used to fight a relatively harmless and proven therapeutic substance toward solving more urgent social problems. George W. Bush's drug czar John Walters, on the other hand, expresses deep concern that people like Nadelmann would use the medical marijuana argument to mislead the public into thinking the drug is entirely harmless and that, by voting to keep it illegal, they would be denying people access to a legitimate medication. Walters maintains that smoked marijuana has no proven medical value. Question 9 passed, making private marijuana use legal in Nevada.

*F*redricka *Whitfield*: The state of Nevada is known for its tolerant stands on prostitution and gambling. Both are legal there. Now, the state is about to take a gamble on another taboo issue—marijuana. This election day, state voters will decide if pot should be legalized for private use. So far, Nevadans are split on the issue. A recent poll by the "Las Vegas Re-

Ethan Nadelmann and John Walters, "Interviews with Ethan Nadelmann, John Walters," *CNN Sunday Morning*, October 6, 2002. © 2004 Cable News Network LP, LLLP. A Time Warner Company. All rights reserved. Reproduced by permission.

view" journal found that 55 percent of likely voters oppose the proposal. Only 40 percent favor it. Ethan Nadelmann supports the measure, and he is executive director of the Drug Policy Alliance, a group that promotes alternatives to the war on drugs, and he joins us from New York. . . .

Ethan Nadelmann: Good morning, Fredricka.

Whitfield: All right. So if Nevadans agree, it would mean that Nevadans could have three ounces of marijuana, and it would be perfectly legal. They wouldn't be sent to jail. Why is that amount the agreed upon amount to be on the ballot, and why even make this push, [Ethan] . . .

Nadelmann: I think basically what you see happening in Nevada is something we're going to see more and more around the United States. It is a lot like what happened during alcohol prohibition in the United States in the late 1920s. You know, a number of states started to repeal their own alcohol prohibition laws on the weight of the repealing the 18th Amendment, the national alcohol prohibition amendment, and at the same time internationally, the United States was increasingly isolated. We were almost alone in alcohol prohibition, and other countries either never adopted it or were turning their back.

It's the same thing today. You look around the world, you see Switzerland is probably going to legally regulate marijuana next year. Last week, the Canadian prime minister said it's time to decriminalize. . . . It's not just the Netherlands anymore, it's a range of countries, and what you see in the United States, in Nevada especially, is more and more people saying that this war on marijuana, it doesn't make any sense, that half of the drug arrests in this country for marijuana doesn't make any sense. I mean, we live in a country where half of all Americans between the age of 20 and 50 have smoked marijuana. We can't even find a presidential candidate who will say that he never smoked marijuana, so the notion of locking people up, having the police waste resources in this area really makes no sense.

Whitfield: But isn't the argument also if you allow the legalization of marijuana, then what stops you from the decriminalization of any other narcotic? Why stop at marijuana if you allow the legalization of one drug, and that means it opens the floodgates for the arguments of all the others?

Decriminalizing Marijuana Would Solve Many Problems

Nadelmann: Fredricka, it's hard to imagine that there's any kind of slippery slope here. I mean, one could have said, you know, 80 years ago that if you legalized alcohol, the next thing you would be doing is legalizing heroin.

The advantage in Nevada is that this is a ballot initiative. It means that the voters have a chance to vote on this. It is a very clear choice for them. Shall marijuana continue to be subjected to criminal prohibitions with people being arrested and thrown behind bars, or not? Will the state government be charged with trying to set up a responsible way for regulating this, or not? Will the medical marijuana initiative that was implemented and voted into effect a few years ago in Nevada, will that be implemented honestly or not?

I mean, I think that's the real question here. Fredricka, the other question, by the way, though, is over the last number of years, almost every state in the West voted to make medical marijuana legal, that marijuana should be legal for medical purposes.

Now, this is something where 70 percent of Americans believe that marijuana should be legal for medical purposes, and the tragedy is that the federal government has refused to abide by the will of the people. Just a few weeks ago in California, federal police agents raided a hospice, 85 percent of the people are terminally ill, arrested paraplegic patients. You know, President [George W.] Bush likes to talk about compassion and compassionate conservatism—we don't see any evidence of that. . . .

Whitfield: Well, is the bottom line of this argument that you feel as though the decriminalization of this amount of marijuana would also help to promote some relief in what are now overcrowded jails and prisons, because a good more than half of the inmates in many of these jails, particularly in your state as well, are dealing with, you know, drug offenses, and is this really the bottom, you know, line of your argument?

Nadelmann: Yeah, because you have to understand most of the people supporting this, this is not a pro-marijuana initiative. This is an initiative to say it's stupid, it's crazy, it's a waste of money, a waste of lives, a waste of police resources to be locking people up.

You know, there's going to be other initiatives as well in Ohio and in Washington, D.C. They are initiatives that have nothing to do with marijuana. They are simply about substituting treatment for incarceration for non-violent drug possession charges.

Whitfield: Critics of this issue are also arguing that it's certainly sending—the legalization of marijuana in any amount is sending the wrong message to young people.

Nadelmann: Well, I'll tell you this, it seems to me that the current policy of, you know, the federal drug czar [John Walters] and the other people in Washington waving the flag and yelling how dangerous marijuana is, I mean, the bottom line is, nobody has better access to marijuana in America today than teenagers. It is true today; it was true 10 and 20 years ago, and in all likelihood, it will be true 10 years from now.

So those who say that it is sending the wrong message to kids, I say the current policy is sending the wrong message to kids. We're telling kids that somehow alcohol and cigarettes are safer? I think we're sending kids a message that it's OK to be hypocritical about drug policy because of the moral prejudices and biases of those people in Washington.

Whitfield: All right, Ethan Nadelmann, thank you very much. I appreciate it.

Nadelmann: OK.

Whitfield: Well, the legalization of marijuana does not have the support of the Bush administration. And joining us live from Washington is John Walters, the U.S. drug czar. He heads the White House Office of National Drug Control Policy. Good to see you.

John Walters: Nice to be with you.

Whitfield: All right, well, is it going to be your concern that if Nevadans do agree that it is OK to possess at least three or no more than three ounces of marijuana, that perhaps this is going to set the tone for the ongoing battle on the federal level, and that perhaps with one state going on board, this might weaken federal law?

Walters: I think our concern is that it's going to weaken the situation in Nevada for people who live there. The federal government's not going to repeal its laws because they are protecting young people, especially. I think we have a lot of ignorance here that I'm trying—my office is responsible for correcting.

Today, of the six million people who need treatment for drug dependency or abuse, 65 percent are dependent on marijuana. Most baby boomer parents, most Americans don't know that. And the charge that our jails are all full of people with marijuana possession—20 percent of the people in state prisons, the largest system in the country, are there for drug charges. Most of them are dealers, and those who are there for marijuana possession who largely pled down [their sentences] are less than .5 percent.

There is a con going on here about, one, marijuana is safe, that we're not controlling it, that it's not a threat. Today, more young people are seeking treatment for marijuana than for alcohol. Today, 60 percent of the people who are teenagers seeking treatment are seeking it for dependency on marijuana. It's more dangerous. The potency of marijuana today, when it was less than 1 percent THC [tetrahydrocannabinol] content, the psycho-active ingredient in the '70s, today it's 7 percent to 14 percent, and with new hydroponically developed strains, it goes up to 30 percent. This is not your father's marijuana. And that's what's causing the problem.

Whitfield: You heard Ethan [Nadelmann], who said that, you know, this mandate is archaic, and at this point the wrong message is being sent to young children because nothing has changed. How do you respond to him when he says that already, you know, there is access, whether you're a teenager or whether you're a young adult, and access is certainly not the problem, but you're sending the wrong message by not allowing the law to evolve with the lifestyles that are evolving?

Marijuana Use Is a Serious Drug Problem

Walters: Well, I think there's two points. One is, first of all, yes, we think that the availability of marijuana is too great, but it's not as available as I think some people like to say. There's a lot of concern that, yes, it's too available, but it's not like alcohol and, yet, today we have a serious problem with marijuana. If we made it more available, do we think the pathology would get smaller, the number of people addicted, the number of teens involved would be smaller? No, it would be larger.

But secondly, it's the attitude. We have to correct the attitude that this is medicine, that this is simply as safe as alcohol and tobacco. I mean, we already have 55 million people who are cigarette smokers and over 100 million who are users of alcohol. We have problem drinkers and certainly are concerned about the health consequences of cigarettes, but we have 16 million people who are users of drugs, most of that is marijuana. Now, would the 16 million grow or would it shrink if we decriminalized it? And secondly. . . .

Whitfield: Well, isn't it—go ahead, sorry, make your second point.

Walters: And secondly, I mean, we try to control cigarettes and alcohol, but still many more kids have access to cigarettes and alcohol. So the way in which the disease of addiction is spread is by non-addictive users. They're the carriers of this disease. If we unleash non-addictive use, we are going to increase the spread of the disease of addiction, so instead of six million people, we'll have something more approximate to the 55 million smokers or the number of problem drinkers we have.

Whitfield: Well, how do you respond to those who say that a mixed message is being sent, if some are allowed to use marijuana for medicinal purposes, then those are going to— you know, those people are going to argue that it's not hurting their bodies. There's nothing wrong with it. It doesn't impair their ability. Then why address this issue to the majority of the population and say, it does impair your abilities, it is dangerous and no one should be using it?

Walters: Yeah, I think that's part of the con here that's frankly going on here. Marijuana is not medicine, and I wish it was because we could eliminate the dispute. We regulate variants of cocaine, variants of opium for medical purposes that are proven.

There is one ingredient in marijuana that is medically efficacious and is allowed to be prescribed, but smoked marijuana is not a medicine. It's failed to meet the criteria we use to have efficacious medical treatment, and we have the best medical system in the history of humankind.

I wish we could say it was, but it's not and it's misleading to tell people that because some people claim it helps them or some people say it makes them feel better when they're dying it's medicine. A lot of people feel better with many things when they're dying. That is snake oil.

Many people who are dying of smoking-related cancers smoke up to the end because cigarettes make them feel better, but it would be outrageous for cigarette companies to claim that makes tobacco medicine and we ought to give it to people.

The fact is, I would like to save smoked marijuana—we're doing research to isolate elements of it that are medicine. But there is a dimension of this issue that is the con and it's extremely cruel, using suffering people to suggest that this is efficacious medicine. It has three to five times as much tar and carbon monoxide as cigarettes, smoked marijuana does. It suppresses the immune system. It is a dangerous carcinogenic substance, and it's not medicine.

Whitfield: All right, well, John Walters, drug czar, thank you very much. And we will find out whether Nevadans are agreeing with you or not because they will be voting on that ballot on the issue, question number nine and it is November 5. All right. Thanks very much. I appreciate it.

Walters: Thank you.

CHAPTER 4

Approaches to Addiction and Treatment

Chapter Preface

Historically, addicts have been stigmatized as weak and immoral. With the creation of Alcoholics Anonymous (AA) in the 1930s and other treatment options however, a more compassionate attitude emerged. Throughout the twentieth century myriad programs arose that were designed to treat addictions rather than condemn the addict. Although it's generally agreed that addicts need treatment, determining the root causes of addiction and what treatment options work best has remained a source of rigorous debate.

For much of the twentieth century, the idea that addiction is a disease reigned. One researcher, E.M. Jellinek, is credited with revolutionizing the dialogue about addiction with the publication of his paper, *The Disease Concept of Alcoholism*. In direct response to Jellinek's work, the American Psychiatric Association and the American Medical Association began to use the term "disease" to describe a person's addiction to alcohol or other drugs. The disease concept maintains that the addict has no control over his or her condition. It also says that though addiction is not curable, it can be kept in remission if a person abstains from alcohol or drug abuse. Proponents of the concept, such as AA and Narcotics Anonymous (NA), have relied on a faith-based treatment model to encourage members to use their faith in God and mutual support to remain abstinent.

In the 1980s, some researchers criticized the disease concept of addiction because they believed it oversimplified a multifaceted, complex, and highly individualized problem. If addiction were truly a disease, they asked, how could some addicts return to moderate consumption at different points in their lives and not lapse into full-blown addiction again? That some addicts seemed to have conscious control over their substance use violated the basic premise of the disease concept.

These critics pointed out that to tell a person she has no control over her addiction can leave her feeling helpless and resigned. Also, they argued that religious treatment alternatives often associated with the disease concept typically are not helpful to people who do not believe in God.

Though many in the treatment community still operate with a disease concept of addiction, a variation of the concept has come into favor recently. It views addiction as a chronic medical condition. It differs from a strict disease model in that, rather than describe addiction as a disorder that progresses through ever-more severe steps, it views it as a chronic medical problem, like diabetes or hypertension, that can be managed with ongoing treatment. As with any medical condition, relapses and setbacks are expected throughout the course of treatment rather than viewed as a failure or lapse of morals on the part of the addict. Just as voluntary behaviors exacerbate the condition of a patient with chronic hypertension, so also will consuming alcohol or drugs cause the recovering addict to experience a setback. Proponents of the chronic medical condition concept say that this fine distinction allows substance abusers to discern that they do, in fact, have control over their condition.

What most in the treatment community are willing to concede is that multiple factors cause substance abuse and that a variety of treatment methods must be available to meet the needs of each individual. For example, where faith-based support groups may work for some people, a strictly medical approach may work better for others. The challenge for countries like the United States is to ensure that a mix of treatment alternatives exists to meet the needs of addicts of all ages, ethnic backgrounds, and socioeconomic status.

Alcoholism Is Not a Disease

Herbert Fingarette

Behavioral scientist Herbert Fingarette numbers among the many who have rejected the idea that alcoholism is a disease. In the following chapter from a 1988 book he wrote to debunk the idea, Fingarette says that the theory that alcoholism is a disease has proven inadequate to explain the many and varied reasons some people cannot drink in moderation. Rather than make alcoholics feel as if they are merely victims of a diseased physical makeup, he says, treatment professionals should help alcohol abusers understand the individual reasons for their drinking, which, he maintains, will help them regain control over their addiction.

Before the classic disease concept of alcoholism was largely abandoned by scientists, a key question among its proponents was, What is the cause of the disease? This question may now seem pointless inasmuch as we have seen that the heart of the classic disease concept, loss of control, is a confused notion that is contradicted by a bookshelf of experimental evidence. But there is so much misinformation abroad—news of breakthroughs in the discovery of the cause or cure of the disease of alcoholism—that one cannot help wondering if there is some fire where there is so much smoke. If we want to sort out the true from the false, we need to examine the theories about the causes of the so-called disease and also . . . the treatments for it.

Despite decades of imminent breakthroughs, the current dominant consensus among researchers is that no single explanation, however complex, has ever been scientifically established as the cause of alcoholism. As one leading research group summarizes the issue: "[the] causes of excessive drink-

Herbert Fingarette, from *Heavy Drinking*. Berkeley: University of California Press, 1988. Copyright © 1988 by The Regents of the University of California. Reproduced by permission.

ing are always multiple and interactive, and . . . any single-factor model of causation is not only wrong in theory, but in practice will lead to inappropriate responses to the individual, and to imperfect social policies."[1] Nor, as we will soon see, has anyone proposed a scientifically accepted multiple-factor explanation.

Alcoholism and Alcoholisms

As one begins to read the literature on the causes of alcoholism, one notices that the words *alcoholism* and *alcoholic* have been, and still are, used to mean many different things. . . . Much the same vagueness obtains in regard to the word *disease*. In medical texts the word has only a loose, ill-defined allusive sense and is not used as a basis for rigorous scientific discussion. Or in [alcohol researcher E.M.] Jellinek's words: "It comes to this, that *a disease is what the medical profession recognizes as such*."[2]

One reviewer summarizes the broad diversity of theories by noting that "the determination of the underlying causes of alcoholism has been even more intensely debated than its definition" and that "at least three major views of the etiology of alcoholism can be identified: (1) medical, (2) psychological, and (3) sociocultural."[3] Which is a scholar's way of saying that every conceivable perspective has been adopted in trying to explain the causes of alcoholism and none of them has achieved general scientific acceptance. The reviewer then proposes that perhaps a little of each brand of hypothesis is true. So we are left with alcoholism as a disease that is "multiple in origin and complex in development." Instead of a single disease and syndrome (cluster of symptoms), we have a continuum of behaviors ranging from teetotaling to chronic heavy abuse.

The Department of Health, Education and Welfare's publication *Alcohol and Health* epitomizes the consequences of the official inclination to use the term *alcoholism* as though it referred to one definable condition: "The causes of alcoholism are so many and appear in such differing constellations from person to person that one cannot consider treating alcoholism as if it were a single illness with an identifiable and specific etiology, a known course, and a proven response to a particular chemical agent or medical treatment."[4]

Despite the fact that there is no general agreement about the definition of alcoholism, hundreds of hypotheses have been proposed about what causes it. In 1980 a monograph published by the National Institute on Drug Abuse discussed a selection of specially interesting theories—forty-three of them.[5] The temptation to doubt that the theories could all be wrong must be balanced by the thought that, however plausible they may seem, at least most of them must be wrong. After all, how many true explanations can there be?

Thus the best answer we have to the question. What causes the disease of alcoholism? is: There is no such single disease and therefore there is no cause. The very proliferation of widely diverging unsupported hypotheses is not characteristic of solid scientific research. It is characteristic of pseudo-science and faddism.

Obviously, we can consider here only a few of the theories that have been proposed, those that contain the most plausible elements of truth, or are the most widely believed, or the most truly informative from a scientific standpoint. At best any of these theories is only a partial explanation of some aspects of heavy drinking.

Genetic Hypotheses

Genetic hypotheses have been widely discussed. On crucial points, however, most of the animal and human studies of genetic influences on alcohol abuse are acknowledgedly indecisive.[6] For example, studies of the children of alcoholic parents have shown that these children are statistically at significantly higher than average risk of becoming alcoholics. But this method of study cannot prove that heredity, rather than family environment, is responsible for the increased risk.

Studies of alcoholism in twins have been far more strongly suggestive of a genetic factor.[7] And several skillfully designed studies of adopted children have provided some insights into the nature versus nurture question. Representative of these studies is the pivotal work of Donald W. Goodwin and his associates.[8]

Goodwin's study is based on a simple idea, though one arduous and complex to implement: Find children who were born to an alcoholic mother or father but who were put up for adoption very shortly after birth and thus were not raised by their biological parents; then see whether these children in later life show a higher rate of alcoholism than a comparable group of adopted infants whose biological parents were not alcoholics. Any difference in the rates of alcoholism between the two groups could be attributed to heredity rather than rearing. And since both groups of children were adoptees, and relationship between alcoholism and being an adoptee should be the same for both groups and will, in effect, cancel itself out in comparisons between the two groups.

Goodwin chose to study only male children, and in 85 percent of the cases the biological alcoholic parent was the father. This experimental design followed the lead of earlier studies, which suggested that father-son relationships were likely to show the strongest genetic influence.

The difference in the incidence of alcoholism for Goodwin's two groups was statistically significant. The rate of alcoholism among the adoptees who had an alcoholic biological parent was 3.6 times greater than that among the adoptees whose biological parents were not alcoholics. What added extra persuasiveness to Goodwin's results was that for the subset of sons whose adopting parents happened to be alcoholics, no statistically significant difference was apparent. It was consis-

147

tently the case that only alcoholism in the biological parents was a statistically significant factor.

Somewhat similar results have been obtained in several other studies.[9] But taken together, these findings do not come anywhere near warranting the conclusion that there is a unique disease of alcoholism which is genetically determined. Besides the question of the differing definitions of *alcoholism* used by the various research teams, at best the studies suggest that heredity is one factor, among many, that pertains in a minority of cases. A second look at the data shows why these qualifications are necessary.

In Goodwin's study, about 18 percent of the sons who had an alcoholic parent became alcoholics, compared to 5 percent of the sons of nonalcoholic parents. The hypothesis is that the difference between these groups is attributable to heredity. But to see the full picture, let's turn the numbers around 82 percent of the sons who had an alcoholic parent—more than four out of five—did not become alcoholics. So if we generalize from Goodwin's results, we must say that about 80 percent of persons with an alcoholic parent will not become alcoholics. Either the relevant genes are usually not transmitted or the genes are transmitted but are usually outweighed by other factors.

A second implication of Goodwin's study is easier to grasp if we construe a hypothetical example based on a ballpark guess about the percentage of alcoholics in the child-bearing adult population. We have no statistics on this issue, but everyone agrees that many more parents are nonalcoholics than are alcoholics. Let us make a very generous round guess that 10 of 100 child-bearing couples have one alcoholic member and that all 100 couples have two sons each. If 18 percent of the 20 sons born to the couples that have an alcoholic partner go on to become alcoholics, we will have about 4 alcoholic sons in this subset. If 5 percent of the 180 sons born to nonalcoholic parents go on to become alcoholics, we will have 9 alcoholic sons in that subset. That is, only one third of the alcoholic sons will have been born of an alcoholic parent.

Granted these are hypothetical numbers, and the proportions will vary depending on the numbers one picks. But his simple example illustrates how from Goodwin's data we can extrapolate the finding that by far most alcoholics have biological parents who are not themselves alcoholics. When we put this together with our earlier observation that by far most children born of an alcoholic parent will not themselves become alcoholics, we see that any genetic factor must be but one possible factor among others and that this genetic factor makes a difference in only a minority of cases.

I do not want to obscure the practical and scientific importance of the data from genetic studies. People whose parents or siblings are long-term heavy drinkers are "at risk" to some unspecifiable degree. And data on heredity are part of the complex total picture for research scientists. But no one should be misled into thinking that alcoholism is genetic. Not only is such a belief incorrect but also it often leads people to become apathetic or defeatist. It is of the highest practical importance for heavy drinkers and their families and friends to understand that whether a given person becomes a heavy drinker or not is not an issue settled by his or her genes. Even when parents or siblings are heavy drinkers, the fate of a particular person is crucially influenced by conduct, character, beliefs, and environment.

Unfortunately, the significance of genetic factors is in general widely misunderstood. When we see very young children who have an exceptional talent for music or art or foreign languages, we rightly suspect that genes play some significant role. But we don't conclude that each person's social destiny and occupation are rigorously and unalterably determined by his or her genes. Many other circumstances of life and personality combine in infinitely many combinations to shape an individual.

By the same token, as one authority explains, "It is common to find that some genetic contribution can be established for many aspects of human attributes or disorders (ranging from musical ability to duodenal ulcers), and drinking is unlikely to be the exception."[10]

A final important point is that even if genetic factors play a role in some drinking behavior, it does not necessarily follow that they play a role in generating the problem behaviors often associated with heavy drinking. How, for example, could genetic factors explain why almost half of adult males in our country who are heavy drinkers have no drink-related personal or social problems while almost half the adult males in our country who have serious personal and social problems associated with their drinking are not heavy drinkers?[11] The link between heavy drinking and serious personal and social problems is much looser by far than is generally supposed.[12] And so, even if heavy drinking is in a minority of cases partly ascribable to genetic factors, such factors would not account for differences between problem and nonproblem drinkers.

Metabolic Hypotheses

We turn now to a group of theories that seek to explain the causes of the supposed disease of alcoholism by looking at human physiology, specifically at the way that our body chemistry reacts to alcohol. The premise is that because of genetic factors or acquired physiological differences, some people's bodies respond to alcohol in an abnormal way that "causes" them to become alcoholics.

One of the physiological hypotheses that made something of a sensation in the 1970s was the proposition that persons who are alcoholics and those identified as at higher than average risk of becoming alcoholics tend to metabolize alcohol in distinctive ways.[13] Some studies measured blood levels of acetaldehyde (an intermediate product in the complex metabolism of alcohol) and reported generally higher levels in alcoholics and alcoholism-prone subjects. But the conjecture that higher acetaldehyde levels somehow produce a physical dependence on alcohol has not been borne out. A review of the literature concludes that "the popular theory that the development of physical dependence upon ethanol [alcohol] is mediated by acetaldehyde is not favored by much experimental evidence."[14]

Other studies have suggested that certain morphinelike substances may be secreted during alcohol metabolism and that these substances significantly affect the way one experiences alcohol intoxication. The facts are so far incomplete; no one has proved that there is a significant difference in the levels of these substances in alcoholics and nonalcoholics. "At present, these findings are only of theoretical interest and will require much more work before their validity can be established."[15] But we can already see that even if a difference were found, it could not account for the drinking patterns of heavy drinkers but only for some aspects of how they experience intoxication. Increased levels of morphinelike substances during the few hours that the body is metabolizing alcohol cannot explain why after a period of sobriety, when the body has been free of alcohol and its metabolic products, an alcoholic will resume heavy drinking.

Tolerance and Withdrawal

We turn next to what may be the most appealing type of explanation of how people become alcoholics. The various versions of this theory all derive from the fact that long-term heavy drinkers often develop a physical tolerance for alcohol and experience physical withdrawal symptoms when they cease drinking. These physical effects are presumed to produce psychological effects that cause an irresistible craving for alcohol.

A characteristic and widely known version of the theory goes like this: At some point the heavy drinker experiences physical withdrawal symptoms (nervous tension, jitteriness, sweating, and a general feeling of discomfort) when he stops drinking. He discovers that alcohol promptly alleviates these symptoms ("a bit of the hair of the dog"). So he takes a drink and the cycle begins again. Of course, this theory cannot explain why, despite the danger signs, a person continued to drink heavily for a long enough time—it can take years—to develop physical withdrawal symptoms. Nor does it explain why after the drinker has had one or two drinks to alleviate the withdrawal discomfort, he doesn't stop or at least moderate his drinking.

To address these questions, a variation of the theory incorporates an element of operant conditioning, the principle that if a behavior or a response is followed by a reward or benefit (positive reinforcement), a person will be more likely to repeat that behavior or response. Since drinking liquor is followed by a positive feeling—relief of distress—drinking reinforces the tendency to drink. As this conditioning repeats itself, the drinking becomes a stronger and stronger habit. But the drinker's ever more frequent intake of alcohol leads to an increasing physical tolerance for alcohol. That is, it takes more alcohol to achieve the same effect as previously. So, over time, the heavy drinker needs more and more alcohol to obtain relief from withdrawal distress. But drinking greater quantities in turn intensifies the withdrawal symptoms when drinking stops.

The upshot is a vicious cycle: Each successive cessation of drinking induces ever greater withdrawal distress; the drinker must drink ever more alcohol to get relief; the relief, in turn, acts as further reinforcement of the conditioned response of drinking, as well as further increasing tolerance, and further intensifying subsequent withdrawal distress.[16] Ultimately, according to this theory, withdrawal distress becomes so severe that it not only activates the automatic conditioned response of drinking but also induces a fully conscious and desperate craving for alcohol in order to dispel the torture of the withdrawal reaction.

This blend of biochemistry and psychology may be appealing, but several kinds of evidence undermine such explanations of alcoholism by reference to tolerance and withdrawal symptoms.

First, a significant proportion of those drinkers classified as alcoholics do not develop tolerance and withdrawal symptoms. One large-scale study found that 36 percent of diagnosed alcoholics did not have these symptoms, even when they were still drinking regularly.[17] Second, ... many experiments have shown that alcoholics do not drink while suffering withdrawal distress. The actual behavior of alcoholics simply does not follow the rigid habitual pattern that conditioning theory would lead us to expect.[18] Third, we cannot go along with the assumption that drinking is a positive reinforcement for the alcoholic because it always relieves tension. Clinical observation has revealed that for alcoholics drinking is often not followed by relaxation or euphoria, but frequently by depression or anxiety. As one specialist in the biopsychology of alcoholism says: "We have developed convincing evidence regarding the complexity of alcohol's effect on the emotions, showing that a simplistic reduction of tension does not explain what occurs."[19]

Fourth, laboratory measurements of blood alcohol levels and withdrawal symptoms do not show the relationships that the theories predict. For example, according to the theory, withdrawal symptoms should decrease as blood alcohol levels rise. But this pattern does not regularly occur. Indeed, blood alcohol levels do not uniformly rise relative to the amount of alcohol drunk. Some drinkers can consume as much as a fifth of whiskey a day and still maintain low blood alcohol levels.[20] And the weight of the evidence shows that "alcoholics do not drink consistently to maintain stable blood alcohol levels."[21]

In sum, the phenomena of tolerance and withdrawal symptoms cannot be viewed as *the* cause of alcoholism. The temptation to save the theory by increasingly speculative hypotheses remains strong, however. Some researchers have proposed that subtle residues of physical withdrawal or related bodily conditions may persist as long as six months after severe withdrawal is over, even if abstinence is maintained.[22] But if there were such subtle residues, it is highly implausible to infer that they would produce an irresistible craving that overwhelms all other motives and that compels abstinent alcoholics to resume drinking.

The search to establish physical tolerance and withdrawal as the decisive cause of chronic heavy drinking has been abandoned by almost all researchers. There is evidence that, like genetic factors, these physical factors may play a role in influencing drinking behavior. But clearly many other factors must also come into play. . . .

At this point we need to clear up some popular misconceptions about the term *physical dependence*. Strictly speaking, physical dependence refers to the development of physical tolerance and withdrawal symptoms in a person who has used a particular substance over time. As we noted earlier, many long-term drinkers do develop a physical tolerance for alcohol and exhibit physical symptoms (tremors, anxiety, etc.) when they stop drinking.

But in everyday conversation, these physical developments are misinterpreted to mean that the substance abuser has an urgent need, an intense desire, a necessary reliance on the substance such that he "can't live without it." There is no scientific evidence whatsoever for this popular redefinition of *dependency*. In no known respect does a person who experiences the physical symptoms of alcohol dependence require—either subjectively or objectively—a drink of alcohol. Rather, abundant studies show that drinkers who suffer physical symptoms of withdrawal will often, and of their own volition, refrain from drinking.

It is true that drinkers who develop the symptoms of physical dependency are, other things being equal, more likely to continue drinking heavily than those who do not. The more severe the symptoms, the greater the likelihood of the drinker continuing to drink, and the lower the likelihood of returning to more moderate drinking. These general patterns have been documented in a four-year followup study of people admitted for inpatient alcohol treatment programs.[23] But while this study suggests general trends, the followup data do not illustrate any hard-and-fast relationships between physical dependency and subsequent drinking behavior. Of those drinkers who showed severe physical dependence symptoms at the time of admission, 12 percent were drinking without any physical symptoms or social problems at the four-year followup, and another 23 percent had been abstinent for at least a year. Among those who on admission had dependence symptoms at low levels, 30 percent were nonproblem drinkers four years later; another 20 percent had been abstinent for a year or more. And of those who on admission were abstinent or without dependence symptoms, about 31 percent were nonproblem drinkers at the followup, and about 16 percent had abstained for a year or more. Despite the statistically significant correlations between physical dependency and subsequent problem drinking, the substantial overlap in all categories indicates that physical dependency, whether severe or mild, is not a trustworthy predictor of how any individual drinker will behave.

A final point about this study raises an issue that always lurks in the background of efforts to relate physical dependency to subsequent behavior. As one might expect, the drinkers who had the stronger symptoms of dependency generally had been drinking much longer and more heavily than those who had mild symptoms or none at all. Thus the statistical correlations reported in this study may have far less to do with the effects of physical dependency than with the simple proposition that people who have been drinking heavily for a long time are likely to have more difficulty in changing their drinking behavior. Habits, associations, and life circumstances would mitigate against the probability of radical change, all quite independently of any physical symptoms. Rather than being a *cause* of heavy drinking, the physical symptoms may be just one more *consequence* of it.

Psychological Hypotheses

Numerous attempts have been made to explain the alcoholic's patterns of drinking by reference to psychological constructs: personality, inner conflict, anxiety, poor self-image, and so on. We need not review all these theories, none of which has been scientifically confirmed and none of which has earned general acceptance in the scientific community.[24] Most are highly speculative, often based on studies of limited samples or clinical interpretations of individual cases.

In the late 1960s and early 1970s there was speculation that men drink heavily in order to hide self-perceptions of weakness, that their drinking represents a reaction against feelings of psychological dependency on others.[25] Other studies suggested that certain personality traits are statistically associated with a higher risk of becoming an alcoholic. But the sorts of traits in question are so broadly defined and are so common among nonalcoholics as well—impulsivity, dependency, inadequate self-esteem—as to be of little practical use. As one reviewer succinctly put it: "Studies of the personality of alcoholics have consistently led to a rejection of an 'alcoholic personality.'"[26]

Several psychosocial studies have, however, provided us with important statistical data on groups likely to be at risk for becoming alcohol abusers. Children of alcoholics are at higher risk in our society: Due to genetic and environmental factors, between 20 percent and 25 percent of males who have an alcoholic parent become alcoholics.[27] The other side of the coin: this finding equally implies that 75 percent to 80 percent of individuals in this high-risk group do not become alcoholics, and that most alcoholics do not have alcoholic parents. So, while this at-risk correlation is statistically significant in predicting national rates of alcoholism, it is useless as a predictor of any individual's destiny, since 75 percent to 80 percent of the time the "prediction" is not fulfilled.

Of equal importance: Even if in some cases genetic factors play a contributing role, whether the child of an alcoholic grows up to become a heavy drinker depends largely on the individual's social environment and life history.

Perhaps the most widely appealing types of psychological hypotheses are those proposing to explain long-term heavy drinking in terms of learning theory. The general premise of this approach is that people persistently drink heavily because they have "learned" to handle certain of life's challenges in this way. We have already discussed, and rejected, an operant conditioning hypothesis. Other applications of learning theory to alcohol abuse emphasize more complex phenomena such as cognition, emotion, and desire.

Although the key behaviors associated with long-term heavy drinking have never been accounted for in rigorous and quantifiable terms derived from learning theory, the jargon of learning theory is loosely adopted in some quarters. One may read of responses, reinforcements, and operant rewards, of learning schedules, cognitive-symbolic correlates, cognitive dissonance, personal attribution effects, and efficacy expectations. Sometimes these terms are used in a reasonably precise way to provide a context for an experiment or a theory. Often they are merely used as professional clichés for describing how people trying to cope with difficult situations adopt and give up various kinds of activities and over time develop preferred and even habitual ways of acting.

Whatever the ultimate adequacy of these theories, we realize that we have left the realm of medicine, disease, and physiological abnormality. All the explanations of alcoholism in terms of learning theory presume that the drinker's basic capacities for learning and unlearning are normal. The "abnormality" consists of the particular things they have learned to do—to repeatedly engage in conduct that has harmful or antisocial consequences—not of any impairment in their mental or physical learning capacities. In this context, *therapy* and *treatment* are medical-looking words that in substance refer to nonmedical procedures: to teaching heavy drinkers to do things other than drinking, and to have them learn to want to avoid heavy drinking.

While some drinkers may be helped by this approach, it is worth noting that we do not have a science of how to teach imprudent people to change and live prudently. And if learning theory should prove to provide a valid explanation for chronic alcohol abuse, then the medical issues of disease and cure, of psychological pathology, will be beside the point.

Society and Culture

It is well established that all the manifold forms and patterns of heavy drinking are substantially affected by social, cultural, economic, and political factors.[28] The more one reads about the very different patterns of heavy drinking in various eras and cultures, the less plausible does it become that there is any one disease—one set of symptoms (a syndrome) uniquely associated with alcohol and its metabolism in the body—that could be the sole causal origin of chronic drinking.[29]

We know, for example, that all drinking patterns, including chronic heavy drinking, reflect cultural and ethnic norms. Relatively high proportions of the Irish, Scandinavian, and Russian populations (especially the adult males) drink a lot with some frequency. The French tradition, in contrast, has been one of drinking modest amounts at any one time but drinking frequently throughout the day, always remaining somewhat under the influence but rarely becoming visibly drunk, and eventually showing such physical signs as withdrawal. All sorts of cultural and subcultural norms, as well as such categories as geography and climate, socioeconomic class, and degree of urbanization have been significantly related to differences in drinking patterns.

Some cultures were first introduced to alcohol by the European explorers and colonists. Others had traditional ritual patterns of drinking and getting drunk that differed markedly from European behavior. For example, among the Chichicastenango Indians of Guatemala, there are two very different ways of drinking heavily. When drinking ceremonially, in the traditional way, men retain their dignity and fulfill their ceremonial duties even if they have drunk so much that they cannot walk unassisted. But when drinking in bars and taverns, where secular and European values and culture hold sway, the men dance, weep, quarrel, and act promiscuously.[30]

Similarly, in America today, we have different patterns for drinking at a formal dinner, at an informal meal in a private home, at a party, at a wedding, in a bar, with a group, and when alone. Social setting influences heavy drinkers as well. For example, one trained observer remarks that, in his experience, "astonishingly few alcoholics drink during their stay in hospital, despite having ample opportunities to do so. Yet an equally astonishing number of treated alcoholics return to drinking within a brief period of discharge."[31]

Another factor not commonly appreciated is economic: Under certain circumstances an increase in the cost of alcohol exerts a downward influence on the amount of drinking, including heavy drinking.[32] The evidence that even chronic heavy drinkers respond to the price of alcohol is that as prices increase, mortality from liver cirrhosis declines. (This is a useful indicator because liver cirrhosis occurs primarily among very heavy, very long-term drinkers, but it is quickly arrested if drinking stops.) . . .

Another point to be mentioned here ... is that political conditions can substantially affect heavy drinking. For example, rates of liver cirrhosis dropped dramatically in France during World War II and in the United States during Prohibition, and heavy drinking rose dramatically in Sweden when more liberal liquor-sale laws were adopted.[33]

Conclusions

Research to date has shown that no one causal formula explains why people become heavy drinkers. Indeed, the attempt to find a single catchall "cause" of a single "disease" has repeatedly led researchers astray. On the basis of all the available evidence, many scientists are challenging *any* theory that assumes "[a] sharp distinction between the determinants of ordinary drinking and harmful drinking."[34]

There are, in short, many kinds of heavy drinking that arise from many different causes and produce many different patterns of associated problems. This recognition, after all these years of research, is not evidence of failure. It is an important and productive discovery, for we now know that we can give up the search for an explanation of a disease that does not exist. We can then look at the realities of alcohol abuse in our society and begin to think constructively about the variety of people and problems associated with alcohol abuse. As one researcher wrote recently, "The greatest advantage of the multivariate perspective is that it complicates the picture of alcohol-related difficulties and in so doing paints a picture that is credible and relevant to the needs of the individual case."[35]

Instead of looking at heavy drinkers as victims of some wayward gene or physical abnormality, we can now see them in a truer light: as a diverse group of people who for diverse reasons are caught up in a particularly destructive way of life. Although this depiction is messier than any single-factor theory, it has the advantage of being true to the observations of clinicians, and to those of many heavy drinkers and their families and friends. Moreover, once alcohol abusers themselves realize that they have not been stricken by some unidentifiable physical or psychiatric condition, they may find new cause for hope and for a more realistic self-understanding.

Endnotes

1. Edwards et al., *Alcohol and Alcoholism* (1979), 22-23. For a sense of the scientific consensus on single-factor models of causation, see Mello and Mendelson, *Alcohol: Use and Abuse in America* (1985), 230; Fingarette, "Philosophical and Legal Aspects of the Disease Concept of Alcoholism" (1983), 11; *Alcohol and Alcoholism* (1979), 89; Armor, Polich, and Stambul, *Alcoholism and Treatment* (1976), chap. 2; National Council on Alcoholism, "Criteria for the Diagnosis of Alcoholism" (1972); American Medical Association, *Manual on Alcoholism* (1967), 11.

2. Jellinek, *The Disease Concept of Alcoholism* (1960), 12. On the use of the term *disease* in relation to alcoholism, see Fingarette (1983), 2-5; Fingarette and Hasse, *Mental Disabilities and Criminal Responsibility* (1979), 144-47; Fingarette, "The Perils of Powell" (1970), 808-12.

3. Saxe, Dougherty, and Esty, "The Effectiveness and Cost of Alcoholism Treatment" (1985), 489.

4. *Alcohol and Health* (1971), 71.

5. Cited in Maisto, Galizio, and Carey, "Individual Differences in Substance Abuse" (1985), 7.

6. For reviews, see Goodwin, "Genetic Determinants of Alcoholism" (1985); Deitrich and Spuhler, "Genetics of Alcoholism and Alcohol Actions" (1984).

7. Partanen, Bruun, and Markham, *Inheritance of Drinking Behavior* (1966); Kaij, *Alcoholism in Twins* (1960).

8. Goodwin et al., "Alcohol Problems in Adoptees Raised Apart from Alcoholic Biological Parents" (1973). Other relevant studies include Cloninger, Bohman, and Sigvardsson, "Inheritance of Alcohol Abuse" (1981); Cadoret and Gath, "Inheritance of Alcoholism in Adoptees" (1978); Schuckit, Goodwin, and Winokur, "A Study of Alcoholism in Half Siblings" (1972).

9. Cloninger, Bohman, and Sigvardsson (1981); Bohman, Sigvardsson, and Cloninger, "Maternal Inheritance of Alcohol Abuse" (1981); Cadoret and Gath (1978); Schuckit, Goodwin, and Winokur (1972).

10. Edwards et al. (1979), 108.

11. Survey data reported by Cahalan and Room, *Problem Drinking Among American Men* (1974), 28 and 74 (table 13).

12. An important line of thought, often labeled "constructivism," proposes an alternative concept of "the problem of alcohol" as a supposed major source of social troubles. As Joseph R. Gusfield has shown, the "problem of alcohol" is a social and symbolic construct that reflects social values and ideologies. For example, automobile accidents that involve a driver who has alcohol in his bloodstream are often perceived as alcohol-caused accidents even when faulty equipment, bad weather, or poor street design may have played a much larger role in causing the accident than the alcohol did. In spite of this, we construe the issue as an alcohol problem rather than a highway safety problem. See Gusfield, *The Culture of Public Problems* (1981); Levine, "The Discovery of Addiction" (1978); MacAndrew and Edgerton, *Drunken Comportment* (1969); Rudy, *Becoming Alcoholic* (1986).

13. Schuckit, *Drug and Alcohol Abuse* (1984), 61; Schuckit and Viamontes, "Ethanol Ingestion" (1979); Lindros, "Acetaldehyde—Its Metabolism and Role in the Action of Alcohol" (1978).

14. Lindros (1978), 159.

15. Schuckit (1985), 61.

16. Ludwig, Wikler, and Stark, "The First Drink" (1974).

17. Polich, Armor, and Braiker, *The Course of Alcoholism* (1980), 39 (table 3.10). See also Fingarette (1983), 7.

18. Mello, "A Semantic Aspect of Alcoholism" (1975), 83; Mello and Mendelson, "Drinking Patterns During Work-contingent and Non-contingent Alcohol Acquisition" (1972), 158.

19. Schuckit, "Charting What Has Changed" (1980), 71. For clinical observations, see Mendelson, "Experimentally Induced Chronic Intoxication and Withdrawal in Alcoholics" (1964), 119. For a summary of the inconsistencies between the positive reinforcement hypothesis and clinical data, see Mendelson and Mello, "One Unanswered Question about Alcoholism" (1979).

20. Pattison, Sobell, and Sobell, *Emerging Concepts of Alcohol Dependence* (1977), 101; Mendelson (1964), 119 and 122.

21. Mendelson and Mello (1979), 11.

22. Kissin, "The Disease Concept of Alcoholism" (1983), 109.

23. Polich, Armor, and Braiker (1980), 59-62.

24. Vaillant and Milofsky's major, influential study concludes: "the etiological hypotheses that view alcoholism primarily as a symptom of psychological instability may be illusions": "The Etiology of Alcoholism" (1982), 494. See also Mello and Mendelson (1985), 237. Here again, however, controversy continues; see Zucker and

Gomberg, "Etiology of Alcoholism Reconsidered" (1986). For a review sympathetic to psychological approaches, see Cox, "Personality Correlates of Substance Abuse" (1985).

25. McClelland et al., *The Drinking Man* (1972); Blane, *The Personality of the Alcoholic* (1968).

26. Tarter, "Etiology of Alcoholism" (1978), 57. See also Polich, Armor, and Braiker (1980), 89-90; Orford and Edwards, *Alcoholism—A Comparison of Treatment and Advice* (1977), 119-20.

27. Goodwin (1985), 82-83.

28. A classic account in terms of the social context is MacAndrew and Edgerton (1969); for a concise review of the literature on cultural and ethnic norms, see Moser, *Prevention of Alcohol-Related Problems* (1980). See also Cahalan, "Subcultural Differences in Drinking Behavior" (1978), 245; Room, "Measurement and Distribution of Drinking Patterns and Problems in General Populations" (1977), 70-72.

29. See, for example, Holden, "Is Alcoholism Treatment Effective?" (1987), 20.

30. Marshall, "'Four Hundred Rabbits'" (1981), 192. For another ethnographical example, from among many, see Hill, "Alcohol Use Among the Nebraska Winnebago" (1987).

31. Heather and Robertson (1981), 143-44, referring to F.M. Canter, "The Requirement of Abstinence as a Problem in Institutional Treatment of Alcoholics" (1968).

32. P. Cook, "Increasing the Federal Alcohol Excise Tax" (1984).

33. Lenke, "Total Consumption of Alcohol and 'Heavy Use'" (1984).

34. Edwards et al. (1979), 23-24.

35. Caddy and Block, "Individual Differences in Response to Treatment" (1985), 354. For a full review, see Caddy, "Towards a Multivariate Analysis of Alcohol Abuse" (1978).

Substance Abuse Treatment Specialists Should Have Credentials

Mark Souder, Melody Heaps, and Eleanor Norton

The George W. Bush administration became concerned that the nation's funding for treatment centers was going to a far too limited number of licensed facilities. To improve access to drug treatment, the administration made funds available to the states to distribute as grants to treatment organizations not previously funded. As a result, Illinois' granting agency, Treatment Alternatives for Safe Communities [TASC], presided by Melody Heaps, was able to award grants to many unlicensed treatment facilities. In the following transcript of a 2004 congressional hearing conducted by Indiana representative Mark Souder, representative Eleanor Norton expresses concern that these unlicensed facilities—many of them affiliated with religious groups—might not be able to provide the same standard of care that a licensed facility would.

M r. [Mark] Souder [Indiana congressional representative]: Ms. [Melody] Heaps [president of Treatment Alternatives for Safe Communities], the State of Illinois got a grant and then you were picked as one of their recipients?

Ms. [Melody] Heaps: State of Illinois asked us to help them come together to design the program because we are a designated agent of the State working with the criminal justice system. The decision was made to target probationers within that system. So we sat down together to design the program.

The funds come to the State of Illinois, a portion of which will come to us for the work we do, the diagnostic assessment,

Mark Souder, Melody Heaps, and Eleanor Norton, hearing before the Subcommittee on Criminal Justice, Drug Policy and Human Resources of the Committee on Government Reform, House of Representatives, 108th Congress, second session, serial no. 108–269, September 22, 2004. www.gpo.gov/congress/house.

the referral to treatment, the case management and the information technology that will trigger vouchers. The State retains the dollars for the treatment and will through the electronic management system be funding the programs that do take our clients.

Souder: And then in setting up the system, are you setting up predominantly for Chicago or for all of Illinois?

Heaps: Because of the vast numbers we are dealing with and obviously limited resources, we targeted Cook County as the primary seat because of the vast numbers of probationers that are there. We also added two [of] what is known as color counties which essentially are suburban/urban areas and then added some rural areas, two rural counties, so that we could see how this pilot would be were it to be expanded statewide.

Souder: In a metro area as big as Chicago, individuals have vouchers, but how many providers would you guess there are in Chicago?

Heaps: Around the State, there are 140 providers with about 462 sites. Probably at least three-fourths of those are within the Chicago metro community. We, at TASC, have developed a provider network with actually every one of the 140 licensed treatment providers and also have been working in terms of recovery with many of the faith-based and other institutions job programs that would help our clients in the past. So we have a network already in existence but it has not been systematized, it has not been fully funded and this gives us an opportunity to do so.

Souder: In addition to those in the system trying to track new people, do you have a process for clearing them for approval to make sure they are adequately licensed?

Heaps: Yes. We have a set of standards we developed with the State. They must be licensed and certified as treatment providers. If they are not direct treatment providers but perhaps recovery support people, do they have a license if they are treating people in terms of safe buildings, etc. Is it a corporation not an individual, do they have a sound fiscal mechanism, do they have a set of standards for providing the service they have, do they have experience in dealing with this population? In order to make sure of that, we will also have and are engaging now an orientation program, a training program for those providers that are not used to being more sophisticated perhaps as you were talking about earlier with Mr. [Charles G.] Curie [Department of Health and Human Services administrator], in dealing with Federal funding. So we will have an ongoing training program actually facilitated by the addiction technology transfer centers that are a part of CSAT [Center for Substance Abuse Treatment] but are locally based.

Souder: Before I yield to [District of Columbia congressional representative] Ms. [Eleanor Holmes] Norton, let me see if I can make one more kind of global picture or sense out of something. The sheer volume of probationers, you said over 125,000 at any given time, not in the course of a year but at any given time?

Heaps: Any given day, right.

Souder: That is Chicago and Cook County or statewide?

Heaps: It is statewide but 80,000 I believe are in Cook County.

Souder: Of those 80,000 probationers, how many would you say are drug and alcohol related?

Heaps: The research suggests that we are dealing with 60 to 70 percent that have some issues.

Souder: So 60,000, it looks like?

Heaps: Exactly.

Souder: So you have 60,000 people there. Do you know how many of the percentage of the mix of 80,000 are juvenile adults?

Heaps: We are dealing with the adult population in that number. We are not dealing with the juvenile population. We will only be focusing on adults courts.

Souder: So in your Chicago area program, you are only going to be dealing with adults?

Heaps: Yes.

Souder: And only dealing with adults on probation?

Heaps: Yes, that is right.

Souder: And only drug and alcohol?

Heaps: That is right.

Souder: So we are probably at around the 60,000 number?

Heaps: Yes, 50,000 or 60,000.

Souder: Do you have a criteria that the person has to have, as we talked about earlier, whether it is some risk or some ability to show an interest or is it that they are high risk? You are not going to have the dollars to do all 60,000?

Heaps: No, we are not.

Souder: If we were looking at 50,000 in the whole Nation, it is unlikely that you are going to get 60,000 in Chicago?

Heaps: That is quite clear. Again, because we have been working with probation for so long and have been working with them in terms of their screening mechanisms, we are going to take advantage of what they do in terms of screens. We are going to use the idea of people want to volunteer for treatment. We are also going to be looking at probation initial screens that suggest there is some activity perhaps in probation compliance, perhaps the hard cases you were talking about that indicate this individual may have a serious drug problem. He then would be referred to us for a full diagnostic assessment and if found drug or alcohol addicted or abusing, move into the treatment of their choice.

Souder: Thank you.

Ms. Norton.

Norton: Thank you, Mr. Chairman.

Ms. Heaps, as I listened to you describe the licenses, I think I heard all kinds of licenses but I am not sure I heard any kind of license or certification for professional proficiency in treating people with drug or alcohol addiction. Is there any such certification of licensing in the State of Illinois attached to your program or to this particular program that is under review here today?

Heaps: By administrative rule in the State of Illinois, all licensed programs must have certified addictions counselors and there is a certification training program and annual training they must comply with. So all licensed programs have individuals treating individuals who are certified in addictions counseling.

Should Unlicensed Programs Be Funded?

Norton: Can programs that are not licensed get the funding that is under discussion today?

Heaps: Absolutely. We estimate that programs that are not licensed, programs that will do the recovery support, whether it is the spiritual counseling or the jobs or education, who will not or may not be licensed as a treatment program will, through our program, be able to get support, will be able to get the voucher paid for their services. We will do so based on a set of standards that I was talking about, bringing them in for training and orientation. In a mechanism, we are projecting that by the end of the second year, almost 40 to 50 percent of the dollars will be going to other recovery support service programs, not simply licensed treatment programs.

Norton: I tell you what, Ms. Heaps, I am very fortunate with my children. If I had a son or a daughter who had an alcohol or drug problem, one of the first things I would look to would be to see the level of professional proficiency . . . I am very troubled by programs that are unlicensed or uncertified, very frankly, because I see them all around. They hover around these communities. The communities that have the greatest drug addiction have all kinds of programs springing up with people who are just like me, they don't know anything except they claim to have the ability to treat people with what I regard as the hardest of all things to treat. Give me cancer or heart disease, the causal relationship I think has worked out there better than an addiction.

I just want to indicate my skepticism not of what you are doing but of the very idea and I speak from seeing the programs that abound. For example, if any religious program can get money, I happen to know that people who are most affiliated with a church are most likely to be able to be drug free. We have many ministers who have mentoring programs here quite unrelated to whether the Federal Government has dollars to hand out or not because they understand the relationship between faith and drawing people from addiction. Alcoholics Anonymous, for example, has often been faith-based.

I have been very troubled by some of these folks who claim to be able to meet standards like this, particularly since the standards seem so amorphous. I just want to indicate that skepticism here because these programs have grown up so often in the African-American community and it is very easy, particularly if you are a religious-based program, to show a tiny group of folks who were affiliated with your church or who you can show in fact met these standards. So much for that.

The most of those affiliated with your two programs come out of the criminal justice system. Do most of them in one fashion or another have some contact with the criminal justice system? ...

Heaps: Under our program, it will be 100 percent. They will be under the jurisdiction of the probation department coming to our program.

I concur with your concern that drug treatment be delivered by licensed professionals and I think the State of Illinois worked very hard to make sure and has a very rigorous licensure program in place. So we are using them for treatment but we also recognize that we are dealing now with partnerships and that there are job programs, faith-based organizations out there that need to welcome these individuals in the community and surround them with support.

Norton: That is very good if you are a job program but if you are in the business of helping people free themselves from addiction, you are in a very tough business and I think you have to be able to show some proficiency. The standard I use for the people in poor communities is the standard I use for my son and I don't see that as the standard if people can get government money who don't have that kind of professional proficiency.

Your 100 percent also tells me that the best way, which I think is very typical, to get drug abuse or alcohol abuse treatment is to knock somebody in the head or commit a crime. I just think we have to face that. There are all kinds of folks waiting in line saying catch me before I kill. I know I am a crack head. In fact, if you are virtually possessed with this addiction, the notion of having to go to jail first is very troublesome. I don't know what to do with that except that they are waiting in line. We can get hold of them but we are not doing that.

Addiction Is Often Caused by Underlying Disorders

John Halpern

Despite the recent widespread rejection of the idea that addiction is a disease, many in the medical community cite research that demands the idea be given another look. Dr. John Halpern, a professor of psychiatry at Harvard Medical School and staff member at McLean Hospital and Brigham and Women's Hospital in Boston, numbers among those defending the idea that certain individuals are genetically predisposed to addiction. In the following article, he maintains that for the medical community to ignore mounting evidence that addiction has a biological component is irresponsible. In telling people their addiction is their own choice, he says, doctors or treatment providers turn their backs on those addicts and on a possible medical cure for their condition.

The practice of medicine obligates physicians to accept the responsibility of promoting the overall health of their patients. When dealing with patients who abuse substances, we can find direct and indirect adverse consequences from such use. Lung cancer, although rare in the general population, is linked to chronic tobacco smoking, for example. Cigarette smokers who begin this addiction in their teen years appear to have a higher incidence of adult depression; so, either early tobacco use is a marker for later mental illness or, more ominously, this legal drug of abuse may promote the development of mental illness. Multiple warning labels describing tobacco's toxicity and other risks to health have been printed for decades on each pack of cigarettes sold, yet more than 20% of Americans continue to "choose" to smoke. Despite the hun-

John Halpern, "Addiction Is a Disease," *Psychiatric Times*, October 1, 2002, p. 55. Copyright 2002 by CMP Media LLC, 600 Community Drive, Manhasset, NY 11030, USA. Reproduced by permission.

dreds of millions of dollars spent in anti-tobacco messages and education, the ever-increasing state and federal "sin" taxes collected on every pack of tobacco product sold, the harsh restrictions on tobacco advertisements by legislative mandate, and the high-profile lawsuits and settlements, the median prevalence figures of current tobacco use in the United States have held steady for the last five years.

Addiction Is Not Just a Choice

Perhaps, then, "choice" has little to do with the decision to continue tobacco use. Cigarette smokers are so concerned about their drug use that each year some 1 million of them attempt to quit; but, sadly, less than 15% succeed in abstinence for a full year. Despite understanding that risks outweigh perceived benefits, addicted individuals compulsively continue their drug use in a chronic, relapsing fashion. It is not that these individuals are devoid of any choice when engaging in behaviors that support and reinforce continued drug use; rather, we must accept that not all choices are equally easy to make, especially when there exists a host of genetic, environmental and non-environmental factors supporting continued drug use.

Clinical research reveals that some individuals may be more vulnerable to drug dependence than others due to genetic and developmental risk factors. The best-validated risks are family history and male gender. Studies of separated, adopted twins, for example, have found the risk for alcoholism and other addictive drugs is greater for those twins whose biological parents also had drug dependence, regardless of drug use status in the adoptive parents. Drug craving and relapse are triggered by exposure to drug-related cues (e.g., photos of drugs and paraphernalia), as well as stress. Neuroimaging studies of former cocaine-dependent individuals have, for example, identified neural correlates of cue-induced craving for cocaine.

Preclinical studies also indicate that repeated exposure to highly addictive substances alters, perhaps permanently, a number of molecular and neurochemical indices, thereby changing physiologic homeostasis. In other words, even after detoxification, an individual may be sensitized to relapse because of changes in the brain from prior repeated use. We know the molecular targets in the central nervous system for most of the addictive drugs. As examples, opioids are agonists at micro opioid receptors; alcohol is an agonist at gamma-alphabutyric acid-A (GABA-A) receptors and an antagonist at N-methyl-D-aspartate (NMDA) glutamate receptors; and tobacco's nicotine is an agonist at nicotinic acetylcholine receptors. We also know that the principal CNS [central nervous system] pathway for processing reward, punishment and reinforcement extends from the ventral tegmental area (VTA) to the nucleus accumbens (NAc), mediated, in particular, by the release of the neurotransmitter dopamine. Preclinical evidence supports the "final common pathway" theory that addictive drugs, despite discordant molecular targets, all result in an increased release and dysregulation of synaptic dopamine in this region of the brain. For example, the same dose of cocaine administered weekly to monkeys results in increased extracellular release of dopamine in the CNS, a phenomenon called neurochemical sensitization. When a second dose of cocaine is administered after the first dose is wearing off, a decreased release of extracellular dopamine is found in the CNS, a phenomenon called acute tolerance. As tolerance builds, increased amounts of the drug are ingested in an attempt to achieve the same rewards, which, in turn, will also further drive molecular changes in the brain. Drug dependence, then, is reinforced at the cellular level as the CNS adjusts to continued drug exposure. Such conditioning may be unmasked by abrupt cessation of drug use, resulting in a period of observable and reproducible symptoms of withdrawal.

Chronic exposure to addictive substances also shifts signal transduction pathways within neurons, thereby altering gene expression. New or different concentrations of regulatory proteins, in turn, are synthesized, directing neurons to form new synaptic branches and altered concentrations of cellular receptor density. Cocaine, for example, has been found to increase spine density and, dendritic branching of neurons in the NAc and prefrontal cortex of rats. The remodeling of neurons involved with the maintenance of the brain's reward center also may continue long after drug use has ceased. There are probably hundreds of transcription factors involved in gene regulation; already the cyclic-AMP [that regulates metabolism and mediates the effects of hormones] response-element-binding protein (CREB) and Delta FosB [a protein] are implicated in addiction. Interestingly, biochemically modified isoforms of Delta FosB appear only slightly after acute drug exposure, but they accumulate over time with repeated drug administration. Other regulatory proteins of the Fos family rapidly break down after synthesis, but Delta FosB is highly stable, persisting for months after drug withdrawal. Here, then, is one example of a molecular mechanism for drug-induced changes in gene expression persisting long after last use. Preclinical models reveal that chronic, but not acute, administration of cocaine, amphetamine, phencyclidine, alcohol, nicotine and opiates induces Delta FosB release in the NAc and dorsal striatum [part of the brain's basal ganglia system].

Drug Abuse Is a Physical and Mental Illness

In short, both human and preclinical data converge to suggest that addiction is associated with frank biological abnormalities that cannot be easily explained by a simple hypothesis of "choice." It is a strange set of societal circumstances that people may still consider the ingestion of some drugs as outside the purview of physicians, when clearly the practice of medicine deals with the impact of exogenous substances upon the human body and mind. Those individuals who abuse drugs do so absent the legal mechanisms for which society provides, i.e., a prescription or recommendation from a physician. Whether legal or not, all addictive substances should be carefully reviewed with our patients precisely because physicians must obtain all information that may assist in the diagnosis and treatment of disease and in the improved preventive health of patients.

Drug dependence changes the lives of users and those around them. Tobacco, for example, is the single greatest cause of preventable death in the United States. Certainly, then, tobacco is a menace to public health and its continued popularity supports nicotine dependence as a chronic, relapsing disease in which volitional choice becomes but one negotiable variable in the struggle to achieve good health throughout the life cycle.

Moral rejectionists mislabel drug dependence as a failure of volition only and, thereby, claim a right to assign judgment and blame. The absurdity of looking through such a narrow lens is that if addiction really were merely a choice, people would stop after experiencing more harm than perceived benefits!

Accepting drug dependence as another mental illness does not typically abrogate responsibility for an addict's actions: Thousands each year are arrested, prosecuted and sentenced to serve jail time for simple drug possession, and, as for mental illness in general, consider that the two psychiatric inpatient facilities in the United States in which the largest numbers of patients reside are the Los Angeles County Jail and New York City Rikers Island Prison. Obviously, such individuals' moment-to-moment decision-making can have long-term consequences that were never wished for or accurately anticipated.

Not all choices can be equally entertained at every given moment either, and sometimes other options are not even known. For example, a young woman, supporting herself and her drug habit through prostitution, may not know of the different "ethical" choices available to her, especially when as a child she had been introduced to both drugs and her career by her mother's example. The reasons for experimenting with addictive drugs, then, may be quite different from the motivations fueling continued use. Relapse is not due to an absolute loss of volitional control but rather to loss of a perspective that cherishes good health and mental well-being above other, less healthy choices. In high-risk situations, this long-term desire for maintaining better health through abstinence is overwhelmed by the cued wish to re-experience a known, anticipated "high" available at that moment.

Stigmatization of illness continues against many patients afflicted with brain pathology. Substance dependence is particularly stigmatized by those who wish to make this illness a debate over volition while denying the biological underpinnings of behavior. Moreover, demands for precise linguistic definitions of addiction and disease, as if they must forever be hermetically sealed within specific denotations of legalese and ethics, is of little value to physicians charged with the observation and treatment of pathology. History reveals many examples of debates over illness versus individual responsibility: Hansen's disease ("leprosy" from Mycobacterium leprae), seizure disorders ("epilepsy"), cancer and major depression are some examples of medical disorders now vindicated with the discovery of effective medications and procedures. Physicians, and psychiatrists in particular, are needed now more than ever to stand up and explain to the lay public how substance abuse and dependence can significantly alter brain function and physical health and that a variety of treatment modalities are available.

Abuse Must Be Managed with Medical Science

Effective management of drug dependence requires a medical model so as to tailor therapy according to the condition of the individual. Faith-based support groups, Alcoholics Anonymous and its affiliates, and long-term residential programs have a long history of assisting people in achieving and maintaining abstinence via a combination of direct therapy, education, cognitive skill-building exercises, expanded non-drug social supports and providing a drug-free environment. Contingency management skills can be taught to provide individuals with extra time to anticipate the high-risk situations and emotions for relapse and then, hopefully, re-script behavior to minimize such exposures. This helps individuals learn to avoid night clubs or other users because such settings and people may make the choice for continued abstinence appear less valuable than the immediate reward anticipated with use.

Current pharmacotherapy for drug dependence includes screening for an underlying psychiatric condition after the patient has successfully completed detoxification. People may choose to self-medicate with an addictive drug, all the while unaware that they have a treatable psychiatric illness. For example, rates for alcoholism and other drug abuse are much higher in people with untreated bipolar disorder and depression. For motivated individuals, disulfiram (Antabuse) may particularly aid in maintaining sobriety from alcohol. Smoking tobacco while on the antidepressant buproprion (Zyban, Wellbutrin) is another aversive treatment, as the drug induces an undesirable taste when some smokers relapse. Agonist replacement medications assist with detoxification and/or offer a stable, safer maintenance therapy for those who repeatedly fail pure abstinence (e.g., methadone for opiate dependence, nicotine gum or patch for tobacco dependence). Many new medications are also in development including more opiate antagonists for the treatment of alcoholism and opiate dependence and NMDA antagonists such as acamprosate [Campral] for alcoholism. One day, perhaps there will even be a vaccine to confer natural immunity against cocaine. . . .

Whether addiction is a disease or merely a choice, the utility of the medical model is needed to address resultant risks to public and individual health. A careful review of this growing body of scientific literature should offer hope that real solutions are possible. All other models for addressing drug dependence have, to date, proven to be costly failures, and doctors are not going to ignore viable treatment options for healing those suffering with drug dependence. Defining addiction as a choice only abdicates our responsibility for seeking health and true healing for our patients and, instead, leaves crushed lives dehumanized by a chronic relapsing condition with no hope for cure. As every doctor knows, "Remember to do some good" should quickly follow the first rule to "do no harm."

Substance Abuse
Is a Personal Choice

Melvin L. Williams

U.S. prisons are full of those arrested for drug-related offenses. Though the country has long made controlling drug abuse a priority, the problem continues to grow. As one drug is regulated or falls out of favor, another waits to take its place. Melvin L. Williams, superintendent of the Willard Drug Treatment campus in New York, says the only way to begin to address the problem with illegal drug use is to take a long, hard look at the facts. He maintains drug abuse is a choice and that if an addict really wants to use a drug, he will find a way to do so despite the legal obstacles in his path. In the following article written in 2004, Williams describes the harsh, disciplined, but often successful treatment that drug-addicted parolees receive at Willard. Williams says that treatment programs like his prove that just as an addict can choose to remain one, he can choose to turn his life around as well.

If there was an easy answer to drug addiction, everyone would use it. Since the evolution of the 1960s, the nation has been faced with the ever increasing use of illegal drugs in society. Of course, this also corresponds with the increase of legal pharmaceutical drugs. In fact, there are drugs for everything from growing hair to improving a person's sexual life. Americans are taught from a very young age that if there is a problem, there is a drug to fix it; yet when unacceptable drugs are used or found, as a nation, citizens become offended and develop high criminal penalties to eradicate this nuisance.

The ever resounding question is, "What is there to do?" The United States uses the latest military technology to pro-

Melvin L. Williams, "Drug Treatment: The Willard Option," *Corrections Today*, vol. 66, April 2004, pp. 106–09. Copyright © 2004 American Correctional Association, Inc. Reproduced by permission.

tect its borders and drug use still increases. There are drug awareness programs in schools, nationally televised programs in household living rooms and drug treatment centers throughout many communities. Yet, people still are being sent to prison for long periods of time for drug charges. Sometimes it appears that correctional staff are so tied up with the law enforcement part of the job that treatment is forgotten. Many people hope that drug abuse will become somebody else's problem or it will simply go away, yet when they open their eyes, they see millions of people who are affected—families are broken and lives are destroyed.

There are certain things about drug abuse that must be understood:

- It is a personal choice, no matter what events led up to it;

- It is a bane on American life and is creating a culture that is subversive and criminal; and

- Throwing money and resources at the problem does not help—a stealth bomber may locate illegal drug sources by using infrared, but if people still want drugs, they will get them.

In drug treatment, everyone, including the client, must recognize that drug abuse is a personal issue. Oftentimes, society needs to place blame on something else—faulting poor neighborhoods, schools, awful parents—yet no one forces a person to continually put drugs into his or her system.

In corrections, by the time a client with a drug problem is incarcerated, the addiction has probably existed for years; it is a developed behavior. There may be many drugs involved and many different types of abuse. This usually results in criminal behavior in the form of obtaining or using drugs, or attempting to get money to buy more drugs. Community treatment centers have been built with the hope that drug abusers could simply be shown the error of their ways, counseled and the problem would disappear. Thus, overnight the client would become a law-abiding citizen with a wonderful job, and the world would be great. When this did not work out, however, the drug abusers were then incarcerated for long periods of time. What this accomplished was the removal of these offenders from the community, but they still had the urge to continue to abuse drugs even while incarcerated. Also, valuable taxpayer revenue was being used to incarcerate many people who still had a problem when they were released. There must be a better way.

In corrections, jails and prisons cannot pick their clients—the clients are sent to them. However, correctional staff must recognize that often, clients are medically and sometimes mentally unstable, they have been abusing drugs and themselves for a long period of time, and many simply enjoy the "street scene" and using drugs.

Treatment Must Involve Consequences

In reviewing these basic factors, treatment staff also recognize that their goals may be different from their clients'. Knowing this, how does corrections proceed? If the nation has laws that make it a criminal offense to possess, sell or use drugs, there must be consequences. Without treating individuals and their drug abuse, the revolving door will continue. The country's prisons are full of these offenders. It would seem that given the nation's history and corrections' observations of the past 40 or so years, many viable treatment programs are available. An accountable treatment approach should include:

- Taking offenders out of the community for a short period of time and putting them in a secure treatment environment;

- Returning clients, after a specific time, to in-patient treatment in the community from which they came;

- Ensuring follow-up after the client completes in-patient treatment; and

- Establishing goals that are attainable and measurable.

By taking offenders out of the community, they will be removed from their environment, which protects not only the clients, but also the community. In addition, by putting the client in a secure environment, the street scene and easy access to addictive drugs are removed, allowing a client's behavior to be addressed. A simple but very important thing can also be accomplished—the client's health can be assessed and improved, both physically and mentally. Through eating controlled, balanced meals, and physical therapy, the client can vastly improve his or her physical health, because without working on the body, one cannot work on the mind. Also, with assessment, the client's mental health needs can be addressed since it is common knowledge that the nation's streets and correctional facilities are filled with people with mental health issues.

A client's stay at a secure environment should be measurable through his or her progress toward achievable goals. Not only do treatment staff want to make their clients' health important, they want to make them more amenable to treatment. Often, a client's greatest incentive for treatment is knowing that by refusing treatment there will be consequences such as prison.

Following their specific treatment program during their short stay in the secure environment, offenders should progress to an in-patient drug treatment program in the community from which they came. This puts them back into the community, which offers certain benefits, including family support, employment opportunities and a continuum of treatment. The program must be licensed and accredited, as well as specific in treatment with attainable goals for the clients. This involves not only getting into their heads, but also dealing

with other issues such as job training and life skills. Throughout treatment, clients must take personal responsibility and be
held accountable for their actions. They also must have a plan
and, after release, follow-up, whether it is parole or some
other type of system that ensures that the clients continue to
meet expectations.

The Correctional Model for Treatment Works

One program that has all of these attributes is the Willard
Drug Treatment Program in Willard, N.Y. Its mission is to
prepare chemically impaired individuals for work release and
to reduce recidivism [repeat offenses]. Run by the New York
State Department of Correctional Services in conjunction
with the New York State Division of Parole and licensed by
the Office of Alcohol and Substance Abuse Services, the program was mandated by the New York State Legislature in 1995
through an initiative by Gov. George Pataki.

Glenn S. Goord, commissioner of New York State Department of Correctional Services, chose a site and model for the
program, using a shock-based model with enhanced treatment. Shock-based is a highly structured program that includes military training and discipline. Everyone who comes
to the facility is either judicially sanctioned directly from the
courts or a parole violator, and is a second-time, nonviolent
felony offender.

This highly structured program mandates 90 days of intensive substance abuse treatment followed by an individualized continuing care plan, which includes intensive parole supervision and continuing treatment needs with providers
licensed by the Office of Alcohol and Substance Abuse. The
program is designed to assist participants to achieve, develop
and maintain recovery.

Phase 1 of the Willard Program is designed to provide
treatment for parolees using the disease model of recovery, in-

tensive substance abuse treatment, cognitive-behavioral and motivational enhancement, as well as the military protocol and therapeutic community structure of the Shock Incarceration Program.

Phase 2 of the Willard Program occurs upon release. All parolees who successfully complete the 90-day residential component at the Willard Drug Treatment Campus (DTC) are released to a period of intensive parole supervision and placed in a community-based treatment program also licensed by the Office of Alcohol and Substance Abuse Services.

Willard DTC clients actively participate in all alcohol and drug treatment, individual and group counseling, physical fitness, academic and GED [general equivalency diploma] preparation, vocational job skills, network decision-making classes, drill and ceremony, and other parole transition activities.

Self-discipline is an important component in overcoming addictions. Participants are expected to know and comply with all the program rules and those of the Division of Parole and the Department of Correctional Services. The major focus of this program is on simplicity of lifestyle and clarity of thought through disciplined behaviors. Parolees are expected to demonstrate responsibility for themselves and for the treatment environment.

This unparalleled program, designed by Cheryl L. Clark, director of the Shock Incarceration Program with assistance from Ronald Moscicki, supervising superintendent of Shock Facilities, uses treatment teams comprised of alcohol and substance abuse counselors and program assistants, teachers and drill instructors from the Department of Correctional Services, and parole officers and parole substance abuse counselors from the Division of Parole. Staff are responsible for providing specific treatment duties for their assigned caseloads. These duties include individual counseling, group sessions, treatment planning, discharge planning, weekly evaluations of treatment progress and assessment duties. Staff facilitate the ancillary programs, which include education, vocational programming, networking and therapeutic work crews.

All Willard DTC staff go through an intensive four-and-a-half-week training program, whether a secretary or the superintendent—everyone is trained. This allows all staff members to understand the entire Willard Program so they can best facilitate it to the parolees. They also are involved with the participants' treatment process, working together to institute this multifaceted, holistic approach to addressing addiction and recovery.

Military Environment Ensures Drug Abusers Learn Discipline

One might ask, how is it possible to do anything in 90 days? Certainly, that is a good question. The answer is, first treatment staff have to have their attention. At Willard, this is done through the military style of the shock model. Parolees are awakened at 5:30 a.m. and march outside to the physical training deck at 5:55 a.m. For the next hour, they participate in group exercises and a company run, which gets them motivated and ready for the rest of their treatment day. After breakfast and showers, there is morning formation and then off to programs. Each group of parolees, or platoon, is involved in all aspects of the program, with a different program for the day, which may include school, vocational training, alcohol/substance abuse treatment, confrontation (the process of helping participants face and change their own nonproblem-solving behaviors), network training, individual counseling, group meetings or therapeutic work program.

The Willard Program was designed to process as many as 3,600 clients per year. Of the 900 beds at the facility, approximately 800 are for males and 100 are for females. All parolees housed in each unit form a platoon. Females are programmed and housed separately from the males, thus alleviating any potential problems.

There is also a medical platoon comprised of many men who have significant medical, physical and/or psychological issues often requiring medication and/or routine monitoring by medical staff. Programming these men on a separate unit allows full exposure to treatment activities while limiting more stringent physical aspects of the program.

Willard accepts adult male and female parolees of any age who are second felony nonviolent offenders, and may have a multitude of physical issues. Willard parolees are sent there for their actions and are expected to dedicate themselves to their treatment.

By working together, staff, both uniform and nonuniform, have created an environment in which treatment can take place. Some people, when they see the shock model, are concerned and confused. They remember images from television of uniformed boot camp facility staff abusing clients. This is not the case in New York. Although staff will confront and hold parolees accountable, they do not put their hands on them. In order for treatment to take place, the parolees must be focused. The shock model, through its military approach, obtains this cooperation and attention in a short period of time. By having platoons work together, there is no time for individual acting out. Everyone wears the same uniform, has the same haircut and goes through the same program.

Through the use of the military approach, parolees form structure and discipline in their lives, which prepares them for treatment. Willard is not easy nor is it meant to be. Outside treatment providers, where Willard parolees go when they leave, consistently say that Willard graduates are the most prepared for treatment and the most successful.

Twelve percent to 14 percent of those who come to Willard DTC either change their mind once they are there or cannot complete the program and are sent to a correctional facility to complete their sentences. In addition, if during the review process a parolee is found not to be living up to the expectations, he or she could appear before an evaluation review committee. There are a variety of sanctions, including keeping them for a longer period of time so that they have a chance to be successful in the program. . . .

Reintegration Is Always the Goal

Parolees begin the community reintegration process and adjustment to parole supervision as soon as they enter the Willard DTC. This process begins with orientation and continues throughout the 90-day program. The treatment team assists parolees at every level.

The assigned treatment team member has specific responsibilities regarding this process. Treatment staff coordinate with the parole substance abuse counselor and the community-based parole officer. This ensures that parolees are tied into the community-based treatment program that is best suited to their needs with no interruption in the continuum of care and treatment.

The treatment team and parole substance abuse counselor work together to make sure that parolees have a clear understanding of the community-based treatment program and scheduled appointments. The treatment team parole officer also ensures that parolees have a clear understanding of the rules and regulations regarding parole supervision and that these standards are adhered to throughout program participation. Each parolee's progress is shared with the community-based parole officer who, in turn, has made the necessary contacts and is ready to take over the reins of parole supervision and assist the parolees upon their re-entry into the community without an interruption in treatment services and with the best possibility of maintaining a healthy, law-abiding lifestyle.

The assigned parole officer meets with parolees to ascertain their desired residence/employment plans upon release. Any shortcomings are discussed and parolees are counseled about any possible problems within the desired residence that could impact negatively on their adjustment. Parolees' past employment history and future vocational/educational goals also are reviewed at this time. If a parolee has no job offers or realistic vocational aspirations, he or she is counseled relative to other job opportunities as well as vocational/educational programs within his or her areas.

At this time, the above information is forwarded to the community-based parole officer for investigation and input. Willard parole staff maintain ongoing contact with the community parole officer to ensure that the proposed parole plan is appropriate and to include the parolee in any needed modifications.

No parolee leaves Willard DTC without a release plan in place. All aspects of that plan are discussed with the parolee prior to graduation. In addition, specific written instructions are provided to parolees to ensure their understanding and best assure a positive reintegration to the community. Immediately after their release, parolees are directed to make an arrival report to the community-based parole officer, at which time both immediate and long-term residence and employment planning are discussed. By working with parole and having parole staff on site, a program continuum is established—from Willard to outside treatment and care.

Certainly, no one will stop their addictive behavior until they decide they want to. Nothing can be accomplished without hard work and Willard parolees and staff do, indeed, work hard, with the goal of addressing addictive behavior. A lot of time is spent having parolees look at themselves and the addictive behavior, which has brought them to where they are now. In only 90 days, parolees become healthier, both in mind and body, and begin the long process of treatment. Through discipline, confrontation, education and care, much can be accomplished.

CHAPTER 5

Drug Abuse Today

Chapter Preface

Though reviewed and revised annually, the United States' National Drug Control Strategy (NDCS) has not significantly reduced drug abuse. Each year the number of chronic users either remains constant or increases. A sharp division exists between policy makers and those in the treatment community over how to alter this trend.

The main thrust of the NDCS has always been aimed at controlling drug supplies, which critics think is the wrong approach. Whenever the supply of one drug is reduced, they say, another equally harmful substance waits in the wings to take its place. It would be impossible for any government or its army to eliminate every supplier or eradicate every supply. Just as there are suppliers anxious to fill another niche with a new drug, there are a whole host of addicts waiting to use it.

Critics also point out that the NDCS's strategy of reducing supply unfairly targets some of the most vulnerable, impoverished people, both at home and abroad. Often small-time domestic drug dealers are themselves addicts, selling to supply their own habit. Also farmers in countries such as Afghanistan, where the United States has launched massive crop eradication programs, have few other opportunities to make a living in an increasingly harsh and dangerous world. Destroying the livelihoods of the poor in other countries, these critics maintain, foments hatred of the United States and leaves people receptive to terrorist recruitment.

Policymakers argue that the NDCS's emphasis on reducing supplies has proven effective in controlling drug abuse. Most recently, the Combat Methamphetamine Epidemic Act of 2005 that restricted the sale of over-the-counter cold remedies containing pseudoephedrine, an essential ingredient in [methamphetamine] meth, led to a drastic reduction in domestic production of the drug. Also, by preventing drugs from crossing

U.S. borders, these NDCS defenders insist they prevent drug dealers and addicts from conducting business as usual. As drugs become more difficult to acquire, addicts in crisis often turn to treatment programs for help. They also say that harsh penalties for drug dealing in the United States have made it a far less attractive business.

Critics of the NDCS say that while it may indeed have led to a few limited successes, the numbers do not lie; a steady or increasing number of U.S. addicts every year is evidence of failed policy. The national focus, they maintain, should shift toward reducing the demand for drugs rather than the supply. An important step toward accomplishing this will be to increase funding for the one aspect of the NDCS that has proven consistently successful: treatment. The argument is that once chronic users enter the treatment environment, they are far less likely to remain consistent users. Another key is to increase funding for educators and counselors who can prevent young users from becoming chronically addicted.

Others believe if lawmakers truly want to reduce the demand for drugs they must make additional, fundamental changes in the NDCS. For example, they would like to see the NDCS address the larger web of social problems of which drug abuse is only a strand. The same problems that make young people abuse drugs—poverty, family dysfunction, and community disintegration—are the same ones that lead them to drop out of school and commit crimes. Another would be to classify all psychoactive substances, including alcohol, caffeine, and tobacco, as drugs, so that an honest discussion of addiction can begin. Finally, opponents believe the NDCS must deemphasize the phrase, the War on Drugs. They say that the military language encourages a harsh view and treatment of the drug abusers rather than of the problem itself.

The Drug War Is Being Waged on Many Fronts

National Drug Intelligence Center

Though the U.S. government's fight against drugs has been effective at controlling the use of certain drugs, it must not rest on these laurels. As one drug becomes more difficult to acquire, addicts turn to other sources for that drug or to another drug entirely. The war against drugs must be fought on international as well as domestic fronts, suggests the National Drug Intelligence Center in this summary published in the 2007 National Drug Threat Assessment. *Also, those who wage this war must constantly reassess the effectiveness of their tactics.*

The trafficking of illicit drugs such as cocaine, heroin, marijuana, methamphetamine [meth] and MDMA [Ecstasy] (the leading drug threats to the United States) is undergoing strategic shifts in response to sustained and effective international and domestic counterdrug efforts. These changes—shifting cocaine and methamphetamine production trends, the increasing influence of Mexican and Asian criminal groups in domestic drug distribution, rising availability of more potent forms of methamphetamine and marijuana, and the substitution of illicit drugs for prescription narcotics—represent great challenges to law enforcement agencies and policymakers attempting to extend recent successes.

Coca cultivation is higher than previously estimated, and cocaine availability and use in the United States has not significantly changed despite record interdictions and seizures. Demonstrable progress in disrupting Colombia coca cultivation since 2001, particularly through aerial eradication, has forced growers to cultivate coca in nontraditional growing ar-

U.S. Department of Justice's National Drug Intelligence Center, *National Drug Threat Assessment*, October 2006. www.usdoj.gov.

eas of Colombia. As a result, intelligence agencies are now challenged to expand their survey areas and reexamine cultivation and production estimates for previous years. Aerial eradication resources will be stretched to cover wider growing areas in Colombia. A lesser concern is the potential for drug trafficking organizations (DTOs) to significantly increase coca cultivation in Bolivia and Peru, where cultivation is much lower than mid 1990s levels but has increased recently in both countries.

Reducing Meth Production Sent Addicts Elsewhere

Recent success in greatly reducing domestic methamphetamine production has also resulted in new challenges for law enforcement. Following a sharp decrease in methamphetamine production nationally (laboratory seizures decreased 42 percent from 2004 (10,015) to 2005 (5,846), and preliminary 2006 data show continued declines), most production and distribution were consolidated under the control of Mexican DTOs producing and distributing higher purity ice methamphetamine, supplanting local independent powder methamphetamine producers and dealers. As a result, Mexican DTOs gained considerable strength and greatly expanded their presence in drug markets throughout the country, even in many smaller communities in midwestern and eastern states. These stronger, more organized, and insulated distribution groups have proven to be much more difficult for local law enforcement to detect and disrupt than the local dealers that they have replaced.

As Mexican DTOs and criminal groups have expanded their control over methamphetamine distribution, many such groups have introduced Mexican black tar and brown powder heroin in southeastern and midwestern states, where Mexican heroin was never or very rarely observed as recently as 2005. Although South American heroin is still the predominant type in most eastern drug markets, Mexican DTOs' ability to advance Mexican heroin beyond traditional western state heroin markets presents new challenges to law enforcement as more groups make the drug consistently available to individuals even in smaller, more rural eastern communities.

Marijuana potency has increased sharply. The production of high potency marijuana in Canada and the United States by Asian criminal groups has been a leading contributor to rising marijuana potency throughout the United States. In fact, average potency of seized marijuana samples has more than doubled from 2000 through 2005, since trafficking by Asian DTOs has increased significantly. Recently, however, Mexican DTOs have also begun producing higher potency marijuana (derived from cannabis cultivated in outdoor plots in California), most likely in an effort to compete with Asian DTOs for high potency marijuana market share. The result may be further increases in average marijuana potency in the United States in the near term.

Since 2004 MDMA trafficking has increased significantly. Canada-based Asian DTOs have also recently gained control over most MDMA distribution in the United States and have expanded distribution of the drug to a level similar to that of 2001, when availability peaked under the control of Israeli DTOs that were largely dismantled by law enforcement. Asian DTOs, however, appear to be stronger than their Israeli predecessors. For example, Asian DTOs trafficking MDMA distribute wholesale quantities of MDMA produced in Canada, and MDMA production by Canada-based Asian groups is increasing. Moreover, Asian DTOs have established much wider distribution networks than did Israeli DTOs. Whereas Israeli MDMA distributors operated primarily in the Los Angeles, Miami, and New York City areas, Asian DTOs have strong distribution networks operating in most states throughout the country.

Rates of pharmaceutical drug abuse exceed that of all other drugs except marijuana, resulting in a high number of pharmaceutical overdose deaths annually. However, recent success within several states in reducing the illegal diversion of pharmaceutical drugs, particularly pharmaceutical narcotics such as OxyContin, through various antidiversion initiatives and monitoring programs has caused some individuals addicted to or dependent on such drugs to substitute other drugs, such as heroin, for prescription narcotics. In some areas, such substitutions among prescription drug abusers have been widespread, creating new challenges for local law enforcement and public health agencies compelled to address a widening local heroin user population.

U.S. regulatory and law enforcement actions, which have made it increasingly difficult for drug traffickers to place illicit proceeds directly into U.S. financial institutions, have resulted in most Mexican and Colombian DTOs avoiding such money laundering methods. Instead, both Mexican and Colombian DTOs transport illicit drug proceeds from U.S. drug markets to other U.S. locations for consolidation. The proceeds often are transported in bulk to an area near the U.S.-Mexico border and are either smuggled into Mexico at Southwest Border ports of entry (POEs), primarily in South Texas, or remitted electronically to Southwest Border locations, where the transferred cash is then smuggled across the U.S.-Mexico border.

U.S. Drug Policy
Needs an Update

Jonathan P. Caulkins and Peter Reuter

*According to public policy experts Jonathan P. Caulkins and Pe-
ter Reuter, the United States needs to revamp its outdated drug
policy. In the following 2006 article, the two say that the large-
scale arrests that occurred in the drug use epidemic of the 1980s
are no longer appropriate. Drug use, they maintain, is more
widespread than in the 1980s. Also, there are more stable numbers of users from year to year. In addition, the United States is
spending huge amounts of money on the high costs of incarcerating large numbers of people for drug offenses, a tactic that has
had no measurable effect on national drug use. The authors insist that much of the money spent on policing and imprisoning
drug offenders would be far better spent on treatment facilities
and programs. Caulkins is a professor of public policy and operations research at Carnegie-Mellon University in Pennsylvania,
and Reuter is a professor of public policy and criminology at the
University of Maryland.*

The United States will soon surpass the half-million mark
for drug prisoners, which is more than 10 times as many
as in 1980. It is an extraordinary number, more than Western
Europe locks up for all criminal offenses combined and more
than the pre-Katrina population of New Orleans. How effective is this level of imprisonment in controlling drug problems? Could we get by with, say, just a quarter million locked
up for drug violations?

Now is an opportune time to consider this issue. The illegal drug problem has fundamentally changed during the past

Jonathan P. Caulkins and Peter Reuter, "Reorienting U.S. Drug Policy," *Issues in Science and Technology*, vol. 23, fall 2006, pp. 79–85. Copyright 2006 The University of
Texas at Dallas. Reproduced by permission.

two decades, in both its nature and its extent. With a few exceptions, the drug problem has stabilized and begun to improve in the United States during the past 15 years. Notably, the number of people dependent on expensive drugs such as cocaine has dropped significantly from its peak. The terrifying spike in drug-related homicides of the late 1980s has long ended. Today, we are dealing with an older, less violent, and more stable population of drug abusers. Despite these changes, the number of drug prisoners continues to increase.

Tough enforcement is supposed to drive up prices and make it more difficult to obtain drugs, and thus reduce overall drug use and the problems that it causes. Yet the evidence indicates that it has had quite limited success at reducing the supply of established mass-market drugs. Thus, even assuming that tough enforcement was an appropriate response at an earlier time, today's situation justifies considering different policy options.

In particular, there is little reason to believe that the United States would have a noticeably more serious drug problem if it kept 250,000 fewer drug dealers under lock and key. Given the social harms that result from imprisonment as well as the considerable taxpayer tab for incarceration, there is a case to be made for working out ways to reduce the number of people in jail and prison for drug offenses.

Among affluent nations, U.S. rates of drug use are not exceptionally high by contemporary international standards. About 1 in 15 Americans aged 12 and over currently uses drugs, a much smaller figure than in, for example, Great Britain. By a wide margin, prevalence is highest among older teenagers and those in their early 20s, peaking at around 40% using within the past 12 months for high-school seniors. Most Americans who try drugs use them only a few times. If there is a typical continuing user, it is an occasional marijuana smoker who will cease to use drugs at some point during his 20s. Marijuana use in the 15- to 26-year-old age group has been at high levels throughout the past three decades, but there have also been notable ups and downs. Usage rose through the 1970s, fell in the 1980s, and bounced back up in the early 1990s, but only among adolescents and very young adults.

What these data from general population surveys do not describe well are the trends in the behaviors that dominate drug-related social costs, which primarily involve drug-related crime, health consequences, premature mortality, and lost productivity. These problems are worse in the United States than they are in most other countries, and they are driven by the number of people dependent on cocaine (including crack), heroin, and methamphetamines, drugs that might collectively be called the expensive drugs to distinguish them from marijuana. Marijuana is by far the most widely used of the illicit drugs, but its use directly accounts for only about 10% of those adverse outcomes, in part because a year's supply of marijuana costs so little that its distribution and purchase engender relatively little crime or violence.

Drug Use Is Passed Between People Like a Virus

The compulsive use of expensive drugs in the United States is a legacy of four major drug epidemics. The notion of a drug epidemic captures the fact that drug use is a learned behavior, transmitted from one person to another. Contrary to the popular image of the entrepreneurial drug pusher who hooks new addicts through aggressive salesmanship, it is now clear that almost all first experiences are the result of being offered the drug by a friend or family member. Drug use thus spreads much like a communicable disease, a metaphor familiar from marketing and new-product-adoption models. Users are "contagious," and some of those with whom they come into contact become "infected." Initiation of heroin, cocaine, and crack use shows much more of a classic epidemic pattern than does marijuana use, although the growth of marijuana use in the 1960s may have had epidemic features.

In an epidemic, rates of initiation (infection) in a given area rise sharply as new and highly contagious users of a drug initiate friends and peers. At least with heroin, cocaine, and crack, long-term addicts are not particularly contagious. They are often socially isolated from new users. Moreover, they usually present an unappealing picture of the consequences of addiction. In the next stage of the epidemic, initiation declines rapidly as the susceptible population shrinks, because there are fewer nonusers and/or because the drug's reputation sours, as a result of better knowledge of the effects of a drug. The number of dependent users stabilizes and typically declines gradually.

The first modern U.S. drug epidemic involved heroin. It developed with rapid initiation in the late 1960s, primarily in a few big cities and most heavily in inner-city minority communities; the experiences of U.S. soldiers in Vietnam may have been a contributing factor. The annual number of new heroin initiates peaked in the early 1970s and then dropped by [about] 50% by the late 1970s and remained low until the mid 1990s. Heroin addiction (at least for those addicted in the United States rather than while in the military in Vietnam) has turned out to be a long-lived and lethal condition, as revealed in a remarkable 33-year follow up of male heroin addicts admitted to the California Civil Addict Program during the years 1962-1964. Nearly half of the original addicts—284 of 581—had died by 1996–1997; of the 242 still living who were interviewed, 40% reported heroin use in the past year and 60% were unemployed.

Cocaine in powder form was the source of the second epidemic, which lasted longer and was more sharply peaked than the heroin epidemic. Initiation, which was broadly distributed across class and race, rose to a peak around 1980 and then fell sharply, by [about] 80% or more during the 1980s. Dependence always lags behind initiation, and cocaine use became more common in the mid-1980s as the pool of those who had experimented with the drug expanded. The number of dependent users peaked around 1988 and declined only moderately through the 1990s.

The third epidemic was of crack use. Although connected to the cocaine epidemic—crack developed as an easy-to-use form of freebase cocaine—the crack epidemic was more concentrated among minorities in inner-city communities. Its starting point varied across cities; for Los Angeles the beginning may have been 1982, whereas for Chicago it was as late as 1988. But in all cities initiation appears to have peaked within about two years and to have again left a population with a chronic and debilitating addiction.

The fourth important epidemic, of methamphetamine use, has gradually rolled two-thirds of the way across the country, from west to east, taking hold where cocaine use was less common. It had already stabilized on the West Coast by the time rapid spread began in the Mississippi and Ohio River valleys; it still has not reached most of the East Coast. There have been other epidemics (for example, ecstasy use), but heroin, cocaine (including crack), and methamphetamine probably account for close to 90% of the social costs associated with illicit drugs in the United States.

What is particularly interesting is that big declines in cocaine and heroin prices (discussed below) have not triggered new epidemics. Initiation goes up when prices go down, but once a drug has acquired a bad reputation, it does not seem prone to a renewed explosion or contagious spread in use. That is a great protective factor, though presumably not eternal.

U.S. Drug War Has Hidden Costs

The United States spends a lot of money on drug control. The drug czar [John Walters] claims that federal expenditures are

$12.5 billion, but that figure excludes big items that everyone else thinks should be included, notably federal prosecution and prison costs. Excluding these figures allows the federal government to claim to roughly balance supply reduction (mostly enforcement) and demand reduction (prevention and treatment). Putting in the full list of programs might take the federal figure to more than $17 billion. State and local governments, which provide most of the policing and prison funding, probably spend even more. So across all levels of government, drug control spending may exceed $40 billion annually.

How well do the different kinds of programs work? Every one likes the idea of preventing kids from starting drug use, but drug prevention is nothing like immunizing kids against drug abuse. The most widely implemented programs have never been shown by rigorous evaluations to have any effect on drug use, and even cutting-edge model programs that fare better in evaluation studies produce reductions in use that mostly dissipate by the end of high school. Even recognizing the historical correlation between delayed onset and reduced lifetime use, projected reductions in lifetime consumption are in the single-digit percentages. Modest effects should not be surprising. It is hard to do anything within 30 contact hours that overrides the impact of the thousands of hours that typical young people spend with peers, listening to music, watching television, and so on. The good news is that the budgetary cost of school-based prevention is low, so prevention appears to still be modestly cost-effective unless one ascribes a particularly high value to the opportunity cost of diverting classroom hours from academic subjects or volunteers' hours from other causes.

Mass-media campaigns are notoriously difficult to evaluate because they are so diffuse; it is hard to find a control group so that one can distinguish the effects of the campaign from other factors affecting drug use. Still, it is sobering that evaluation. . . of the federal government's high-profile media campaign suggest that it has had no effect on drug use.

Treating those with drug problems is the one kind of intervention for which there is a fairly good empirical base to judge effectiveness. About 1.1 million individuals received some kind of treatment for drug dependence or abuse in 2004, plus another 340,000 for whom alcohol was the primary substance of abuse. Federal expenditures on that amounted to about $2.4 billion; the states may add about as much again. Heroin addicts mostly get methadone, a substitute opiate. Everyone else gets, in some form, counseling. Even though the majority of clients entering treatment drop out and of those who complete their treatment more than half will relapse within five years, it is easy to make the case that the intervention is cost-effective. This comes from the fact that many of those who enter treatment, certainly those with heroin or cocaine problems, are very high-rate criminal offenders. During treatment, their drug use goes down a lot and that cuts their crime rates comparably. These crime-reducing benefits from treatment help the community as well as the patient.

It is disappointing that the number in treatment at any one time ([about] 850,000, including 500,000 who also abused alcohol) is only a modest fraction of the 3 to 4 million who are dependent on cocaine, methamphetamine, or heroin. There are a similar number who are dependent only on marijuana, which is the single most common primary substance of abuse for those treated; however, those dependent only on marijuana are less likely to be frequent offenders or to suffer acute health harms, so the social benefits of treating them are quite different and much smaller. (Most marijuana-only users who are compelled into treatment by an arrest are low- to medium-rate users.)

Most U S. drug efforts go to enforcing drug laws, predominantly against sellers; oddly enough, that is also true for other less punitive nations, including the Netherlands. Although eradication and crop substitution programs overseas in the source countries, primarily in the Andes [mountains in South America], get a lot of press coverage, they account for a small share of even the federal enforcement budget, about $1 billion. More money—about $2.5 billion in 2004—is spent on interdiction: trying to seize drugs and couriers on their way into the country.

Neither source-country programs nor interdiction has much promise as a way of producing more than a transitory reduction in drug consumption in the United States. They focus on the phases of the production and distribution system at which the drugs are still cheap and easily replaced because there is plenty of land, labor, and routes available to adapt to government interventions. In addition to creating occasional transitory disruptions, interdiction (in contrast to source-country interventions such as crop eradication) has long made drug smuggling surprisingly expensive, but it has not managed to raise smugglers' costs further in a long time.

The majority of all drug control expenditures go to the enforcement of drug laws within the United States. Between 1980 and 1990, dependent drug use and violent drug markets expanded rapidly, and the number of people locked up for drug law violations increased by 210,000. Between 1990 and 2000, drug problems began to ease, but drug incarcerations increased by still another 200,000. Simply put, incarceration has risen steadily while drug use has both waxed and waned.

The great majority of those locked up are involved in drug distribution. Although a sizable minority were convicted of a drug possession charge, in confidential interviews most of them report playing some (perhaps minor) role in drug distribution; for example, they were couriers transporting (and hence possessing) large quantities or they pled down to a simple possession charge to avoid a trial.

Society locks up drug suppliers for multiple reasons. Drug sellers cause great harm because of the addiction they facilitate and the crime and disorder that their markets cause. Thus there is a retributive purpose for the imprisonment. Still, sentences can exceed what mere retribution might require. Perhaps the most infamous example is that in federal courts the possession of 5 grams of crack cocaine will generate a five-year mandatory minimum sentence, compared with a national average time served for homicide of about five years and four months, even though that $400 worth of crack is just one fifty-millionth of U.S. annual cocaine consumption, or about two weeks' supply for one regular user.

Is the United States' Tough Policy Working?

An important justification for aggressive punishment is the claim that high rates of incarceration will reduce drug use and related problems. The theory is that tough enforcement will raise the risk of drug selling. Some dealers will drop out of the business, and the remainder will require higher compensation for taking greater risks. Hence the price of drugs should rise. It should also make drug dealers more cautious and thus make it harder for customers to find them. So the central question is whether the huge increase in incarceration over the past 25 years has made drugs more expensive and/or less available.

The science of tracking trends in illicit drug prices is not for purists; there are no random samples of drug sellers or transactions. However, the broad trends apparent in the largest data sets (those stemming from law enforcement's undercover drug buys) are confirmed by other sources, including ethnographic studies, interviews with or wire taps of dealers, and forensic analysis of the quantity of pure drug contained in packages that sell for standardized retail amounts (for example, $10 "dime bags" of heroin). During the past 25 years, the general price trends have gone more or less in the opposite direction from what would be expected. Incarceration for drug law violations (primarily pertaining to cocaine and heroin) increased 11-fold between 1980 and 2002, yet purity-adjusted cocaine and heroin prices fell by 80%. Methamphetamine prices also fell by more than 50%, although the decline was interrupted by some notable spikes. Marijuana prices unadjusted for purity rose during the 1980s and 2000s but fell during the 1990s. Declining prices in the face of higher incarceration rates does not per se contradict the presumption that tougher enforcement can reduce use by driving up prices. Other factors may have driven the price declines. Drug distributors might have been making supernormal profits in the early 1980s that were driven out over time by competition, or "learning by doing" might have improved distribution efficiency within the supply chain. Hence, it is possible that prices would have fallen still farther had it not been for the great expansion in drug law enforcement. . . .

With a few exceptions (notably oxycontin and methamphetamine), the drug problem in the United States has been slowly improving during the past 15 years. The number of people dependent on expensive drugs (cocaine, heroin, and methamphetamine) has declined from roughly 5.1 million in 1988 to perhaps 3.8 million in 2000, the most recent year for which figures have been released. The residual drug-dependent populations are getting older; more than 50% of cocaine-related emergency department admissions are now of people over 35, compared to 20% 20 years ago. The share of those treated for heroin, cocaine, and amphetamine dependence who were over 40 rose from 13% in 1992 to 31% in 2004. Kids who started using marijuana in the late 1990s are less likely to go on to use hard drugs than were kids who started in the 1970s.

What we face now is not the problem of an explosive drug epidemic, the kind that scared the country in the 1980s when crack emerged and street markets proliferated, but rather "endemic" drug use, with stable numbers of new users each year. The substantial number of aging drug abusers cause great damage to society and to themselves, but the problem is not rapidly growing. Rather, it is slowly ebbing down to a steady state that, depending on the measure one prefers, may be on the order of half its peak.

Rising imprisonment probably made some contribution to these trends. Some of the most aggressive dealers are now behind bars; their replacements are no angels but may be both less violent and less skilled at the business. However, the discussion above raises doubts about whether incarceration accounts for much of the decline. If prices have not risen and if the drugs are just as available as before, then it is hard to see how tough enforcement against suppliers can be what explains the ends of the epidemics and the gradual but important declines in the number of people dependent on expensive drugs.

Drug Policies Have Not Kept Up with the Times

This provides an opportunity. Changed circumstances justify changed policies, but U.S. drug policies have changed only marginally as the problem has transformed. The inertia can be seen by examining why the number of prisoners keeps rising even as drug markets get smaller. Drug arrests have been flat at 1.6 million a year for 10 years, and more and more of them are for marijuana possession (almost half in 2003), which produces very few prison sentences.

Three factors drive the rise in incarceration. First, today's drug offenders are not just older; they also have longer criminal records, exposing them to harsher sentences. Second, legal changes have made it more likely that someone arrested for drug selling will get a jail or prison sentence. Third, the declining use of parole has meant longer stays in prison for a given sentence length. On average, drug offenders who received prison sentences in state courts in 2002 were given terms of four years, of which they served about half. Is it a good thing that those being convicted are now spending more time behind bars?

Any case for cutting drug imprisonment should not pretend that prisons are bulging with first-time, nonviolent drug offenders. Most were involved in distributing drugs, and few got into prison on their first conviction; they had to work their way in. The system mostly locks up people who have caused a good deal of harm to society. Most will, when released, revert to drug use and crime. They do not tug the heart strings as innocent victims of a repressive state.

Still, would the United States really be worse off if it contented itself with 250,000 rather than 500,000 drug prisoners? This would hardly be going soft on drugs. It would still be a lot tougher than the [Ronald] Reagan administration ever was. It would ensure that the United States still maintained a comfortable lead over any other Western nation in its toughness toward drug dealers. Furthermore, incarcerating fewer total prisoners need not mean that they all get out earlier. The minority who are very violent or unusually dangerous in other ways may be getting appropriate sentences, and with less pressure on prison space, they might serve more of their sentences. Deemphasizing sheer quantity of drug incarceration could usefully be complemented by greater efforts to target that incarceration more effectively.

There is no magic formula behind this suggestion to halve drug incarceration as opposed to cutting it by one-third or two-thirds. The point is simply that dramatic reductions in incarceration are possible without entering uncharted waters of permissiveness, and the expansion to today's unprecedented levels of incarceration seems to have made little contribution to the reduction in U.S. drug problems.

Drug treatment as an alternative to incarceration has become a standard response, more talked about than implemented. Drug courts that use judges to cajole and compel offenders to enter and remain in treatment are one tool, but they account for a modest fraction of drug-involved offenders because the screening criteria are restrictive, excluding those with long records. Proposition 36 in California [passed by voters in 2000], which ensured that most of those arrested for drug possession for the first time were not incarcerated, seems to have been reasonably successful in at least cutting the number jailed without raising crime rates or any other indicator one worries about. These, though, are interventions that deal with less serious offenders, most of whom will only go to local jail rather than to prison.

A more important change would be to impose shorter sentences and then use University of California at Los Angeles Professor Mark Kleiman's innovation of coerced abstinence as a way of keeping them reasonably clean while on parole. Coerced abstinence simply means that the criminal justice system does what the citizens assume it is doing already, namely detecting drug use early via frequent drug testing and providing short and immediate sanctions when the probationer or parolee tests positive. The small amount of research on this kind of program suggests that it works as designed, but it is hard to implement and needs to be tested in tougher populations, such as released parolees.

A democracy should be reluctant to deprive its citizens of liberty, a reluctance reinforced by the facts that imprisonment falls disproportionately on poor minority communities and that many U.S prisons are nasty and brutalizing institutions. Further, there is growing evidence that the high incarceration rates have serious consequences for communities. A recent study suggests that differences in black and white incarceration rates may explain most of the sevenfold higher rate of HIV among black males as compared to white males. If locking up typical dealers for two years rather than one has minimal effect on the availability and use of dangerous drugs, then a freedom-loving society should be reluctant to do it.

Yet we are left with an enforcement system that runs on automatic, locking up increasing numbers on a faded rationale despite the high economic and social costs of incarceration and its apparently quite modest effects on drug use. Truly "solving" the nation's drug problem, with its multiple causes, is beyond the reach of any existing intervention or strategy. But that should not prevent decisionmakers from realizing that money can be saved and justice improved by simply cutting in half the number of people locked up for drug offenses.

Prescription Drugs Rival Others for Addictive Power

Joli Jensen

Doctors tell millions of Americans they have "neurochemical imbalances" that can be corrected to make them feel better and think more clearly. Because the drugs do indeed make them feel better, these people believe that something was inherently wrong with their neurochemistry. Many develop emotional and chemical dependencies on these prescription drugs that, as critics point out, are as problematic as any other addictions. Professor of communications at the University of Tulsa and recovered alcoholic Joli Jensen agrees. In the following 2004 article, she asserts that in the doctor's hurry to make her patient feel better, she may be helping that patient begin an addiction every bit as strong as the one Jensen had to overcome. She suggests that people may need to return to nonmedicinal means of dealing with anxiety and depression. In the process of taking mood-altering medications, people may in fact be numbing the "true self" and the "normal" their doctor promised to restore.

In modern life, we each get to choose how to act and whom to be. This freedom can also be a curse, because we must make our choices based on approaches to doing and being that may be persuasive but are often in conflict. Our choices are centered on the stories we tell ourselves and the stories we are told; our challenge is to find good ways to choose among contradictory stories.

Such decisions are among the most basic challenges we face, because they become the foundation for a succession of other choices we make throughout our lives, often with no clearly right answers yet with long-term consequences. When we want to make the "right" decision about education, child rearing, or medicine, we must first sort out conflicting claims about what is true.

But while modern life offers us an abundance of compelling stories about what is best for us to do, it offers little guidance for finding our way through a thicket of equally plausible but often mutually contradictory points of view.

There are as many compelling illustrations of this issue as there are choices to make. The example I will use centers on a personal medical decision, but it involves far broader issues: social norms, approaches to choice, even identity. It is about mood medication.

I'm a prime candidate for such medication—female, entering menopause, with a full-time job and two active children. I've long been prone to bouts of sadness and lethargy. I usually answer yes to most of the depression screening questions found in women's magazines and drug company pamphlets. On top of my symptoms of depression, I have lots of anxiety; I'm definitely a worrywart, imagining disasters of many kinds befalling me, my loved ones, and the world.

Plenty of experts have tried to convince me that I need mood medication. In the last 10 years my primary care physician, my gynecologist, and even my allergist's assistant have offered to get me prescriptions. I'm also being targeted by pharmaceutical companies with magazine and TV ads that describe me exactly and tell me that I can greet the dawn with gusto, romp with my children, smile at myself in the mirror, and be productive, cheerful, and optimistic ("like myself again") if I take their drugs. Why am I resisting taking mood medications, an option that millions of my fellow citizens have already chosen?

One reason I'm hesitant to take Prozac, Zoloft, Xanax, Celexa, Wellbutrin, or their like involves a related but complicating issue: alcoholism. Years ago, I quit drinking because I believed I was an alcoholic, and if this is true it makes taking even doctor-prescribed drugs problematic. When I was first struggling to control my alcohol use, I strongly resisted the *alcoholic* label. But my resistance was interpreted by a counselor as denial, which is a key element in the diagnosis of alcoholism. And as with those depression screening questions, I could answer yes to well over the minimum number of questions required for an official diagnosis of alcoholism.

Since even with my best efforts I was unable to control my drinking, I finally adopted the language and beliefs—what we in academic life call the *discourse*—of alcoholism recovery, including the conviction that the only way to control my addiction was to abstain completely from alcohol and other mood-altering substances. I've successfully abstained from these, one day at a time, for more than 20 years.

Many in 12-step recovery circles believe that mood medication—20 years ago it was Librium, Valium, and tricyclic antidepressants—is just alcohol in pill form. In the 1980s, lots of recovering alcoholics (more women than men) considered themselves dual addicts because they both drank and took pills. Recovering addicts were therefore considered to be one drink or drug away from active addiction. So if these beliefs are true, antidepressants are (for me, if I am indeed an addict) not useful medicine but dangerous drugs. Even everyday medicine—cough syrup, pain pills—could lead me back into active addiction, at least according to some members of the 12-step recovery community. So perhaps I am right to be especially wary.

Yet today many recovering alcoholics make exceptions for doctor-prescribed medications. Even as they consider themselves recovering alcoholics, they are taking and feeling better on mood medication such as Prozac and stimulants such as Ritalin (taken for "adult attention deficit disorder" [or ADD]). These people believe they are treating medical conditions, not feeding their addiction. They believe prescription medication, taken when recommended by a doctor to treat a real illness, is not dangerous and does not lead to relapse.

Are they right? Previous generations of doctors happily prescribed the tranquilizers and pep pills—the Mother's Little Helpers—that brought many women into what they defined as active addiction. In my early sobriety, I heard harrowing tales of how hard it was for these women to learn to live without the pills that their doctors had prescribed for the same kinds of symptoms I struggle with today. And it turns out that today's new and improved mood medications are also difficult to quit, requiring a gradual weaning process much like other addictive drugs. How are Paxil, Zoloft, and Xanax any different from Miltown, Librium, and Valium, the pills many critics now denounce as addictive drugs used to keep women of the '50s and '60s passive and complacent?

What Is Normal?

If you believe the media coverage of the 1990s, the newer selective serotonin reuptake inhibitors (SSRIs) are unlike the drugs of the past because these new medications treat a chemical imbalance that causes the diseases of depression and anxiety. Many who take these medications believe they are correcting a brain chemical deficit. But this is a marketing model that misrepresents what neuroscientists currently know about brain chemistry and the reasons these drugs may work. On top of that, depression, anxiety, and even alcoholism aren't diseases like cancer or diabetes, even if it may be helpful to think of them this way.

There is plenty of controversy about whether alcoholism even exists or, if it does, if it really is a disease. The original use of the term *disease* in Alcoholics Anonymous [A.A.], was metaphorical, aimed at destigmatizing the condition and describing its relentless course if untreated. But alcoholism, along with anxiety and depression, has come to count as a disease in the diagnostic manuals used by psychotherapists and physicians. This means that, at least for prescription and insurance purposes, they *are* diseases. Yet this pathologizing of elements of human experience begs the question: What makes heavy drug or alcohol use, long-term sadness, or heightened anxiety a disease?

And what constitutes addiction? Most of us are dependent on something, and in the last few decades people have learned to define themselves as gambling addicts, sex addicts, food addicts, exercise addicts, television addicts, and so on. For all the claims about how "nonaddictive" current mood medications are, the mounting evidence suggests otherwise, since most long-term users feel dependent on them and cannot easily stop using them. And although the American Psychiatric Association says withdrawal effects like those experienced by people who abruptly stop using SSRIs are neither necessary nor sufficient for a diagnosis of "substance dependence," such symptoms traditionally were seen as the hallmarks of addiction.

Furthermore, for all my commitment to continued sobriety, I'm far from "drug free" today if you count caffeine, as we should, as a mood-altering substance. I carry a Thermos of strong tea with me every day, carefully doling out my cups to avoid getting a pounding headache. How is this different from carrying a small flask of medicinal whiskey? Aren't caffeine and nicotine as addictive (if addiction exists) as alcohol and heroin, if not more so?

So are popular products like Prozac, Paxil, Zoloft, Xanax, and Celexa best understood as drugs that change us or as medicines that cure us? What makes them one or the other, beyond social convention and a doctor's prescription?

There's another twist. I have spent most of my life learning how to cope with my moods. I'm deeply invested in figuring out how to glean something useful from my depressions as well as learning how to manage and make the most of my periods of elation. I have found ways to minimize the damage and disruption that my periods of gloom and nameless grief can cause. My moodiness is—and has always been—my "self." Perhaps there's some benefit to living with, rather than medicating, my temperament. I've certainly learned a lot about the range of ways reality can feel. What does it mean for me to start defining myself as "mood-disordered" or "chemically imbalanced" or "borderline personality disordered" or "ADHD" [attention deficit hyperactivity disorder]?

By whose story should I live? Am I simply an especially emotionally responsive person, or have I squandered most of my life trying to compensate for biological dysfunctions that modern medicine now allows me to correct?

When it comes to deciding if I should medicate my moods, I am, as we say in my academic field, situated at the intersection of conflicting discourses. But this is true for all of us, with or without mood swings, possible addictions, or persuasive physicians. The invention and marketing of medications that seem to alleviate symptoms of depression and anxiety make it possible for every one of us to choose to take what some would call drugs and others would call medicine, to become (depending on your point of view) an addict, or your old self, or even a preferable self. We are all faced with this choice, as well as many others. How do we choose well?

Three overlapping but conflicting discourses operate whenever we think about taking pills to influence our emotions— discourses of addiction, of neuroscience, and of mental health. Each of these has its own opposition, a discourse that challenges all its premises. If I want to choose wisely about taking or not taking antidepressants, I have to find my way not only through each of these three discourses, each with different evidence and assumptions, but through three additional discourses—the ones that challenge that evidence and those assumptions.

This is a daunting project, but I think it is fairly typical of what modern life asks of each of us. We are always being asked to choose among conflicting stories. The dominant challenge of the modern age is figuring out how to make wise choices.

Is It All for Our Own Good?

Most of the stories we are told serve some purpose: to sell a product, support a belief, sustain a social position. The first thing to ask of any contemporary story is the obvious one: Who benefits? In a mass-mediated world, many different self-interested groups are offering us stories we seem to want to hear. In the case of mood medication, the pharmaceutical industry is spending and making stunning amounts of money selling us a story of "chemical imbalances" that their product can safely correct. The recovery community and the mental health industry are both telling us a story of epidemic levels of disorders that require their particular kinds of treatment. And the medical establishment believes it is now better able to "do something" for the many patients who are stressed, anxious, and unhappy.

Those who take mood medication often report that they are now much better able to cope with their stress, anxiety, and unhappiness. They are grateful, even if they are simultaneously uneasy about relying on pills or about various side effects. As Peter Kramer's 1993 bestseller *Listening to Prozac* describes so compellingly, many even celebrate the "new self" that cosmetic psychopharmacology seems to make possible. But even the most fervent celebrators of the possibilities of self-enhancement through medication express ambivalence about going too far with self-transformation. We may have the chemical ability to create and sustain ever more resilient and productive and desirable selves. Should we take that option?

If we are surrounded by contradictory stories, whose stories count? Clearly, we have every reason to be skeptical of the stories told to us through advertising. Is this also true of the stories told to us by politicians and journalists? What about the stories told to us by the medical community, grassroots organizations, teachers, religious leaders, scientists, family members, or even those that emerge from our own gut? People with good intentions and no desire to make money from us can still have a vested interest in persuading us to their way of thinking. But how can we know if it is also in our interest?

Because it is all too easy to fall for plausible but damaging stories, we need to find ways to figure out which stories to believe. We aren't as good as we think we are at using evidence to make wise decisions. As Michael Shermer points out in *Why People Believe Weird Things* (1997), we fall into logical fallacies and superstitious beliefs with amazing ease. In his analysis of pseudoscientific thinking, Shermer identifies a number of characteristics that bolster faith in our current practices of medicating depression and anxiety.

For example, we are too easily persuaded by anecdotal evidence, by scientific language, and by bold statements, all of which have abounded in media coverage of mood medication. I've reviewed news coverage of mood medication since the early 1990s, and Shermer's caveats describe perfectly their heady mix of personal success stories, accounts of scientific breakthroughs, and hyperbolic language of personal, social, and cultural transformation.

We also succumb to emotive words ("depression is a disease . . .") and false analogies (". . . to be treated like diabetes"). And we tend to over-rely on authorities ("neuro-scientists believe . . ."). We like to split the world in two (well or sick, normal or abnormal, functional or dysfunctional). We eagerly deploy circular reasoning ("I feel better now that I'm taking this medicine, which I'm told is treating a chemical imbalance; therefore my brain is imbalanced and I must need the medication"). Why do we fall for hokum? Shermer believes we are vulnerable to false beliefs because we want certainty, especially in an increasingly complex society. . . .

We Must Trust Our Own Instincts

What is normal mood, anyway? The antidepressant ads suggest that the products they tout help you "feel like yourself again." But who is this "self," and should he or she be the vibrant, active, zest-filled person the ads depict? What makes us so sure that mental health is about feeling good most of the time? There are those who argue convincingly for the value and worth of the darker emotions, who are highly critical of a modern American propensity to make everything sunny.

There are also social critics who argue that it benefits capitalism to keep workers cheerful and productive, and that it benefits patriarchy to keep women chipper and docile. From their perspectives, taking antidepressants prevents the kind of legitimate anger and motivated action that social inequalities require; it makes us all into Stepford employees and partners. But is this argument disrespectful of the genuine suffering these new medications supposedly alleviate? Sorting out what constitutes reasonable and unreasonable emotionality is a highly charged, and often highly personal, endeavor. Whose experiences and beliefs count here? Should we consult the social critics, mental health professionals, our family and friends, or our own preferences?

Your way through this thicket of contradictory, plausible, and interdependent discourses will no doubt be different from mine. All I want to do here is show how I've made my way, trying to evaluate evidence in ways that help me assess the consequences of believing in some stories instead of others. We can never know for sure if we are making the "right" decision. As Shermer notes, I will probably remember only the evidence and arguments that confirm my choice, and ignore or dismiss the evidence that contradicts it. But at least we each have the opportunity to try to sort things out for ourselves.

So: My own sense of the neurochemical evidence is that the medications so many are taking are far riskier and offer far less benefit than we now realize. So I believe in the "counter-discourse" of neuroscience—that the dominant serotonin story is misleading and potentially dangerous, and that the critique of the dominant story has it mostly right. The model of chemical imbalance sells drugs but doesn't have much to do with how brain chemistry actually functions in mental states. We still know very little about how (or even if) particular brain chemicals connect with particular moods, feelings, or perceptions, and neuroscientists are constantly revising their always-contingent models.

Evidence is accumulating that suggests much of the anecdotal evidence of successful mood alteration may be due to a placebo effect. Some recent controlled studies do not consistently show positive effects from these medications, and other studies suggest that side effects, including suicidal thoughts and actions, are more prevalent than previously publicized. The effects of the medicine on the brain may be structural, long-term, and not very beneficial. To me, that sounds like an unacceptable level of risk.

But maybe I really do have something wrong with my brain, and my heavy drinking in adolescence and early adulthood was my feeble attempt to deal with a condition these new medications could finally treat. Maybe my belief that I'm selling out my sobriety by taking legal drugs is ludicrous. There are certainly compelling critiques of the recovery industry and 12-step programs . . . that would suggest I have been propagandized and brainwashed. Critics of A.A. and related programs rightly note the ideological rigidity, lack of empirical evidence, cult-like qualities, hypocrisy, illogic, and cliché-ridden aspects of what has been called "the recovery movement." Have I fallen for an ideology that means I "keep coming back" for lies?

I am also plenty skeptical of the late-20th-century boom in insurance-funded rehabilitation institutions, and I am very much opposed to requiring those arrested for drunk driving to attend A.A. meetings or go into treatment if they want to avoid jail. I get uneasy around the clichés and psychobabble that flourish in some recovery settings. But I am also impressed by the democratic, self-supporting nature of A.A. and inspired by the sanity and wisdom of the people who sustain it. So in relation to this discourse, I (in the language of recovery) take what I need and leave the rest, and I am grateful to be able to hang around with people committed to recovery discourse. Nonetheless, I don't really believe alcoholism is a disease. Taking one drink or pill might not lead me back into active alcoholism, but it's just not worth the risk to me. So I'm choosing to live by the alcoholism discourse, even as I doubt many elements in it and agree with many elements of the critique of it. . . .

I've long been drawn to the grouchy and the eccentric. There is something enlivening about being a crank, and something scary about how easily difference is labeled pathology these days. The relentless emphasis on "adjustment" that sociologists criticized in the 1950s is now so commonplace as to be almost invisible. But what's so great about being adjusted to systems I don't always believe in or support?

So here's where I end up: Mood medication is too risky for me to take or want to give to my kids, although I'm happy to let other people take whatever legal or illegal drugs they want as long as they realize what they are doing. I don't want my friends, family, or fellow citizens to get sucked into believing they are treating a chemical imbalance with medicine when what they are actually doing is taking drugs to feel better.

I think we make too much of being "normal." Variety and difference are good things. I want people to stop falling for stories about diseases and imbalances that make them eager consumers of expensive, possibly dangerous, and possibly ineffective drugs. Taking drugs to feel better may be just fine for you, but I am betting that the option is particularly dangerous for me. So far, living without most drugs (I'm keeping the caffeine) has worked out pretty well.

Club Drugs Can Kill

Kate Patton

Ecstasy users and nonusers alike often dismiss it and other club drugs as relatively harmless. Kate Patton, in the following 2002 congressional testimony, says otherwise. After she lost her teenage daughter Kelley to an Ecstasy overdose, Patton made it her life's goal to make sure that her daughter's life and death would have meaning. She successfully lobbied the legislature in her home state of Illinois for the creation of Kelley's Law, which metes out harsh fines and sentences to those profiting from the sale of Ecstasy in clubs. Since the law took effect in January of 2002, there has been a marked decrease in Ecstasy use in Illinois.

Chairman [Mark] Souder, I thank you for inviting me here today to testify on what has become an ever growing problem across the country, Ecstasy abuse.

It has been two years and ten months since I was told the four words that are every parent's worst nightmare, "your child is dead," I lost my daughter to an accidental overdose of Ecstasy, more correctly I lost Kelley three times to Ecstasy, first when she started using it, secondly when she started selling it and lastly when she died from it. I am here today to put a face to the devastation that Ecstasy can have on a family. The day Kelley was born I saw her take her first breath, I wrapped my arms around her and gave her, her first hug. But I wasn't there for her last breath and I was robbed of hugging her good-bye. My life is forever changed as is that of my young daughter, who lost her only sister to a drug that so many people feel is harmless.

Before the death of Kelley I had never heard of club drugs let alone Ecstasy. I now know more about the drug that took

Kate Patton, "Ecstasy: A Growing Threat to the Nation's Youth," hearing before the Subcommittee on Criminal Justice, Drug Policy, and Human Resources of the Committee on Government Reform, House of Representatives, 107th Congress, second session, serial no. 107–229, September 19, 2002. www.gpo.gov/congress/house.

my daughter's life than I ever thought possible. Ecstasy took my daughter but it will not take me! A year ago I started a foundation in her memory. The Kelley McEnery Baker Foundation for the Prevention, Education and Awareness of Ecstasy Use. I speak to high schools and youth groups and share Kelley's story with hope the kids will learn from Kelley's deadly mistakes. I also speak to parents' groups and town hall meetings to encourage parents to become what I now call "information junkies" when it comes to knowing all you can about the many drugs that may cross paths with their children. I tell parents that we so often go to the grocery store very prepared with a grocery list in hand but are we as prepared when it comes to sitting down and talking to our children about drugs. My goal is to re-inform the misinformed and to enlighten those who know nothing.

Parents Must Join the Fight

During the past year I've talked to well over 3,000 kids, I use a Power Point program to help with Ecstasy facts and figures but I mostly talk from my heart. I have found the reception that I am greeted with has been one of warmth and respect. I encourage questions and I have plenty [of] questions of my own to ask as well, one question I never fail to ask is how many parents have sat down and had a "drug talk" with them, sadly all too few hands are raised. At one particular school I visited I went further and asked how many of them knew someone who had overdosed on drugs, surprisingly far more hands went up, they then went on to share the stories with me. It is my experience that there is a huge population of parents that don't talk to their children about drugs, perhaps they themselves aren't informed of the many different drugs or maybe they feel as many parents do "my child is not the type to try drugs." I know of what I speak, I was one of those parents. The time is now to find a way to impress upon parents how important it is to become knowledgeable about all drugs and then to share that important information with their children. Drug awareness and education starts in the home.

I was recently asked by my Congressmen Mark Kirk [Illinois Republican, 2001-present] to join a drug task force that he has assembled after realizing there was a need to address the growing concern that we are facing regarding club drugs in Illinois. This task force is made up of a group of knowledgeable professionals which includes former DEA [Drug Enforcement Administration] Director Peter Bensinger. Also represented is an Illinois State Senator and State Representative, along with several Metropolitan Enforcement Group officers and many leaders in the drug prevention field. A major goal of the task force is to increase drug awareness which with hope will lead to a decrease in drug use in the Chicago area. I am proud of the State of Illinois and it's lawmakers for taking a hard stance against Ecstasy and club drugs by introducing and passing House Bill 126. It was a labor of love for me to have lobbied for this law. It is now known as "Kelley's Law."

Kelley's Law targets criminals who seek to profit from illegal club [drugs], it took effect January 1, 2002. People convicted of selling from 15 to 200 doses of Ecstasy with intent to distribute will face Class X felony penalties of six to 30 years in prison with no chance of parole. It is the toughest law of its kind in the country. Without Kelley's Law a person would have to sell more than 200 grams (approx. 900 pills) in order to be charged with a Class X felony in Illinois. Chicago DEA supervisor George Karountzos recently told me through intelligence information that he has gathered since the inception of Kelley's Law there has been a marked decrease in people wanting to get involved with dealing Ecstasy due to these very stiff penalties.

There is much to be done on many fronts in order to put a significant dent in the war that we have waged against drugs. I believe that our priority should be education and awareness, which should start in the home and continue with the support of our school system and faith based organizations (church, synagogue). The phrase "it takes a village to raise a child" is a good metaphor in that [for] drug education and awareness to be effective [it] should be approached from many different directions. It is a fact that we must learn to accept that drug abuse/addiction is a medical illness, and is deemed so by the AMA [American Medical Association]. There are many repeat drug offenders who land in jail repeatedly with no help for their illness, they should be treated for their illness with the help of drug programs and drug courts. Illinois and Kelley's Law has set an example that stiffer club drug penalties work. I feel every state should review their drugs laws and update them accordingly. This is a bipartisan issue and is of paramount importance in order to help protect every child in this country.

I will close today as I close my presentation to the kids I speak to, I ask for a volunteer to read a poem. This is a poem that I selected and was read at Kelley's funeral by one of her high school classmates.

Remember me
    To the living I am gone.
    To the sorrowful, I will never re-
    turn.
    To the angry, I was cheated.
    But to the happy, I am at peace.
    And to
    the faithful I have never left.
    I cannot be seen, but I can be
    heard.
    So as you stand upon a shore,
    gazing at a beautiful sea . . . re-
    member me.
    As you look in awe at a mighty
    forest and
    it's grand majesty . . . remember me

As you look upon a flower and
admire its
simplicity . . . remember me.
Remember me in your heart, your
thoughts and
your memories of the time we
loved, the times
we cried, the times we fought, the
times we laughed
For if you always think of me,
I will have never gone. . .

After this poem has been read I ask the kids if they could possibly imagine reading this poem at the funeral of one of their friends or worse yet having it read at their own funeral; the silence is deafening. I am hoping this exercise drives home the point that drugs not only may harm them, send them to jail or worse yet kill them. Thus far my point has been very well taken.

I want to thank this subcommittee and all members of Congress from the bottom of my heart for all your efforts in the fight against drugs.

Fighting Methamphetamine Requires New Strategies

Mark Souder

By the turn of the twenty-first century, methamphetamine, or meth, had become the new drug of choice. Many people easily made meth from the over-the-counter cold and headache medicine ingredient pseudoephedrine. The problem was especially severe in rural areas where these home-based labs were easy to conceal from the authorities. Indiana congressman Mark Souder led the charge against meth use and production by crafting the Combat Methamphetamine Epidemic Act of 2005. In the following interview with the PBS newsmagazine Frontline, *Souder criticizes the George W. Bush administration and its drug czar John Walters for failing to see the meth problem for what it was and then for failing to adapt old drug-fighting strategies to combat it when meth use reached a crisis. He also faults pharmaceutical companies for refusing to voluntarily regulate the sale of pseudoephedrine. The Combat Methamphetamine Epidemic Act now requires all pharmacies to keep the drug behind the counter. Consequently, meth production and use has significantly decreased.*

Frontline: *Tell me about the impact that crystal meth has had on your constituents.*

Representative Mark Souder: In my district, like most of the country, it started as a rural problem, a few isolated cases. You didn't think you had as much of a problem. It was kind of an aggravation of law enforcement. Then they started to see house trailers catching on fire, firemen going in and wondering whether it was going to explode and blow them all up,

Mark Souder, "Frontline Interview with Mark Souder," November 2, 2005. www.pbs .org. Copyright © 2005 WGBH Educational Foundation Copyright © 1995–2007 WGBH/Boston. Reproduced by permission.

whether there were children involved. Pretty soon it starts to get into the child custody system as the problem starts to spread. You see more and more pollution questions as the problem spread—particularly in one county, Noble County, which has had the most labs in Indiana. It's a rural and small town, and [meth] has overwhelmed their police force.

Their drug task force will go out there, the officers will sit there, wait for the state police to come in, seal the site. Then they'll wait for the DEA [Drug Enforcement Administration]-contracted people to come in and clean it up. So their local police guys are tied up there, and now they're out of overtime hours. They don't know how to pay for their police depart-ment. They're only dealing in many of these cases with two or three [offenders], so it means lots of bigger drug busts or other types of crime are going unprotected because these few people have tied up the system.

Then they hit the treatment system. The treatment system has been only moderately effective. Since this problem has been mostly in rural areas, at least the mom-and-pop-type labs, those treatment centers have the least money, the least training, the most underfunded staff, and are the least able to execute the complicated treatment strategies you need. Thus, a typical thing would be that somebody goes into treatment, and as soon as they're done with treatment, they're back into the problem again. We have that [problem] in [treating] drugs in general, and that seems to be even more the case [with meth]. . . .

I just heard recently of a particular case where the person got picked up three times for [operating meth] labs and still hadn't been processed for his first prosecution. It has just overwhelmed local law enforcement and treatment providers. And it has a different impact than any other kind of drug be-cause of this multiplicity of effect: of endangerment to fire de-partments, endangerment to the policemen, endangerment to children. The fires associated with it, the environmental cleanup associated with it, the length of time at the site—all those things complicate it more than other narcotics.

The Federal Government
Has Been Slow to Respond

I was just amazed by the number of people that we're dealing with here, that county jail systems are overwhelmed, and foster care systems. Can you talk about the lack of resources for treating this problem?

Where meth has hit, whether it's crystal meth or mom-and-pop-lab meth, it overwhelms the entire judicial system. In St. Paul, Minn., in Ramsey County, which is an urban area, from a standing start to nine months later, 80 percent of the kids in child custody were there because of meth. In a rural area, as much as 80 to 90 percent of the cases, in some cases 100 percent, are meth-related. . . .

And whether it's crystal meth or mom-and-pop meth, both types of meth are very addictive. So we see it in the rural areas, where . . . it takes up 80 to 100 percent of their jail space, because these criminals are more likely to be violent, more likely to endanger other people, more likely to commit multiple crimes. They can't just release them like they can others. So even if there are other criminals, they have to concentrate on the meth criminals. . . .

The astounding thing about this is you can have one county where you have 80 percent of the kids in child custody [because of] meth, 100 percent of the people in jail because of meth, and in the county next [to] it, [it] would be 10 percent. It is one of the unusual phenomena of this drug.

And so given that places like St. Paul or Indiana or out West have had such serious problems, why do you think it took so long for the East Coast establishment to take the meth problem seriously?

One reason that the Washington [D.C.] establishment and our narcotics establishment has been slow to respond to meth is that it started in isolated, rural areas, usually around where there are national forests or open lands where people can hide, where there's not as much patrolling, where you don't have as much local police presence. It only has in the last six months to a year started to hit cities the size of Omaha [Nebraska] or Portland [Oregon] or St. Paul.

A second thing is, particularly with mom-and-pop labs, which are what endanger local police [and] children the most—[they] don't work through the normal criminal organizations, and our narcotics efforts are set up to deal with large trafficking organizations, so they're better at tackling crystal meth. Not that they're great on crystal meth, but they're better on crystal meth than they are on the mom-and-pop labs. It's a totally different type of phenomenon.

And do you think that there is some element of regionalism, that Washington only cares about what's going on in Washington?

That is tough speculation. . . . I believe that it's more of a rural/urban phenomenon than a regional phenomenon. The rural areas of America do not have as many congressmen in the House as the urban areas. Even in a state like California, meth has been in the more rural areas, and the numbers aren't as great in Los Angeles and San Francisco, where they don't seem to have a meth problem.

While on the surface it looks like it's just West versus East or rural versus urban, it's complex. Even in a home state like mine, Indianapolis has no meth problem. Six of the nine [congressional] districts are mostly related to the city of Indianapolis, so that leaves three congressmen out of the nine in Indiana who have a [regional] meth problem. Of those three congressional districts, like mine, the biggest city is Fort Wayne, Ind., and [it] has one lab. The rural areas in my district, which represent less than 30 percent of my district, have a huge meth problem. So even in districts where there's a meth problem, it isn't in your population center, so it's been harder to get the political establishment to focus, because even in my district, which is one of the hardest hit meth districts, meth isn't the number one problem in the biggest urban area. So it has been an unusual challenge to try to get the attention of public policy-makers, because the majority of their voters, even in a meth-hit district, aren't affected by meth.

Now, as the problem has moved, and as it moves to places like Omaha, St. Paul and Portland, you start to see more and more congressmen start to get the noise up. Plus, the Senate starts to respond because they're dealing with it statewide. And that's moving West to East, because it hasn't hit the East yet, which still has the biggest chunk of the population. It hasn't quite crossed the threshold, but with all the media coverage, with all the members of Congress in the outer areas starting to [feel the] squeeze, we're starting to see some response. I think that partly explains why it's been so long in coming.

The Bush Administration Must Change Battle Strategies

What's your assessment of how the current administration and its drug czar [John Walters] has handled meth over the last few years?

My first frustration is that they don't seem to understand that the war on narcotics changes from year to year. . . . I believe when you're fighting illegal narcotics that the target changes during different periods and that if you stay on the same theme year after year, the people wear out and you start to get an immunity to the message. . . . When you have an issue like meth, where everybody can see that the person starts by thinking that they're going to be able to be more productive at work, it's easy to convince people [of the dangers of the drug]. So why wouldn't we shift our tactics in prevention, for example, to try and educate people on that? Then if it moves to [the prescription drug] OxyContin two years from now, move to OxyContin and convince people on that.

So part of [the problem is], where has our prevention been? Why can't you see the advantage overall in the narcotics movement to say, "Look, meth is a hot drug of choice right now. It's destructive. We can sell this message. Don't just stick in what you were doing two years ago"?

Secondly, my biggest argument with the administration is that [this] new drug came up in a different way than the traditional systems. It's devastating to local law enforcement, local judicial systems, local treatment systems. When you see a new drug come through with a new kind of devastation, why don't you come up with a new strategy? It's like in war: We [don't] still think people are going to line up and fight us like at the Battle of Waterloo [a final defeat] and not do insurgencies. Why don't we adjust our strategies? In narcotics you have to have flexible strategies when new challenges come up, and there's been a refusal out of the drug czar's office in particular to grant that it's a threat, and it's a threat that requires a different type of strategy.

What is your assessment of what their approach has been, what their public statements have been?

I believe the office of the drug czar has had a laughable position that meth is only a minor problem, that it's not an epidemic and it only represents eight percent of drug use in America. I believe the number is higher. I believe the impact is higher. I believe it's catastrophic in regional areas and that the statistical methods that they're using, focusing on youth, focusing on traditional busts, are wrong. And when you combine this together, it's led them to miss what is probably the biggest drug epidemic in the last couple years, because their whole models and constructs are wrong.

So over the last 20 years, the pharmaceutical industry has lobbied at every turn to prevent regulation, to open loopholes, to keep ephedrine and pseudoephedrine on the market. What's been your experience of that kind of lobbying in Congress?

My subcommittee has been tracking this issue of regulation of pseudoephedrine since even before the first state law was put into effect.... That said, I've been frustrated that the pharmaceutical industry has not shown much willingness to work with us, and at this point I have moved to say, "Look, we're going to go behind the counter." ...

Starting with the state of Oklahoma, the battle over regulation of pseudoephedrine has been a state-by-state battle. Some states have been able to pass a very strict control law for pharmacies to put [products containing psuedoephedrine] behind the counter. In other states, it's been defeated.... So we have a mixed bag at the state level.

What is clear is [that meth] can't be regulated effectively without a national law. In the state of Indiana, where they put it behind the counter, [users] now just go over to Ohio and Michigan, so we clearly need a national law. The pharmaceutical companies have been resisting that, and the strategies for how they resist it vary. Sometimes they use the grocery stores as a front; sometimes they use the divisions in law enforcement; sometimes they'll use different types of arguments. But clearly they have held up our ability to move the bill.

Pharmaceutical Companies Have Put Up a Roadblock

And so what's your opinion of how the pharmaceutical industry has conducted itself through this debate?

With the invisible hand of the pharmaceutical companies, it's hard to say that the pharmaceutical companies as a whole are doing such-and-such. What we have is different pieces and different types of problems.... But the bottom line is ... [that] there are very few [pseudoephedrine-] manufacturing companies in the entire world, so why don't we get accurate data out of them?

The second thing is, clearly the Mexican border is where most of the pseudoephedrine is pouring in through. We have a flood of pseudoephedrine and super lab meth coming through Mexico. It has been very difficult to agree on how to do border strategies.

Then, once it gets into the United States, the question of what goes behind the counter, of whether it goes in a pharmacy or whether it's regulated at all, has varied by the type of company and their willingness to work with us. So you have big retail operations like Wal-Mart, Target being willing to put in certain controls, but they have management systems that can do that. A little grocery store in a small rural town does not have the type of systems that Wal-Mart and Target have, and they are in danger of being run out.

So the pharmaceutical companies will often use the divisions between the small and big retailers, between the different members of Congress. . . . That's why the invisible hand of the pharmaceutical companies is hard to figure out in this. We know they're there, but they haven't directly led the fight against regulation.

One thing that's happening is now that companies are losing shelf spaces because their products with pseudoephedrine must be placed behind the counter. They are bringing out products with phenylephrine [which, unlike pseudoephedrine, cannot be turned into crystal meth]. But phenylephrine has been around for about 50 years. Why do you think it took so long?

As I understand it, the alternative products are not as effective in treating pain or symptoms as the products that had the pseudoephedrine in them, and it isn't clear whether something can come to market that will replace that. But the plain truth of the matter is that in order to tackle the meth problem, at least in the short term, we are probably going to have some reduction in some quality of impact of some products. The question is, are we better off as a nation to have a little bit less effective headache medicine or cold medicine in order to get rid of meth?

But why has it taken so long to introduce these products?

I believe in America we've reached a tipping point. If it [were] just in rural Nebraska, it would be a fair political debate to say, "Should we restrict a grocery store in New York City from having the most effective headache product in their choices from 120 choices to 20?" But if the problem moves beyond just Nebraska—and it's now in 40 states, quickly heading to 50 states, and it's devastating costs to law enforcement, to treatment, to environmental impact—so you say, "OK, the marginal change here in headache medicine is worth it."

Some say the pharmaceutical industry has had to be dragged kicking and screaming here.

I believe that any industry wants to maximize the profits of a previous product rather than having to put new research into a product that they hope can replace the restricted one, so it's not unnatural for any industry to resist change. But our challenge as public policy-makers is to say, "When is that change necessary?" and to force them to change their products. They can come up with other alternatives. Eventually they'll come up with other alternatives that may even be better. It's just that every company's goal is to maximize their profits, which is a fine goal as a society, but that's why we have public policy lawmakers, to try to say, "OK, this is a balance. There's a tipping point here. You've got to change."

Controlling International Suppliers Is Crucial

The international side of this problem is much bigger than most people realize. Can you talk specifically now about the problem in Mexico?

For the last 20 years, Mexico has become the primary conduit of illegal narcotics in the United States. [Drugs] from the Andean region [of South America]—the heroin, the cocaine— come up through Mexico. And now Mexico itself is starting to provide much of the heroin and the marijuana that comes through the border. . . . It is a more or less open border in many parts of the United States, . . . so we have a general border problem. So as we crack down in California and other places on the super labs, they're going to move to Mexico. . . .

So we simultaneously have to have a border control strategy here. That basically means we have to have some kind of reasonable immigration strategy in this country, or we'll never control our borders. And so one issue will plunge us right into one of the most controversial issues in America—immigration—and how do we deal with the fact that we have 12 to 15 million people working in America who we don't acknowledge are here?

And another angle of this problem is that Mexican pharmacies are importing vastly more pseudoephedrine than is their legitimate need for cold medicine. . . . We know that Mexico is importing far more pseudoephedrine than they need, probably 50 percent more than they need—tons more than they need—and that's headed for the United States, either processed through super labs or in raw form to be then turned into methamphetamine in the United States. We have to get control of the Southwest border, where it's pouring through Mexico.

I don't know if you know that there's an international regime for codeine, and that every country on Earth has a quota over how much codeine they can import. They can import that much and no more. Don't we need to somehow come together to solve this problem internationally and come up with a plan, as they did with codeine?

It would be ideal if we could come together internationally and come up with a plan. . . . I believe we should have some sort of a buy-what-you-use type of program around the world. But the fact is that rogue nations aren't going to follow it anyway. . . . Mexico has a clear choice here: . . . Are they going to be a responsible member of the world, or are they going to be a rogue nation?

And lastly, what about this whole business [that] there are only a few factories that make this stuff? Why can't we get a handle on who these factories are selling it to?

Almost every aspect of trying to get a coordinated strategy on meth has been incredibly frustrating, but this seems like an elementary building block. . . .

What I realize is, the forces at international politics are tougher even than local law enforcement. It's like, we don't want to hurt our trade with India; we don't want to hurt our trade with China. We have all these other big issues to deal with. Hey, I understand that. I'm a member of Congress. . . . But look, if these countries want to be responsible, international countries, all we want is basic data, basic control.

And, our State Department doesn't want to cooperate. I've talked to [Secretary of State Condoleezza] Rice about this, as have other members, and we need a more aggressive policy out of our State Department to put the pressure on China and India and say, "Regulate this stuff. Track it. Give us the data—not only the raw stuff, but the pills. Report where it's going, who your shipping companies are, because this is devastating the families and children of people all across America and across the world."

There are basically nine major factories in the whole world that make the key ingredient in meth. It would seem that the logical way to tackle this would be to go there, because once it gets out of there and it moves to Mexico, or it moves to other places around the world, [it's] about impossible to control. Then it comes out of the Southwest border, and it goes into every state. It goes into little towns, into big cities, and you lose it. So why wouldn't we focus the traffic to see where it's coming out of there, to try to regulate it there, to watch it there, to get counts there, so that we can see where it's moving in the shipping lanes, then watch where it's moving around the world? . . .

The way we've dealt with cocaine is to say, look, it grows in the Andean region, and that's the number one source, so let's try to get to the cocaine there. If we fail there, let's try to interdict it. If we fail there, let's try to get it at the border. If we fail there, let's try to get it at the cities. But we understand that if we can get it when it's in the ground in Colombia and Peru, then it's easier than once it gets into the United States. Why not methamphetamine? If the key ingredient is pseudoephedrine, and there's only nine plants in the world, and most of those are in India and China, why wouldn't you focus there and have the same strategy that we employ in every other narcotic in the world, like we do with heroin in Afghanistan? What's our first strategy? We go to the ground. We try to get it there. Then we try to interdict it as it's moving out of the ground, because if you wait to fight heroin till it's in process and somebody's using it, all you're doing is picking up users. What you have to do is get back to the source and have multiple cracks at this. It's the only way you can reduce a drug on the street.

Methamphetamine Attracts More than Teenagers

Teresa Jones

This self-described soccer mom had a debilitating addiction to methamphetamine, or meth. Like many women, Jones initially used the drug to lose weight but then became unable to function without it. In the following piece from an anti-meth Web site she designed and hosts, Jones describes how, at the height of her addiction, she nearly lost her family and her life. She is convinced that without her faith in God and drug treatment, she would have died. Since her recovery from meth addiction, she has dedicated herself to keeping others off the drug.

My name is Teresa, I'm a 33-year-old wife and mother. I have lived in North Georgia most all of my life. I'm a recovering meth [or methamphetamine] addict and I have been clean for almost 4 years. At the time I first started meth, I was a Girl Scout Cookie Mom, a wife, a homemaker, and worked part-time in website development.

In the beginning I tried Crystal Meth [another form of methamphetamine] for weight loss. I was extremely overweight and was desperate to try anything after many failed diets. I really wasn't into the drug scene. I drank some and tried marijuana as a teen, but never got into drug use. At first using crystal-meth was fun, so I did it all the time and I was losing the weight fast! I was looking so great, slimmer than I was in High School! But before too long I needed Meth to feel "normal" and needed it to function in my everyday life.

My addiction led me to leave my husband and 2 daughters, which at the time were only toddlers—3 and 5 years old. I have missed 12 months of their lives because of my past addiction to meth. Those bonds are being mended everyday.

Teresa Jones, "Meth Testimonial," *Anti-Meth.org*, 2007. Reproduced by permission.

Becoming Trapped Is Easy

I became close with my drug dealer and moved to Miami Beach, Florida, with her, to live the fun, and big life. I left all my friends and family behind, I didn't need them anymore. Crystal Meth was all I needed. My new found friend and drug dealer assured me, that in Miami, Meth flows like honey, and it's not the crappy stuff they make here in the mountains but it's the "pure form" called "ICE." My family was terrified for my safety. They tried to help me, but did not know what to do, I was so far away. I never cared or thought about how my actions affected them, especially my daughters that were so young and without a mother. I only cared about how I felt and getting that next hit of Meth. I turned into a person that I never wanted to be, a person I hated and despised.

Before too long I became so depressed, I didn't want to live any longer. Most of my family had given up on me because I wouldn't return phone calls or come home to visit my daughters or family. (I hadn't seen them in 6 months.) I lived in a Penthouse 3 blocks from the beach . . . but rarely ventured out, because Meth had made me so paranoid that I feared of being arrested, and I thought people were out to kill me. This paranoia led me to stay in our penthouse for weeks at a time, becoming a hermit and never leaving. What kind of life is that?? I was supposed to be here living the ideal life in Miami Beach. Partying and having the time of my life! Meth paints a pretty picture in the beginning. It tricks you, lies to you. It's very clever. That's why it's called the devil's drug. So instead of living this ideal life in Miami Beach, I was fearing for my life everyday, I was paranoid, suicidal, lonely and in deep depression.

During my 8 month addiction I tried killing myself, and was admitted to a rehab center in Florida, as soon as I got out, I went back to using Crystal Meth (ICE), the most potent and addictive form of Meth. I didn't go home to see my children or family; I went back to the love of my life . . . Crystal Meth.

My final straw came one day after seeing something very terrible. The image will stay in my mind for the rest of my life. Let me say this. Miami is everything the movies and the news say it is. Top of the chart in Crimes and Drugs. That day, I answered a phone call from my 5 year old daughter. Her birthday was coming up, and I asked her what she wanted for her birthday, and she replied in tears, "I want my mommy to come home". That did it. I didn't hesitate, I didn't pack anything, I just got on a plane with my wallet and the clothes on my back and flew home to Georgia. I never looked back. I didn't even go back to get all my belongings that I had moved there in a U-haul. I wanted as far away as possible from Crystal Meth. I admitted myself to a detox center here in North [Georgia], and have been 100% drug free ever since. I have turned to *God* as my higher power, and give all the credit of my recovery to prayers and my faith in *God* and the friends and family that *Did Not* give up on me. You know which ones you are. Thank you for loving me enough not to give up hope and continuing to pray. Most of all I thank my Merciful God for watching over me, loving me and protecting me when I came so many times near death.

Addicts Can Free Themselves from Meth

Now I want to help fight the war against Methamphetamine. Every time I see a news report or watch a show on meth, I get angry and now I want to fight back. . . .

Today I live a happy, peaceful, drug-free life. My life has changed 100%. My morals, goals and outlook on life are opposite from where they used to be—selfish, angry, suicidal and destructive. They are now happiness, giving, helpful and positive. My dreams and goals are coming true and my anger, sadness and hopelessness has subsided. I am happily re-married to a wonderful, sweet & caring man and have a wonderful family with my 2 daughters and 3 step-children. I am a Soccer-Mom, Home schooling Mom and work part time in my business designing websites.

I am presently on the committee for The White County Meth Task Force and plan to continue to fight this war against drugs in our community. I don't dare think of what my life would be like if I had not had the desire to live for the sake of my daughters, and became clean of Meth. I just thank God every day that I am alive and free of the devil's drug *Meth*.

I pray my story encourages or helps anyone that is struggling with the addiction to Methamphetamine. I want you to know I didn't stop this drug alone, I needed help. I found that help in God, treatment and in myself. Also from my experiences, what I've witnessed, and thinking of the people I love. This all helped me beat the addiction. I want to say to all those reading this, *Do Not Try It*, and if you are using it, *Stop*. Get help, before it destroys you. I did it. . . . And you can too! *Let Go . . . Let God!*

Chronology

1551

South American missionaries condemn the use of coca at the first Ecclesiastical Council in Lima, Peru.

1561

The French ambassador to Portugal brings tobacco back to France, where it is quickly adopted as a cure-all for wounds, headaches, venereal disease, and other ailments.

1604

King James I of England taxes tobacco in an attempt to discourage smokers.

1611

Marijuana is first cultivated in Virginia.

1642

Pope Urban VIII issues an encyclical condemning tobacco smoking.

1805

Morphine is first extracted from opium poppies.

1827

Merck & Company begins commercial manufacture of morphine.

1839

The Opium War begins when the Chinese authorities try to keep British merchants from importing opium from India. Victorious Britain forces China to end trade restrictions.

1853

The hypodermic needle is invented. Morphine is first injected.

1860

German chemist Albert Niemann isolates cocaine from the coca plant.

1863

Cocaine-laced tonics become a popular digestive aid.

1864

Barbiturates are synthesized.

1868

First commercial tobacco cigarettes are produced in the United States.

1868

The Pharmacy Act of 1868 requires testing and registration by those who dispense drugs such as morphine, cocaine, and barbiturates.

1869

The National Prohibition Party is organized and wins seats in state legislatures.

1874

British researcher C.E. Wright synthesizes heroin.

1875

San Francisco passes the first U.S. ordinance against smoking opium in opium dens. Within a few years, many other cities and states follow suit.

1882–1901

Under the advisement of the Women's Christian Temperance Union, the United States passes Temperance Education Laws that require teachers to inform students about the harmful effects of alcohol and narcotics.

1884

Austrian neurologist Sigmund Freud publishes "On Coca."

1887

Amphetamines are synthesized.

1898

Heroin is synthesized.

1903

Coca-Cola removes cocaine from its soft drinks.

1904

Smoking opium is banned in the United States with passage of the Opium Exclusion Act.

1906

The U.S. legislature passes the Pure Food and Drug Act, which requires that all drug ingredients be listed on the label of patented medicines.

1914

The Harrison Narcotics Act is passed. Among other things, it limits the quantities of opium and morphine that can be included in over-the-counter drugs.

1919

Methamphetamine is synthesized.

1920

Prohibition begins with passage of the Eighteenth Amendment to the Constitution.

1922

The Narcotic Drug Import and Export Act restricts the use of narcotics except for legitimate medicinal use.

1924

Passage of the Heroin Act makes it illegal to manufacture heroin in the United States.

1925

The Supreme Court in *Linder v. United States* makes it legal for doctors to prescribe small doses of narcotics to ease withdrawal symptoms.

1932

The amphetamine Benzedrine is sold commercially in inhalers, which leads the way for amphetamines to be prescribed for depression and obesity over the next few decades.

1933

Prohibition is repealed by the Twenty-first Amendment to the Constitution.

1935

Alcoholics Anonymous (AA) is founded.

1937

Marijuana Tax Act is passed to regulate its production and distribution.

1938

Swiss chemist Albert Hoffmann synthesizes LSD.

1938

The United States passes the Food, Drug and Cosmetic Act, which gives the Food and Drug Administration (FDA) control over drug safety and redefines drugs as substances having an effect on the body even in the absence of disease.

1942

The Opium Poppy Control Act is passed to prevent people from growing poppies without a license.

1943

LSD is used on humans.

1949

The amphetamine Benzedrine is removed from inhalers because it causes addiction and potential for overdose.

1950

A report in the *Journal of the American Medical Association* links smoking with cancer.

1951

The Boggs Act imposes mandatory sentences for narcotics violations.

1956

The Narcotics Control Act imposes even stiffer penalties for narcotics violations.

1959

PCP is developed as an anesthetic.

1962

The Supreme Court decides in *Robinson v. United States* that addicts who agree to be committed to drug treatment facilities can avoid incarceration.

1964

Insurance companies begin providing coverage for alcohol abuse treatment.

1964

Methadone is developed as a maintenance treatment for heroin addiction.

1965

Warning labels are required on cigarettes manufactured in the United States.

1969–1971

The heroin epidemic peaks.

1970

The Controlled Substances Act divides drugs with the potential for abuse into five categories called schedules.

1970

TV ads for cigarettes are banned in the United States.

1971

President Richard Nixon appoints the National Commission on Marihuana and Drug Abuse and rejects the findings of its report that marijuana use should be decriminalized.

1973

The Drug Enforcement Administration (DEA) is created.

1973

Opiate receptor sites on the brain are discovered and lead to research attempts to address addiction.

1973–1979

Eleven states decriminalize possession of small amounts of marijuana.

1977

President Jimmy Carter encourages the decriminalization of marijuana.

1980

First Lady Nancy Reagan launches her Just Say No campaign designed to discourage drug use in America's youth.

1981

Crack cocaine appears.

1981

The human immune system disease AIDS is discovered and its transmission linked to intravenous (IV) drug use.

1984

The Drug Offenders Act sets up special programs for offenders and emphasizes treatment.

1984

Uniform Drinking Age Act withholds federal transportation funds from states that refuse to raise their drinking age to twenty-one.

1985

MDMA (Ecstasy) use is officially banned in the United States.

1986

The Surgeon General declares that secondhand smoke causes lung cancer.

1986

The Controlled Substances Analogue Reinforcement Act makes the use of substances with similar effects and structure to existing illicit drugs illegal.

1986

President Ronald Reagan declares an official War on Drugs.

1988

The Anti-Drug Abuse Act vastly increases antidrug spending, strengthens the government's ability to confiscate property in drug-related crimes, reinstates the death penalty for traffickers, and establishes the Office of National Drug Control Policy.

1989

The Drug-Free Workplace Act requires all U.S. employers to adopt a formal drug-abuse policy and notify employees of its requirements.

1992

A needle-exchange program is organized in New York City to stem the spread of the HIV virus that causes AIDS.

1992

The United States overturns approval of marijuana as an experimental treatment for glaucoma and nausea, saying that other, safer alternatives exist.

1993

President Bill Clinton cuts the number of employees in the Office of National Drug Control Policy.

1996

President Clinton increases the international narcotics control budget by 43 percent, allocating money for crop eradication and alternative crop development programs and initiatives aimed at reducing foreign drug trafficking.

1996

The Safe and Drug-Free Schools and Communities Program is formed to develop and maintain long-term prevention strategies.

1997

The Drug-Free Communities Act authorizes grants for community groups to develop drug abuse treatment and prevention programs for youths.

2000

Massive funding is allocated for addressing the socioeconomic issues that made Colombia a major supplier of drugs to the United States. Money is also set aside to discourage coca crop development in the country and prevent cocaine traffickers from establishing bases in Colombia.

2003

Funding for the National Youth Anti-Drug Media Campaign is cut, but funding for the Drug-Free Communities Act is increased.

2003

President George W. Bush's Access to Recovery Initiative provides a voucher system that those in treatment could use to select a treatment program, even a faith-based program, if that suited their individual needs.

2005

Funding is provided to investigate and control poppy farming and distribution in Afghanistan.

2005

Congress refuses to fully fund President Bush's Access to Recovery Program.

Organizations to Contact

The editors have compiled the following list of organizations concerned with the issues debated in this book. The descriptions are derived from materials provided by the organizations. All have publications or information available for interested readers. The list was compiled on the date of publication of the present volume; the information provided here may change. Be aware that many organizations take several weeks or longer to respond to inquiries, so allow as much time as possible.

American Civil Liberties Union (ACLU) Law Reform Project
125 Broad St., 18th Floor, New York, NY   10004
(888) 576-2258
Web site: www.aclu.org/drugpolicy/decrim

Long a champion of civil rights, the ACLU formed this branch of its organization to work to end punitive drug policies that challenge the constitutional and basic human rights of drug users. The organization publishes a wide variety of drug policy publications that are available for download on its Web site. Recent titles include "Making Sense of Student Drug Testing: Why Educators Are Saying No" and "Caught in the Net: The Impact of Drug Policies on Women and Families."

Drug Policy Alliance (DPA)
70 W. 36th St., 16th Floor, New York, NY   10018
(212) 613-8020 • fax: (212) 613-8021
e-mail: nyc@drugpolicy.org
Web site: www.drugpolicy.org

Committed to ending America's War on Drugs, DPA envisions new drug policies based on science, compassion, health, and human rights. It also works to create a society that will not incubate the fears and prejudices that lead to harsh treatment of drug users. The alliance makes a large number of publications available to the public via its Web site. Some recent publications include "Safety First: A Reality-Based Approach to Teens and Drugs" and "Beyond Zero Tolerance."

Drugtext Foundation
koninginneweg 189, 1075 cp, Amsterdam
  Netherlands
e-mail: mario@lap.nl
Web site: www.drugtext.org

The Drugtext Foundation was established to provide a clearinghouse of current and accurate information about substance use, addiction, harm reduction, and domestic and international drug policy. It maintains a list of some of the latest articles, books, legal developments, and other related topics.

Faces and Voices of Recovery
1010 Vermont Ave. Suite 708, Washington, DC   20005
(202) 737-0690 • fax (202) 737-0695
Web site: www.facesandvoicesofrecovery.org

This organization was founded by an alliance of treatment professionals and recovering addicts to give a policy voice to those most intimately acquainted with the devastation of drug abuse: the users themselves. It publishes *Faces and Voices of Recovery*, a bimonthly e-newsletter, and *Rising: Recovery in Action*, a biannual magazine.

Interfaith Drug Policy Initiative (IDPI)
PO Box 6299, Washington, DC   20015
(301) 270-4473 • fax: (301) 270-4483
e-mail: TylerSmith@idpi.us
Web site: www.idpi.us

Established in 2003, IDPI is a nonprofit coalition of religious groups committed to drug policy reform and helping craft drug policies that emphasize education and treatment. The organization makes available a number of fact sheets on topics such as medical marijuana use and mandatory minimum sentences for drug offenders. It also provides doctrinal drug policy positions from the major denominations across the United States.

Leadership to Keep Children Alcohol Free
e-mail: leadership@alcoholfreechildren.org
Web site www.alcoholfreechildren.org

Founded by a coalition of governors' spouses, federal agencies, and public and private parties, Leadership to Keep Children Alcohol Free is the only organization dedicated to keeping children from nine to fifteen from becoming addicted to alcohol. With a grant from the Robert Woods Johnson Foundation, the organization published *Drinking It In*, a CD-ROM that illustrates how children are surrounded by messages to drink. They also publish *Science, Kids and Alcohol*, an online compendium of the latest scientific information about the effects of alcohol on children.

Marijuana Policy Project (MPP)
PO Box 77492, Capitol Hill, Washington, DC   20013
(202) 462-5747
e-mail: info@mpp.org
Web site: www.mpp.org

The largest marijuana policy reform organization in the country, MPP works to debunk myths about the dangers of marijuana. The group maintains that the greatest danger associated with marijuana use is unnecessary incarceration of users. It advocates for people who want to use marijuana for medical purposes. Subscribers may sign up for legislative e-mail alerts pertaining to recent developments in marijuana policy in their state.

National Drug Intelligence Center (NDIC)
319 Washington St., 5th Floor, Johnstown, PA   15901-1622
(814) 532-4601 • fax: 814-532-4690
e-mail: NDIC.Contacts@usdoj.gov

Web site: www.usdoj.gov/ndic

The NDIC was founded in 1993 as a branch of the U.S. Department of Justice and a branch of the U.S. intelligence community. The NDIC worked with President George W. Bush to develop the General Counterdrug Intelligence Plan, which designated the organization as the main center for strategic domestic counterdrug intelligence in the United States. Recent NDIC publications include the "National Drug Threat Assessment 2007," the "National Methamphetamine Threat Assessment 2007," and the "Domestic Cannabis Cultivation Assessment 2007."

National Organization for the Reform of Marijuana Laws (NORML)
1600 K St. NW, Suite 501, Washington, DC   20006-2832
(202) 483-5500 • fax: (202) 483-0057
e-mail: norml@norml.org
website: www.norml.org

For the past thirty years, this public-interest lobby has spoken out against the prohibition of marijuana. Its mission is to defend the interests of the millions of responsible marijuana users in the United States and to work to change a governmental policy that declares any use of marijuana is a crime. NORML publishes a monthly e-newsletter and maintains a library of information about marijuana decriminalization and reform.

National Youth Anti-Drug Media Campaign
PO Box 6000, Rockville, MD   20849-6000
(800) 666-3332 • fax: (301) 519-5212
Web site: www.themediacampaign.org

Founded by the Office of National Drug Control Policy in 1998, the National Youth Anti-Drug Media Campaign has dedicated itself to reaching parents, teens, and communities with education and support that will help them fight teen drug use. Among many pamphlets on keeping children off drugs, the organization offers an annual *Parenting Tips* e-newsletter.

For Further Research

Books

Dan Baum. *Smoke and Mirrors: The War on Drugs and the Politics of Failure.* New York: Little, Brown, 1996.

Philip Bean and Teresa Nemitz. *Drug Treatment: What Works?* New York: Routledge, 2004.

Martin Booth. *Opium: A History.* New York: St. Martin's, 1996.

Herbert Covey. *The Methamphetamine Crisis: Strategies to Save Addicts, Families, and Communities.* Westport, CT: Praeger, 2007.

George B. Cutten. *Should Prohibition Return?* New York: Fleming H. Revell, 1966.

Gary L. Fisher. *Rethinking Our War on Drugs,* Westport, CT: Praeger, 2006.

Erich Goode. *Marijuana.* New York: Atherton, 1970.

Richard Hammersley, Furzana Khan, and Jason Ditton. *Ecstasy and the Rise of the Chemical Generation.* New York: Routledge, 2002.

Institute of Medicine. *Dispelling the Myths About Addiction.* Washington, DC: National Academy, 1997.

E.M. Jellinek. *Phases in the Drinking History of Alcoholics.* New Haven, CT: Hillhouse, 1946.

Andrew C. Kimmens. *Tales of Hashish.* New York: William Morrow & Co., 1977.

John Kobler. *Ardent Spirits: The Rise and Fall of Prohibition.* New York: G.P. Putnam's Sons, 1973.

Mark Edward Lender and James Kirby Martin. *Drinking in America: A History.* New York: Free Press, 1982.

Andy Letcher. *Shroom: A Cultural History of the Magic Mushroom.* London: Faber & Faber, 2006.

Marsha Manatt. *Parents, Peers and Pot II: Parents in Action.* Rockville, MD: National Institute on Drug Abuse, 1983.

Joel Miller. *Bad Trip: How the War Against Drugs Is Destroying America.* Nashville, TN: WND, 2004.

David F. Musto. *The American Disease: Origins of Narcotic Control.* New Haven, CT: Yale University Press, 1973.

Steven B. Nock. *The Costs of Privacy: Surveillance and Reputation in America.* New York: Aldine De Gruyter, 1993.

James Orcutt and David R. Rudy, eds. *Drugs, Alcohol and Social Problems.* New York: Rowman & Littlefield, 2003.

Robert E. Popham, ed. *Alcohol and Alcoholism.* Toronto: University of Toronto Press, 1970.

Eric Schlosser. *Reefer Madness: Sex, Drugs, and Cheap Labor in the American Black Market.* Boston: Houghton-Mifflin, 2003.

Thomas Szasz. *Our Right to Drugs.* New York: Praeger, 1992.

Geraldine Woods. *Drug Abuse in Society.* Santa Barbara, CA: ABC-CLIO, 1993.

Periodicals

American Druggist and Pharmaceutical Record, "History of Narcotic Legislation," July–December 1910.

Robin Blummer. "Drug War Invades State Elections," *St. Petersburg Times*, June 1, 2003.

William F. Buckley. "Legalization of Marijuana Long Overdue," *Albuquerque Journal*, June 9, 1993.

Tom Burke. "Warning: Drugs Cost the Earth. If You Want to Do Your Bit for the Environment Stop Snorting and Stop Inhaling," *New Statesman*, June 30, 2003.

Chicago Sun-Times. "Suffering Patients Deserve Access to Medical Marijuana," March 2, 2006.

John J. Dilulio Jr. "Two Million Prisoners Are Enough," *Wall Street Journal*, March 12, 1999.

David Henderson. "Supporting the Drug War Supports Terrorists," *Reason*, July 2002.

Bob Holmes. "Quick Fix: Just a Single Dose of an Asian Folk Remedy Can Free Drug Addicts from Their Cravings, So Why Aren't Doctors Welcoming It with Open Arms?" *New Scientist*, Spring 2001.

Journal of the American Medical Association "The Cocain Habit," January–June 1901.

Robert MacCoun. "O Cannabis! Pot Decriminalization in Canada Highlights U.S. Isolation," *San Francisco Chronicle*, June 11, 2003.

David McDowell. "Club Drugs and Their Treatment," *Psychiatric Times*, January 1, 2006.

Ethan Nadelmann. "Switzerland's Heroin Experience," *National Review*, July 10, 1995.

———. "There Must Be a New Approach That Is Not Grounded in Ignorance or Fear But in Common Sense," *Los Angeles Times*, September 19, 1999.

Ethan Nadelmann, Kurt Schmoke, Joseph McNamara, Robert Sweet, Thomas Szasz, and Steven Duke. "Symposium," *National Review*, July 1, 1996.

New Scientist "No Smokescreen: If a Drug Can Save Lives, We Shouldn't Withhold it Without Good Reason," October 4, 2003.

Robert Patton. "Drugs Legislation," *Freeman*, January 1973.

San Diego Union-Tribune "Give Drug Addicts Treatment, Not Syringes," July 29, 2005.

Robert Sharpe. "Drug War Fuels Crime," *St. Louis Post-Dispatch*, March 25, 2006.

Thomas A. McLellan, David Lewis, Charles O'Brien, and Herbert Kleber. "Drug Dependence, a Chronic Mental Illness," *Journal of the American Medical Association*, October 4, 2000.

Milan Vesely. "Heroin Trade on the Increase: Since the Fall of the Taliban Afghanistan's Multi-Billion-Dollar Drugs Trade Has Soared," *Middle East*, November 2002.

Joey Weedon. "Drugs and Crime Are Linked," *Corrections Today*, July 2005.

William L. White. "Addiction as a Disease: Birth of a Concept," *Counselor*, January 2000.

———. "Recovery: The Next Frontier," *Counselor*, January 2004.

Li-Tzy Wu, Daniel Pilowsky, and William, E. Schlenger. "Inhalant Abuse and Dependence Among Adolescents in the United States," *Journal of the American Academy of Child and Adolescent Psychiatry*, October 2004.

Web Articles

"A Friend of Mine Committed Suicide the Other Day," www.lifeormeth.com/testimonials.

American Civil Liberties Union. "Testimony of Executive Director Ira Glasser on National Drug Policy," www.aclu.org/drugpolicy/decrim/10858leg19990616.htm, June 16, 1999.

Rev. Arnold W. Howard. "Drug War Addiction," Interfaith Drug Policy Initiative, www.dpi.us/dpr/writings/writings _dwaddiction.htm.

"Pushing Back Against Meth: A Progress Report on the Fight Against Methamphetamine in the United States," www.nattc.org/resPubs/meth/FINALPushingBack AgainstMethReport.pdf

William L. White. "Treatment Works! Is It Time for a New Slogan?" www.addictioninfo.org/articles/1361/1/Treat ment-Works-Is-it-time-for-a-new-slogan/Page1.html.

Index